FIC STAR

P9-CJF-485

JAN 30 2014

DISCARD

The Tainted Coin

The Tainted Coin

The fifth chronicle of

Hugh de Singleton, surgeon

MEL STARR

MONARCH
BOOKS

Oxford, UK & Grand Rapids, Michigan, USA

Copyright © 2012 by Mel Starr

This edition copyright © 2012 Lion Hudson

The right of Mel Starr to be identified as author of this work has been asserted by him in accordance with the Copyright, Designs and Patents Act 1988.

All rights reserved. No part of this publication may be reproduced or transmitted in any form or by any means, electronic or mechanical, including photocopy, recording or any information storage and retrieval system, without permission in writing from the publisher.

Published by Monarch Books
an imprint of
Lion Hudson plc
Wilkinson House, Jordan Hill Road, Oxford OX2 8DR, England
Tel: +44 (0)1865 302750 Fax: +44 (0)1865 302757
Email: monarch@lionhudson.com
www.lionhudson.com

ISBN 978 0 85721 250 4
e-ISBN 978 0 85721 401 0

First edition 2012

A catalogue record for this book is available from the British Library.

Printed and bound in the UK, August 2012, LH27

For Peter and Muriel Horrocks
Thanks for the wonderful memories of days spent at
Trethevy Farm

Acknowledgments

Several years ago when Dan Runyon, professor of English at Spring Arbor University, learned that I had written an as yet unpublished medieval mystery, he invited me to speak to his fiction-writing class about the trials of a rookie writer seeking a publisher. He sent sample chapters of *The Unquiet Bones* to his friend Tony Collins. Thanks, Dan.

Thanks to Tony Collins and all those at Monarch who saw Master Hugh's potential. Thanks especially to my editor, Jan Greenough, who excels at asking questions like, "Do you really want to say it that way?" and "Wouldn't Master Hugh do it this way?"

Dr. John Blair, of Queen's College, Oxford, has written several papers about Bampton history. These have been invaluable in creating an accurate time and place for Master Hugh. Tony and Lis Page have also been a wonderful source of information regarding Bampton. I owe them much.

Ms Malgorzata Deron, of Poznan, Poland, has offered to update and maintain my website. She has done a wonderful job. To see the results of her work, visit www.melstarr.net

Glossary

Alaunt: a large hunting dog.

All Saints' Day: November 1st.

All Souls' Day: November 2nd.

Almoner: monastic official in charge of charity and care of the poor.

Aloes of lamb: lamb sliced thin and rolled in a mixture of egg yolk, suet, onion, and various spices, then baked.

Angelus Bell: rung three times each day; dawn, noon, and dusk. Announced the time for the Angelus devotional.

Apples in compost: apples cooked with a sauce of malmsey wine, sliced dates, sugar cinnamon, and ginger.

Bailiff: a lord's chief manorial representative. He oversaw all operations, collected rents and fines, and enforced labor service. Not a popular fellow.

Baxter: a professional baker, usually female, who often sold on the streets.

Beadle: a manor official in charge of fences, hedges, enclosures, and curfew. Also called a hayward, he served under the reeve.

Blanc de sire: ground, cooked chicken, thickened with rice flour and cooked in almond milk.

Boon work: the extra hours of labor service villeins owed the lord at harvest.

Bruit of eggs: an egg-and-cheese custard.

Buttery: a room for storing beverages, stored in "butts" or barrels.

Cabbage with marrow: cabbage cooked with bone marrow, breadcrumbs, and spices.

Calefactory: the warming room in a monastery. Benedictines allowed the fire to be lit on November 1st. The more rigorous Cistercians had no calefactory.

Capon farced: chicken stuffed with hard-boiled egg yolks, currants, chopped pork, breadcrumbs, and various spices.

Cellarer: the monastic official in charge of food and drink.

Chapman: a merchant, particularly one who traveled from village to village with his wares.

Chardewarden: pears cooked in wine sauce with breadcrumbs and various spices.

Chauces: tight-fitting trousers, sometimes of different colors for each leg.

Compline: the seventh and last of the daytime canonical hours, observed at sunset.

Coney in cevy: rabbit stewed with onions, breadcrumbs, and spices in wine vinegar.

Coppice: to cut a tree back to the base to stimulate the growth of young shoots. These were used for anything from arrows to rafters, depending upon how much they were permitted to grow.

Cotehardie: the primary medieval outer garment. Women's were floor-length, men's ranged from thigh to ankle.

Cotter: a poor villager, usually holding five acres or less, he often had to work for wealthier villagers to make ends meet.

Cresset: a bowl of oil with a floating wick used as a lamp.

Cyueles: deep-fried fritters made of a paste of bread crumbs, ground almonds, eggs, sugar, and salt.

Demesne: land directly exploited by a lord and worked by his villeins, as opposed to land a lord might rent to tenants.

Deodand: an object which had caused a death. The item was sold and the price given to the King.

Dexter: to the right hand. Also a large, powerful war horse.

Egg leech: a thickened custard.

Extreme Unction (or Last Rites): a sacrament for the dying. It must not be premature. A recipient who recovered was considered as good as dead. He must fast perpetually, go barefoot, and abstain from sexual relations.

Farrier: a smith who specialized in shoeing horses.

Farthing: one fourth of a penny. The smallest silver coin.

Fistula: An abnormal passage developed between two organs, sometimes from an abscess to the body's surface.

Gentleman: a nobleman. The term had nothing to do with character or behavior.

Gersom: a fee paid to a noble to acquire or inherit land.

Groom: a lower-rank servant to a lord, often a youth and usually assistant to a valet.

Haberdasher: a merchant who sold household items such as pins, buckles, hats, and purses.

Habit: a monk's robe and cowl.

Hallmote: the manorial court. Royal courts judged free tenants accused of murder or felony. Otherwise manor courts had jurisdiction over legal matters concerning villagers. Villeins accused of murder might also be tried in a manor court.

Hamsoken: breaking and entering.

Infangenthef: the right of the lord of a manor to try and execute a thief caught in the act.

King's Eyre: a royal circuit court, presided over by a traveling judge.

Kirtle: the basic medieval undergarment.

Lammastide: August 1st, when thanks was given for a successful wheat harvest. From "loaf mass".

Leach lombard: a dish of ground pork, eggs, raisins, currants, and dates, with spices added. The mixture was boiled in a sack until set, then sliced for serving.

Leech: a physician.

Liripipe: a fashionably long tail attached to a man's cap.

Lychgate: a roofed gate in a churchyard wall under which the corpse rested during the initial part of a burial service.

Maintenance: protection from punishment for misdeeds; provided for knights who served a powerful lord and wore his livery.

Mark: a coin worth thirteen shillings and four pence.

Marshalsea: the stables and their associated accoutrements.

Maslin: bread made from a mixture of grains, commonly wheat and rye or barley and rye.

Mews: stables, often with living quarters, built around a courtyard.

Nones: the fifth canonical office, sung at the ninth hour of the day – about 3 p.m.

Page: a young male servant, often a youth learning the arts of chivalry before becoming a squire.

Palfrey: a riding horse with a comfortable gait.

Pannaging: turning hogs loose in an autumn forest to fatten on roots and acorns.

Passing bell: ringing of the parish church bell to indicate the death of a villager.

Pomme dorryce: meatballs made of ground pork, eggs, currants, flour, and spices.

Pottage: anything cooked in one pot, from soups and stews, to simple porridge.

Pottage of eggs: poached eggs in a sweet sauce of honey, sugar, and cinnamon.

Reeve: the most important manor official, although he did not outrank the bailiff. Elected by tenants from among themselves, and often the best husbandman, he had responsibility for fields, buildings, and enforcing labor service.

Reredorter: the monastery toilets.

Runcey: a common horse of lower grade than a palfrey.

Sacrist: the monastic official responsible for the upkeep of the church and vestments, and time-keeping.

St. James's Wort: ointment from this plant was used for wounds, and a syrup was added to wine for easing pain.

Sinister: to the left hand.

Solar: a small private room in a castle, more easily heated than the great hall, where lords preferred to spend time, especially in winter. Usually on a castle's upper floor.

Soul cakes: small cakes given to children and the poor on All Saints' Day and All Souls' Day.

Stockfish: inexpensive fish, usually dried cod or haddock, consumed on fast days.

Surcoat: an overcoat.

Tenant: a free peasant who rented land from his lord. He could pay his rent in labor on the lord's demesne, or (more likely by the fourteenth century) in cash.

Terce: the canonical office at 9 a.m.

Toft: land surrounding a house. Often used for growing vegetables.

Valet: a high-ranking servant to a lord – a chamberlain, for example.

Vigils: the night office, celebrated at midnight. When the service was completed Benedictines went back to bed. Cistercians stayed up for the new day.

Villein: a non-free peasant. He could not leave his manor or service to his lord, or sell animals without permission. But if he could escape his manor for a year and a day, he would be free.

Wattle: interlacing sticks used as a foundation and support for daub (plaster) in building the walls of a house.

Whitsuntide: Pentecost; seven weeks after Easter Sunday.

Yardland: about thirty acres. Also called a virgate, and in northern England an oxgang.

Yeoman: a freeholder below the rank of gentry, generally more prosperous than a tenant.

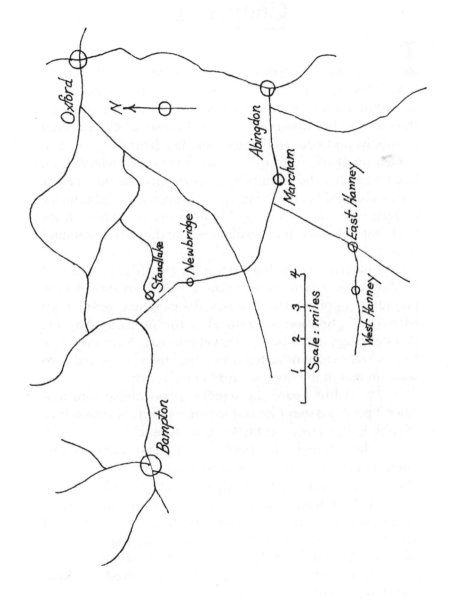

Oxford

N

Abingdon

Marcham

East Hanney

Newbridge

Standlake

West Hanney

Scale : miles
1 2 3 4

Bampton

Chapter 1

I would have preferred to remain in bed a while longer. The October morn was cool, my bed warm, but Bessie stirred in her cradle and Kate was already up and bringing the coals to life upon our hearth. I arose, clothed myself hurriedly, and bent to lift my daughter from her cot. She smiled up at me from the woolen layers into which Kate had tucked her the night before. Elizabeth was now nearly a year old, and beginning to sleep through the night, much to Kate's joy, and my own. Children are a blessing from God, but not when they awaken before dawn and demand to be fed.

I had placed the babe upon my shoulder and turned to the stairs, when from below I heard an unwelcome pounding upon Galen House's door. When some man wishes my attention so soon after the morning Angelus Bell has rung, it can be to no good purpose. A window was near, so rather than hasten down the stairs, I opened it to see who was at my door so early in the morn.

My visitor heard the window open above him and when I peered down I looked into the gaunt, upraised face of John Kellet, curate at St. Andrew's Chapel.

"Master Hugh," he shouted, "you must come at once. There is a man wounded and near dead at St. Andrew's Chapel. Bring your instruments and make haste!"

I did so. Kate had heard Kellet's appeal and awaited me at the foot of the stairs. She took Bessie from me, and over her shoulder I saw my breakfast awaiting upon our table – a loaf and ale. It must wait. I filled a sack with instruments and herbs from my chest, unbarred the door, and stepped into the foggy dawn.

"Quickly, Master Hugh," the skeletal priest urged,

and set off down Church View Street at a trot, his bare, boney feet raising puffs of dust from the dry dirt of the street. I flung my sack over a shoulder and followed. I had questions about this abrupt summons, but Kellet was already too far ahead to allow conversation. I loped after the priest, the sack bouncing against my back.

Kellet led me to the High Street, thence up Bushey Row to the path to St. Andrew's Chapel. The parish Church of St. Beornwald is a grand structure, but the chapel is old and small. 'Tis little more than a quarter of a mile from Bampton to the chapel, and soon the ancient building appeared in the fog. Kellet plunged through the decrepit lychgate and led me to the porch. There, upon the flags, I saw a man. The priest had placed the fellow upon a pallet so he did not rest upon the hard stones. I bent over the silent form and thought Kellet's trouble unnecessary, for the man before me seemed insensible, if not already dead.

"Found 'im here at dawn, when I rose to ring the Angelus Bell. I heard a moan, so opened the door an' found the fellow under the porch roof, just where he now lies. Put a pallet 'neath 'im an' sought you. I could see 'e was bad off, even in so little light as in the porch."

The curate lived in the chapel tower, in a bare room but four paces on a side. He need not go far from his bed to ring the bell of St. Andrew's Chapel, for the bell-rope fell through a hole in the center of his chamber to the base of the tower at ground level.

The porch lay in shadow, so the nature of the man's wounds was obscure. I asked Kellet to take one end of the pallet, and I grasped the other. Together we lifted the unconscious stranger to the churchyard where the rising sun was visible through the thinning fog and his wounds and injuries became apparent.

The man had been beaten senseless. His nose was broken and askew, his scalp lacerated just above an ear where a blow had found his skull, his lips were purple and swollen, and it seemed sure his jaw was broken and teeth were knocked loose.

"You heard him moan when you rose to ring the Angelus Bell?"

"Aye," Kellet replied.

"Did he say anything when you found him?"

"Nay. He was as you see 'im now."

Whoever this man was, he had used the last of his strength to reach sanctuary, as I think he assumed the ancient chapel to be. I looked closely at the face, but could not recognize him as any man I knew. I asked the priest if he knew the fellow.

"Nay. 'Course, he's so abused, he might be someone I know. In his state his own mother'd not know 'im, I think."

I silently agreed with the priest, then bent to examine the man's injuries more closely to learn was there anything I might do to save his life and speed healing of his wounds.

I am Hugh de Singleton, surgeon, trained at the University of Paris, and also bailiff to Lord Gilbert Talbot at his lands in Bampton. Many would find the work I must do as surgeon disagreeable, repairing men's bodies when they have done themselves harm, but I find my duties as bailiff, collecting fines and dealing with obstreperous tenants, more irksome.

With my dagger I cut away the wounded man's cotehardie and kirtle, the better to inspect his hurts, and as I did so considered that the supine form presented me with two tasks: I must treat his injuries, and discover who had dealt with him so.

The man's body presented as many wounds as his head. So many bruises covered his ribs that they might have been one great contusion. I tested one purple blemish and felt the ends of a broken rib move beneath my fingertips.

My examination roused the unconscious fellow. I saw his eyelids flicker, then open. Perhaps he saw my face above him, perhaps not. His eyes seemed not to focus, but drifted about, hesitating only briefly when they turned to me. Did he take me for a friend? Who can know? He surely did not think me one of his assailants, else he would not have spoken as he did.

With pain and effort he opened his swollen lips and said, so faintly I had to ask John Kellet if he heard the same words, "They didn't get me coin."

I had learned two things: whoso attacked the fellow had sought a coin, or perhaps many coins, and more than one had done this evil. I would learn no more from him, for as I began to inspect a bloody laceration between two ribs, his chest heaved and was then still.

"Dead?" Kellet asked after a moment.

"Aye. You must think back on finding the fellow. Is there anything you can remember of this morn which might tell who he is and who has done this?"

"I will think on it while I ring the Passing Bell. I have already offered Extreme Unction, before I sought you. I could see how ill used he was, even in the dark of the porch, and feared he might not live till I returned."

"While you do so I will fetch the coroner. Hubert Shillside must convene a jury here before we may do any other thing."

I heard Kellet ring the bell of St. Andrew's Chapel as I left the churchyard and its tumbled-down wall. I noted several places where someone – Kellet, I presume – had replaced fallen stones so as to halt the decay. My eyes traveled to a section of the wall where, three years past, I had hidden to escape Thomas atte Bridge and the priest, who intended my death. Kellet, for this felony and others, was sent on pilgrimage to Compostela. He returned a transformed man, and was assigned to assist the almoner at the Priory of St. Nicholas, in Exeter. There he was so assiduous at seeking the poor that he came near to impoverishing the priory, it not being a wealthy house, and the prior beseeched the bishop to be rid of him. As no curate had been found for St. Andrew's Chapel, Kellet was reassigned to the place. He left it three years past a corpulent hedonist, but returned a year ago an emaciated pauper, who wore no shoes at any season and gave to the poor nearly all of the meager living he was awarded as curate. I have never seen a man so reformed, and indeed, when first I learned of the change, doubted it was truly so. May the Lord Christ forgive me for mistrusting the alteration He can work in a repentant man's life. All saints were once sinners, and any sinner may become a saint.

Hubert Shillside, Bampton's haberdasher, was no more pleased than I had been to open his door so early, but accepted his duty as coroner, and when told of the death at St. Andrew's Chapel, set out to assemble a jury while I walked to Church View Street and Galen House.

I told Kate of events at the chapel, hurriedly gobbled the loaf she had set out for me, swallowed a cup of ale, then set out again for the chapel. I arrived with Shillside and his coroner's jury. The haberdasher asked of the priest what he knew of the corpse, and was told what I had already heard. Kellet could think of nothing more to explain the dead man's condition.

All who viewed the corpse agreed that the death was murder, not misadventure, and so Shillside did readily declare. No weapon was to be found, so the coroner, no doubt hungry to break his fast, absolved himself and his jurymen of further responsibility in the matter and turned the death over to me.

As the coroner's jury departed the place, I told Kellet to once again take in hand an end of the pallet. Together we carried the corpse through the porch, into the chapel, and deposited it on the flags before the altar.

"I'll say a mass, have a grave dug, and bury the man this day," the priest said.

I wished to know where this stranger had been attacked, to see if there might be at the place some evidence of his assailants. It could not have been close to the chapel, for he would have cried out when attacked, and Kellet would have heard him. But the dead man had been so badly injured that he would not have crawled far. I searched the grass of the churchyard for blood and found traces which led to the lychgate. The curate saw, and followed. Beyond the gate was the path, dry from absence of rain for the past fortnight. In the dust it was easy to follow the track of a crawling man back to the east, for the sun was now well up over the fields and meadow which bordered the narrow road. Nearly two hundred paces to the east the path entered a wood, and a few paces beyond that the marks of a crawling man disappeared into the verge.

I studied the place where the man had crawled from the forest. Why did he struggle to leave the place and crawl to St. Andrew's Chapel? In his battered condition this required much effort. Was he familiar with Bampton, so that he knew help might be found could he reach the chapel?

John Kellet had followed from the chapel and with me studied the path where marks in the dust told of the man's entry upon the road.

"Look there," the priest said, and pointed a few paces beyond. Between road and forest was a swathe of dry grass and across this patch of vegetation two parallel tracks of bent-down foliage showed where a cart or similar wheeled conveyance had turned from the road and entered a narrow opening which led into the forest. Marks of the cart wheels and a horse's hooves, and the footprints of men were visible in the dust of the path where the vehicle entered the wood, but although we searched for many paces in both directions from the place, neither Kellet nor I could find any mark where a cart might have left the wood and regained the road. Whatever had entered the forest was yet there.

The priest followed as I traced the path of the cart into the wood. Fallen leaves covered the forest floor, so the track was soon obliterated, but it was possible to guess the way by seeking openings between the trees and bushes large enough to admit passage of a horse and cart.

We had walked perhaps fifty paces from the road when I heard a horse whinny. Another forty paces brought us to a shaded clearing in the wood where before us stood a horse, harnessed to a cart, its reins tied to a small beech. The horse neighed again, no doubt pleased to see men who might offer it water and food.

"Why is this beast here, so distant from the road?" Kellet wondered aloud. "And did it belong to the man now lying dead in St. Andrew's Chapel?"

My mind had posed the same questions, and I thought it likely the answer to the second question was "yes." An inspection of the cart might confirm this. It was well made, with two wheels. A waxed cloth had covered the cart, but was drawn aside and hung from the cart to the forest floor. I peered into the cart and saw there several chests, open and upended. Their contents were strewn about. There was a packet of combs, some of wood and cheaply made, but others of fine ivory. Another small chest had held an assortment of buckles, pins, buttons, and a package of needles. These were all tossed about in the cart. A larger chest had held several yards of woolen cloth in a variety of colors. This fabric was flung about, and one bolt lay partly over the side of the cart, dragging upon the leaves. Here was a chapman's cart. The owner made his living selling goods in villages too small to have haberdashers and suchlike merchants.

I began to form an opinion of what had happened here. The chapman, I thought, had decided to sleep the night under his cart, the weather being yet mild. He led his horse deep into the wood, away from the road and felons who might prowl the countryside, but was followed. Perhaps men saw the track his cart made in the dust of the road, as did the priest and I, or mayhap he was trailed from the last town where he did business.

Here in the forest men surprised the chapman and demanded his purse. He refused to give it up, so they set upon him with a club, but yet he would not tell them where it was hid. They beat him senseless, near to death, ransacked his cart, then left him in the forest to perish.

Kellet had inspected the contents of the cart from over my shoulder. As I pondered the discovery I saw him reach for a sack and untie the cord which closed it. He examined the contents, then poured some into a wooden bucket which lay in the cart beside the sack. The horse smelled the oats, and neighed in anticipation. The priest took the bucket to the beast, which plunged its muzzle in eagerly. No doubt the animal was thirsty as well.

A fallen branch next caught my eye. It lay at the edge of the clearing, three or four paces from the cart, and seemed freshly broken. One splintered end was white in the dappled sunlight, and the limb lay atop the fallen leaves, not under, as should be had it occupied that place for a day or more.

I lifted the broken limb and saw a thing which caused me to recoil. At a place where a twig had broken from the branch and left a raised and thorn-like barb was the dark stain of blood and what appeared to be a bit of flesh. The priest saw me examining the club, and when the horse had consumed his ration of oats Kellet joined me in studying the cudgel.

"Broke it over 'is 'ead, I'd say," Kellet said.

The limb was as large around as my arm, and as long. Blows from it would easily break a man's ribs or skull.

I was not optimistic that I could find the felons who had done this murder. Had they taken goods from the chapman's cart, I might seek in villages nearby for men who had wares to sell, or whose wives wore new buttons upon their cotehardies or bragged of ivory combs. But if the villains did take goods from the cart, they left much behind. Why so? Unless some men boasted of this attack, I would have no clue which might lead to the assailant.

Even the horse and cart might be carried away to some town and sold. The beast would fetch ten shillings, perhaps twelve, and the cart another eight or ten shillings, for it was well made and sturdy. Whoever murdered the chapman had left here in the woods goods to the value of as much as three marks. Did the chapman cry out loudly as he was attacked, so as to frighten the felons away? Kellet had heard no such screams, but I could think of no other reason thieves might leave such loot here in the forest.

"Whose goods are these now?" Kellet asked.

"Unless we can discover some heir to the dead man, they become Lord Gilbert's possession, being found upon his land."

"Oh, aye. There is much wealth here. I had thought

some might be sold to help the poor through the winter to come."

"Lord Gilbert is not a greedy man, no more so than most of his station. Some of the buttons and buckles of the meaner sort he will give to his grooms and valets, but there may be some he will allow to be sold. I will speak to him about it."

I replaced the waxed cloth atop the cart, then led the horse through the wood to the road. Here I halted to again study the dust of the road to see if it might tell me more of what had happened here. Many men had walked this way since the last rain, and horses also. It was impossible to tell which of the tracks might have been made by the men who had slain the chapman.

We walked to St. Andrew's Chapel, where Kellet left me to set about his duty to bury the chapman in the hallowed ground of the churchyard. I led the horse and cart through the town and under the Bampton Castle portcullis to the marshalsea, where I told a page to unharness and care for the beast, but to leave the cart where it stood. I then sought John Chamberlain and requested of him an audience with Lord Gilbert. I awaited John's return in the hall, but was not long abandoned. John returned with announcement that Lord Gilbert was at leisure and would see me in the solar.

That chamber, smaller and more easily warmed than the hall, was Lord Gilbert's choice when the weather turned cool and damp. The day was mild, but a fire blazed upon the hearth when I was ushered into the solar. A great lord cares little for use of firewood, as he will always have supply. And, in truth, the warmth was pleasing. If I had such resources to hand I would this day have a blaze in all of the hearths in Galen House.

"Hugh, what news?" Lord Gilbert said, looking up from a ledger. Lord Gilbert is a bearded, square-faced man, ruddy of cheek and accustomed to squinting into the sun from atop a horse. Unlike most lords, he desires to keep abreast of financial dealings within his lands. Each year

I prepare an account for his steward, Geoffrey Thirwall, who resides at Pembroke. Thirwall visits Bampton once each year, for hallmote, when he examines my report. Most nobles allow their stewards final say in matters of business, as, in truth, does Lord Gilbert. But, unlike most, Lord Gilbert wishes to keep himself informed of profit and loss first hand, rather than rely only upon the accounts of bailiff and steward. Many great lords have lately been reduced to penury, and must sell lands to pay debts. The plague has taken many tenants, and dead men pay no rents. Lord Gilbert is not in such straightened circumstance. Perhaps his inspection of my accounts and those of his other bailiffs is reason why.

"A dead man was found this morning upon your lands," I said. "Well, he was not dead when found, but died soon after."

"A tenant, or villein?"

"Neither, m'lord. A chapman, I think. We found a place in the wood where the man was attacked, and a horse and cart were there."

"We?"

"Aye. John Kellet found the man moaning and near dead under the porch roof of St. Andrew's Chapel. I have brought horse and cart to the castle. Neither I nor Kellet recognize the dead man, nor did Hubert Shillside or any man of his coroner's jury. If no heirs can be discovered the goods in his cart are yours, m'lord."

"Oh, aye... just so. What is there?"

"Two chests of combs, buckles, buttons, pins, and such like, and another of woolen cloth of the middling sort."

"A traveler, then," said Lord Gilbert.

"Aye. 'Tis why he is unknown in Bampton. Hubert Shillside sells much the same stuff. The man has probably passed this way before, perhaps traveling from Cote to Alvescot or some such place, and this may be why he sought St. Andrew's Chapel when men set upon him."

"If thieves," Lord Gilbert wondered aloud, "why did

they not make off with his goods?"

"Before he died he looked at me and said, 'They didn't get me coin.' Poor men might find it impossible to hide possession of ivory combs for their wives. Even selling such things would raise eyebrows. But coins... even a poor cotter will have some wealth. Perhaps whoso attacked the chapman thought disposing of his goods might point to them as thieves, so wished only for his purse."

"Did you find it?"

"Nay. He had no purse fixed to his belt, nor was there one in the cart or the forest, unless it is well hid."

"Then why, I wonder, did he say the fellows had not got his coin?"

"This puzzles me, as well. Perhaps the purse was in his cart, and he was too knocked about to know that the thieves made off with it."

"Aye," Lord Gilbert agreed. "Let us have a look at the cart, and see what is there."

"John Kellet has asked, if the chapman cannot be named, and no heir found, some of the goods found in the cart might be sold and the profit dispensed to the poor, to help them through the winter to come."

Lord Gilbert is not an unjust man, but the thought of surviving a winter, or possibly not, does not enter his mind, nor do any nobles give the season much thought other than to make ready a Christmas feast. That many folk might see winter as a threat to their lives and the survival of their children was an unfamiliar thought to my employer.

"Oh, uh, well, let us see what is there and I will consider the matter."

Most great lords need an extra horse or two, even if the beast be of the meaner sort. Lord Gilbert ordered the chapman's horse placed in an empty stall, and after inspecting the contents of the cart, commanded two grooms to take the goods to John Chamberlain's office, where he might hold them secure while I sought for some heir to the unidentified chapman. The empty cart was placed beside the castle curtain wall, behind the marshalsea, there to await disposition.

My stomach told me 'twas past time for my dinner, and as I departed the castle gatehouse the noon Angelus Bell rang from St. Beornwald's Church tower to confirm the time. Kate had prepared a roast of mutton, which I devoured manfully, though such flesh is not my favorite. I have never told this to Kate, as I dislike disappointing her. So I consumed my mutton and awaited another day and a dinner more to my pleasure.

I decided after dinner, of which a sizeable portion remained for my supper, to revisit the clearing in the forest where John Kellet and I found the cart, then travel east to Aston and Cote. Perhaps the chapman did business in the villages and some there would know of him, or perhaps his murderers lived there and might be found out.

The path to the forest took me past St. Andrew's Chapel, and as I approached the lychgate I saw the curate and another man leave the porch, the dead chapman between then upon the pallet. In a far corner of the churchyard was a mound of earth where a grave lay open to receive its unidentified tenant. I turned from the road, passed through the rotting lychgate, and became a mourner at the burial.

Kellet lifted his eyes from his task when I approached and this caused him to stumble as a toe caught some uneven turf. He tried to regain his balance while maintaining a grip on his end of the pallet, but was unable to do either. The priest was a man who, three years past, could draw a longbow and place arrows in a butt as well as any. It is unlikely he could do so now, or even break an arrow shaft across his knee. Kellet's gaunt frame seems hardly robust enough to keep him upright, much less sustain a burden, and the chapman had been a sturdy man.

Kellet had provided no shroud for the corpse. The priest gives away so much of his living that he probably had no coin with which to purchase a length of even the coarsest hemp. So when he dropped his end of the pallet the chapman rolled uncovered to the sod, face down.

GIBSONS AND DISTRIC
PUBLIC LIBRARY

I hastened to help Kellet to his feet, and together with his assistant we lifted the corpse back upon the pallet. But when the chapman's face was raised from the grass I saw there a thing which arrested my attention and caused his dying words to return to my mind. A small coin lay upon the turf where a moment before the corpse had lain face down.

When the dead man was again upon his pallet I searched in the grass and retrieved the coin. It was worn and corroded, and looked like no coin I had before seen. It was of tarnished silver, smaller than a penny, very near the size of a farthing.

Kellet and his assistant watched as I inspected the coin. The priest finally spoke, "How did that come to be here in the churchyard?"

"It fell from the dead man's lips when he was turned onto the grass," I replied.

"Is that what he meant when he said the felons had not got his coin? He had hid it in his mouth?"

"Perhaps."

"'Tis an odd thing," Kellet said.

"Aye. Words are inscribed upon it, and the profile of a king, but they are so worn I cannot make them out."

"Why would men do murder for a small silver coin?" the priest asked.

I shrugged and said, "That is the service Lord Gilbert requires of me, to find who would do such a thing on his lands, and why."

Chapter 2

When the chapman was properly buried I walked to Aston and Cote and learned there two things. The man was named John Thrale, and he visited Cote and Aston three or four times each year. October was the latest month he was likely to appear, as roads would soon be ankle-deep in mud and travel would be cold, wet, and unpleasant. No one knew of a certainty where he made his home. A crone of Aston thought he was of Abingdon, but I mistrusted her memory.

Shadows lay long upon the ground when I returned to Bampton and Galen House. Bessie had discovered that, with proper use of arms and legs, she could explore her surroundings. Without constant supervision she is likely to cause herself some harm, as the fire is warm and inviting upon the hearth on a chill autumn day. So it is with men, who must be guided by the Lord Christ, else they harm themselves with the appealing but perilous things of the world. Kate was pleased at my return, as she then had an assistant to contain our daughter's explorations, while she busied herself at the work of the house.

Kate asked what news, and I told her of the silver coin and learning the chapman's name. I showed Kate the coin, and lamented that the letters stamped upon it were illegible. Kate took the coin from me, studied it, then turned to the hearth. From a corner of the fireplace she took a dead, blackened coal, then lifted the lid from my chest and drew from it a sheet of the parchment upon which I record accounts of events in Bampton. She placed the coin upon our table, laid the parchment atop it, then lightly brushed the coal across the two. An imprint of the coin appeared, and some of the letters circling the coin became readable.

"CA_A_SIV ET F_ATR_S S_I" were discernible. With some study I was able to construe the letters which were worn away. The inscription read, "CARAVSIVS ET FRATRES SVI" – "Carausius and his brothers".

Such words I had never seen on a coin, but I knew their meaning. No wonder the letters were worn, for lying upon my table was a Roman coin more than one thousand years old. How had the murdered chapman come by it? And why would two or more men murder him for it? The coin was not likely of pure silver, and was small, so its worth to a silversmith would be slight. Few merchants would exchange goods for it as they would not know its value. Had the chapman done so, receiving the coin in trade for buttons or a comb? Mayhap, but such dealing would not lead men to slay him for possession of a coin of so little worth.

I voiced these thoughts to Kate as she bustled about, preparing our supper. I would find more mutton upon my trencher this evening, but for this I was prepared. Perhaps on the morrow Kate would prepare a custard. Hope is a dish near as tasty as any other.

"Would a man perish to save a coin from falling into the hands of thieves?" Kate asked when I had concluded my musing and fallen silent.

I had been considering why men would murder to possess such a coin. Kate wondered why a man would risk a beating and death to keep it. I could discover no ready answer to either question, for as I would not attack another man for such small gain, neither would I risk wounds from those who demanded it of me if I refused to give it up.

It is useful in solving a felony to be able to set one's self in the place of felon or victim. I could do neither.

Bessie awoke in the night, hungry, and so roused Kate from her sleep, but not me. I was already lying awake, sleepless, considering why possession of a small silver coin might lead to a man's murder. There must be, I thought, more to this death than I suspected.

The old woman of Aston had suggested Abingdon

as the chapman's home, and as this was my only clue as to his residence, I resolved next day to claim Bruce at the castle marshalsea and seek what information I might of John Thrale. The old horse was given to my use when I accepted Lord Gilbert Talbot's offer to serve as his bailiff at Bampton, and had carried me many miles in Lord Gilbert's service, once all the way to Exeter. The elderly beast seemed pleased to leave his dark stall this day, but I think he was equally happy when our journey ended at the New Inn on the market square in Abingdon.

I had warned Kate that my task would require two days to travel to Abingdon and to search for some kin of the slain chapman (if, indeed, he had made his home there), then return, for Bruce is grey at the muzzle and will not be hurried. Bruce had carried Lord Gilbert at Poitiers, twelve years past.

I thought John Thrale might be best known among competitors and those who sold goods like his own, so I saw Bruce quartered in the mews behind the New Inn, and after I had consumed half of a roasted capon from the kitchen, I sought some business which sold items similar to those I found in the chapman's cart. I discovered such a shop and manufactory but a hundred paces from the inn, on Bridge Street, and when I asked of John Thrale my search was ended. The proprietor knew Thrale, and was, in fact, the chapman's supplier for the buttons and buckles he sold in villages about the shire.

This haberdasher of Abingdon was not pleased to learn of the death of a reliable customer, and was full of questions regarding the chapman's demise. As there was information I desired of the man, I thought the exchange of information a fair bargain. In return for my recitation of what was known of John Thrale's death, the shopkeeper pointed me to his house which, I was informed, was but a short distance away, upon East St. Helen Street.

John Thrale's house differed from most on the street in but one way: behind, in a small toft, was another structure. This was the stable where Thrale kept horse and cart when he was not upon the roads seeking custom.

I had not thought to ask if Thrale was married, so thumped upon the door of his house to see if a wife would respond. Eventually a wife did, but not the chapman's. From the next house on the street, where a sign identified a pepperer's business, a woman appeared at the door, a child upon her hip, and said, "Ain't 'ome. On 'is rounds, is John."

"Is there no other, then, at home?" I asked.

The woman's eyes narrowed in suspicion at this. Why, she was clearly wondering, did some well-dressed man, who knew so little of John Thrale, seek him?

"Nay," she finally said. "What d'you want of 'im?"

I walked to the woman's door and replied, "I seek nothing of John Thrale. The man is dead. I am bailiff of the lands where he was found, and seek any wife or children so the goods discovered with him might be returned to them."

"Dead?" the woman frowned. "'E seemed well enough when 'e went off a week past."

"His health did not cause his death. Brigands set upon him on the road and murdered him."

The woman crossed herself at this news, and she whispered, "Murdered?"

"Aye. Had he a wife, or children?"

"'Ad a wife, but she and a child died o' plague near twenty years past, so 'e said. 'E was always on the road at 'is business an' never wed again. 'Though I have seen a woman about 'is place the past weeks. My Alfred told John 'twas dangerous work, to be on the roads alone with the goods in 'is cart. Said evil would come upon John soon or late."

"Had the chapman a brother or sister?"

"Aye, sisters, I think."

"Do they reside hereabouts?"

"Don't know. 'E never said much of 'em. Poor John only lived 'ere on the street since Lammastide. Didn't talk much, an' was never 'ome for long."

I thanked the woman for her time and turned my attention to the chapman's house. Perhaps within the dwelling there might be some evidence of the sisters to whom the contents of the chapman's cart might now belong. The windows were small, and covered by shutters which seemed fragile and easily torn aside. Prosperous families lived on East St. Helen Street, but John Thrale's house was one of the meanest, and in need of some repair.

I did not wish to call to myself the attention which pulling down a shutter would bring, so tried the door. It was securely shut, as I expected, even though there was no lock. It was barred from within. This being so, there must be another door, with a lock, at the rear, in the toft, else there would be no means of entry to the place.

I circled the house and saw my assumption correct. The rear of the house had but one small window, shuttered like those in the front, and in the middle of the wall was a door secured with a heavy iron latch. A large keyhole was centered in this lock, and when I tried the latch handle it would not move.

I had found no key in the chapman's cart, nor did Thrale carry it upon his person. Who would? Such a key is as long as my hand and the iron would weigh heavily upon a man.

My eyes found the barn at the rear of the toft and I left the house to search the place for a key. If I was the chapman, I thought, where would I hide a key that no man might discover it?

I would not hang it upon a nail, no matter how well hidden it might be. Such a place would surely be sought first.

The interior of the barn – which, in truth, was little more than a shed – was dark, stinking of manure, and shaded from the setting sun by the roof of the neighboring house. My eyes did not readily conform to the shadows, but when they did I surveyed the interior before moving to seek a key.

I saw a rusted nail, driven part-way into a corner

post, which in such place could serve no purpose but to hang upon it some object. But no key was there. Perhaps some time past Thrale, or some earlier inhabitant of the house, had hung a key there and some miscreant found it and looted the house while the owner was away. I saw no key in any other place, so began to search under beams and in hidden, shadowy places. I found no key.

Was the chapman a careless, slovenly fellow? Or had he allowed his beast's manure to accumulate upon the befouled straw so as to ensure no man was likely to plunge in his hand seeking a key beneath the filth? In a corner of the small barn I saw a shovel and rake, which tools the chapman must have used when he did clean the stable. I seized the rake and began to pull aside the fouled straw. Half-way across the shed I felt the wooden teeth of the rake strike some solid object. It was the key.

A moment later I entered the chapman's house. The interior was near pitch-black, for the autumn day was fading and the shutters over the windows were closed, permitting only narrow slivers of light to illuminate the place. The house was like those of most of King Edward's more prosperous subjects, however, so I did not require much light to find my way about.

The house had two rooms upon the ground floor, and the larger of these could be warmed by a fireplace. This was a puzzle, for itinerant chapmen do not usually possess such wealth as to afford a house of two floors, complete with fireplace, even if the house was in some disrepair.

In one corner of the larger room was a table, upon which rested a small chest and a cupboard. In another corner was the chapman's bed. A larger chest, complete with iron hasp and lock, occupied a third corner, close to the fireplace. Closer inspection of the table showed a cresset, and resting nearby, flint and steel for striking a fire.

I sought no heat, but desired more light, so unraveled a few threads from Thrale's bed covering, set these alight with sparks from the flint and steel, then transferred the flame to the wick of the cresset.

I opened the small chest. I sought there some document or letter which might lead me to Thrale's sisters. Likely he could not read, for I found nothing written there. Or perhaps he kept such things in his large chest. If so, I would not see them unless the chest was not locked, or I could find another key.

The chest was locked. The key for this box would not be so large as the one which opened Thrale's door, therefore easier hid. I returned to the small chest and inspected its contents. No key was there. I removed the bed covers and shook them out, to no purpose. I inspected the mattress, to see if some seam might show where a key was hid in the straw, and pounded upon the pillow to learn if a key might be among the goose feathers. I found nothing.

Next I overturned the bed to see if a key might be fixed somewhere under the frame. None was there. I moved the table and cupboard from the wall. Perhaps Thrale had hidden the key behind the cupboard. He had not, and running my fingers under the table showed no key there. I found only a splinter from the crudely made table.

I sucked upon the offended finger and surveyed the room. Did the chapman have this smaller key with him, and it lay now buried with him in his grave, or was it yet in his cart, and I had overlooked it when I took inventory of Thrale's possessions?

I next inspected the smaller ground-floor room, beyond the stairs. It was empty – no bench or chest or bed or cupboard was there. I climbed the stairs and with the flame of the cresset examined the two upper rooms. They were as bare as the small ground-floor room. John Thrale lived in but one room of this house. Why, at Lammastide, had he moved to a house much larger than his need?

I returned to the ground floor, studied again the larger room, and saw another place a man might hide a key. I bent to the hearth and from it drew a footed iron pot. Inside the pot I found the key. Whatever the chapman had stored in the larger chest, he had taken some pains that no man would open the box and discover his secret.

The key fit the lock poorly, and I thought at first it was a key to some other lock. But eventually, after some twisting and force, I made the key to work and drew open the chest. I was stunned at what I found there.

No letters or documents lay in the chest, but I found three leather pouches, a hammer near as large as a smith might use to pound out a horseshoe, a small, hand-operated bellows, and a tiny iron box, open at its top, narrow at the base, which was about the length of a finger and half as wide and deep.

I could not guess why such objects might be hid securely in such a chest, but thought the contents of the sacks might explain. They did so, for one sack contained thirty or more coins similar to the one which had dropped from the chapman's lips in St. Andrew's Chapel churchyard. Another sack held jewelry of various and wondrous designs: wrist bands, rings, and necklaces of gold, some of these studded with precious stones.

The third sack was smaller, and when I untied the thong which closed it I found within five small ingots of silver and one of gold, and seven small stones, one of which was green and much like an emerald. One glance at the small iron box told me whence these ingots had come. I took an ingot and fitted it to the box. It was a perfect match. After prising out the jewels, the silver and gold had been melted to fit the iron mold.

A bench lay against the wall beside the cupboard. I sat upon it and pondered this discovery. Much wealth was in this house. Why was this so, and where did the gold and silver come from? The silver and gold ingots were made of coins and jewelry like that found in the other two sacks. The chapman had used the bellows to create a fire upon his hearth hot enough to melt the coins and jewelry found in the other two sacks. What then did he do with them?

Some men had followed John Thrale and beat him to death in the forest to the east of Bampton. I now knew why. They knew of his secret wealth and desired to have it for themselves. They did not know all, else they would have come to this house and entered it while the chapman was away, as I had done. Unless they did not know where Thrale lived when he was not about the shire. But surely they knew some of what I had discovered, and battered the chapman to make him tell of what they did not know. This they had failed to do. Or had they?

Had they succeeded, this house would hold no gold or silver for me to find. No, John Thrale had died rather than give up his secret. And what was this secret? I understood some small part of the reason for the chapman's death, but there was more to know.

The day was near gone and little light now entered through the cracks between the ill-fitting shutters. Only the cresset gave illumination to the chamber. I took the three leather pouches from the larger chest, then locked it and replaced the key in the iron pot.

I then set in order the bed and its covering. When all was as it had been I departed the house with the three sacks, locked the door, replaced the key under the manure and straw, then set off for the marketplace and the New Inn. It was near time for curfew, and dark enough on the streets that the three pouches were invisible against my brown cotehardie.

I slept fitfully that night. You would have also with ten or twelve pounds' worth of gold and silver under your pillow, and a half-dozen other fellows snoring in the shared chamber. I was pleased when dawn showed through the cracks in the shutters, and I was able to rise and see to Bruce's preparation for returning to Bampton.

I fixed the three pouches to a belt under my cotehardie. This caused me to appear a trencherman, but seated upon Bruce, the effect was diminished and I was reassured that no man would guess the wealth I carried. I would return to Abingdon to seek John Thrale's sisters, but I was not prepared to leave the chapman's hidden wealth either at his house or at the inn while I searched for his family.

I drew Bruce to a halt before Galen House just past midday. The old horse would have continued down Bridge

Street, to the castle and his stall, so I was required to yank firmly upon the reins to turn him into Church View Street. Perhaps no harm would have been done had I gone first to the castle, then walked home with the three sacks. Or perhaps I might have left the bags with John Chamberlain, but I felt uneasy about doing so, for no reason I can now explain.

So I entered my house with three sacks of silver and gold, much to Kate's surprise, and took a moment to tell her how I came by such riches before I placed the pouches in my chest.

Kate was not much pleased when I told her that I had planned to return to Abingdon again on the morrow. Bruce would likely be unhappy about it as well. The old beast often seemed pleased to set out upon a journey, but was happiest when he entered the castle forecourt and knew a stall and bucket of oats awaited him. I was not enthusiastic about the journey myself. Had you spent a night amongst the snoring residents of the abbey's New Inn, you would understand. But a man was dead, murdered upon Lord Gilbert's land, and it was my duty to seek those who slew him, and return his possessions to his heirs, could they be found.

Chapter 3

Next day was Friday, so when I arrived at the New Inn there was no roasted capon for my dinner, but boiled stockfish. The fish had been poorly salted, or had been too long in the barrel, for no matter how hot the pot from which it was drawn, it stank of age. I could manage but a few bites, then completed my meal with two maslin loaves which, unlike the fish, seemed fresh.

I sought again the haberdasher who had supplied John Thrale with some of his wares, and questioned the fellow about the chapman. He knew of Thrale's sisters, but knew not of their abode. One, he thought, had wed a cobbler of some nearby town, but he could not remember that the chapman had ever named the place. The other sister lived nearby, he thought, perhaps in Abingdon, but he could not say of a surety. He thought their names were Julianna and Edith, but which lived near and which had wed a cobbler he knew not.

This information was not of much use, but was more than I had known when I picked at my stockfish. I next walked to East St. Helen Street, intending to again visit the pepperer's wife, to see if the two names might spur her memory. She answered my knock upon her door readily, probably assuming a customer, with her infant yet propped upon her ample hip. I saw recognition in her eyes. "You again?" she said.

"I have learned that John Thrale indeed had two sisters," I began. "Julianna and Edith. Do you remember him speaking of them? Where they might reside? His goods should be surrendered to them."

"Why would you need to know? He's nothing left now

for any kin, but for the house. You said 'e was murdered for 'is goods."

"Not so. The goods found in his cart are safe in Bampton Castle. And some possessions are in his house."

"No more. The night after you was last here two men entered John's house. My Alfred heard 'em in the toft, long past curfew. He thought to stop 'em, but saw there was two of them and but one of 'im, so come back to bed. Went out come morn yesterday an' saw they'd broke into the place."

"What was taken? Could your husband see in the night what they were about?"

"Nay, an' didn't stay to watch."

"Did he or any other inspect the house after the men had gone?"

"Nay. But them fellows come back the next day. Thought one was you. Tall, skinny fellow with, beggin' your pardon, a big nose."

"For what did they return?"

"Didn't find whatever they sought, I suppose. Asked of John, if he had kin nearby, just like you, an' wanted to know had 'e left goods with us for safekeeping. I told 'em, 'Nay,' on both counts, an' they went to every house on the street. Askin' the same questions, I'd guess."

"You can describe the men?"

"Oh, aye. Like I said, one was as tall as you an' slender, an' wore a beard trimmed short, like you. The other was not so tall, an' had more belly than a man ought. His beard needed trimming."

"What of their clothing?

"The tall one wore a brown cotehardie, much like yours, an' the fat one wore grey."

"What color was their hair?"

"Brown, both of 'em."

"Of what color were their caps?"

"Tall one wore red, the other wore blue."

I was about to thank the woman for her assistance when she added, "Told 'em another had been here day before, seekin' the same knowledge."

"What did they say when you told them this?"

"Asked who 'twas. Told 'em I knew not, that 'twas some bailiff where John was found murdered."

Here was a distressing announcement. If the two who had entered John Thrale's house were the men who had murdered him, they knew who it was who sought them, and if they knew of and coveted the gold and silver from his chest, they now knew where it might be if it was not found in Thrale's house. But of these villains I knew nothing but a description which might match a quarter of the men of Oxfordshire. I began to wish I had taken the three pouches to John Chamberlain in the castle for safekeeping.

I went to three other houses on East St. Helen Street to learn if any resident knew of Edith or Julianna. Only one resident had heard their names, and did not know more of them.

Before I returned to the New Inn I decided to see what damage was done to the chapman's house. I walked behind the place and saw that the shutters had been torn from the single small window which looked out upon the toft. The oiled skin which had closed the window to the chill October nights was ripped asunder. Likely the two men climbed in through the torn window.

I sought the shed, and with the rake tested the filthy straw until I found the key, where I had returned it two days past. Here was evidence that my assumption was correct, for thieves would not trouble themselves to replace a key, and had they found it they would not have awakened a neighbor by forcing entry to Thrale's house.

I opened the door farther, entered the chapman's house, and saw before me a scene of ruin. The bed was overturned and mattress and pillow were torn apart. Straw and feathers littered the floor. The table and cupboard were likewise displaced, and the table stood askew, missing a leg. The small chest was gone from the table, but I soon found what remained of it.

When the felons had failed to discover a key they chose to force the large chest open. This they must have done by battering it with the smaller chest and a leg from the table. Splintered remains of the small chest littered the floor about the larger chest, which lay open, its top demolished. The fractured table leg lay propped in the ruins of the chest. I peered into the chest and saw there the hammer and the small iron box. The bellows lay apart, near the opposite wall of the room, as if it had been thrown there in disgust. No wonder the neighbor had been awakened in the night. Breaking open such a chest would rouse all the street, but none had intervened. Violence heard in the night will keep most men behind their own barred doors. The destruction they heard might be visited upon them if they thought to meddle in the business.

I left all as it was, shut the door behind me, and left the place. I did not trouble myself to dig the key from the straw to relock the door. To what purpose?

If neither a man with whom John Thrale had done business, nor the chapman's neighbors, could direct me to his kin, I had no other thought as to how I might discover them. This concern occupied my mind as I returned to the inn, and so distracted was I by this failure that I came close to encountering a man upon the street before the inn whom I preferred to avoid. It was not yet dark, so I saw clearly a group of four men walking twenty or so paces before me. Much banter and laughter accompanied them. One of the four was taller than most, and wore a yellow cap with a long liripipe coiled stylishly upon his head. His friends also wore fashionable clothing. These young gentlemen entered the New Inn and as they did so I got a better view of the taller man's misshapen ear, which I recognized with a shock.

I remembered the man's profile as well, and his great, hawk-like nose. The ear was familiar to me, as I had sewn it to the fellow's head when Odo Grindcobbe had come near to knocking it loose from his skull, supposing the man to be me. It was Sir Simon Trillowe who walked before me into the New Inn.

Sir Simon is a vengeful sort. He blames me, I think,

that an ear juts from the side of his head in unsymmetrical fashion. 'Tis not easy work to stitch a man's torn ear in place, and his was the first I had ever attempted. Perhaps I will do better should the need arise again.

Sir Simon also harbors a grudge against me because I won Kate Caxton, when he had set his cap for her also. I was outnumbered four to one, so decided prudence would be a virtue. Perhaps some would call it cowardice, but I passed by the door, walked through a gate to the mews, and made my bed that night in the straw beside Bruce. He seemed glad of the company, and unlike others who occupied the upper story of the inn, Bruce did not snore.

I thought it unlikely that Sir Simon would yet be found in the public room of the inn, but entered cautiously next morn in case it might be so. He was gone, and I wished to be away from the place myself, so I downed a cup of ale, then visited the baker across the marketplace for a fresh loaf which, after I had saddled Bruce, I ate as the horse ambled from the town.

Once again I arrived in Bampton just past the hour for my dinner. But this day I first left Bruce in the hands of the castle marshalsea, and so could enjoy my meal with no other obligation to intrude. That was not precisely true, for as I consumed the stewed capon which Kate set before me, my eyes traveled to my iron-bound chest and I remembered the three pouches there.

Lord Gilbert wishes to be kept informed of events upon his lands, so I kissed my Kate and left Galen House for the castle. I found my employer entertaining guests in the hall, and decided he was not likely ready to hear a complete recitation of my travels and discoveries, slight as those were. So I told him the rudiments of what I had learned, then bowed my way out of the presence of this noble entourage.

For the remainder of the day I occupied myself with manor business. John Holcutt, Bampton's reeve, is competent to oversee these affairs, but he would be employed upon his own land and I might relieve him of some of his labor if I saw to manor concerns.

Final plowing of fallow fields was nearly complete, and upon Monday villeins would begin to sow wheat and rye upon Lord Gilbert's demesne lands. It is a risk to sow crops so late in the year. If no rain fell soon, the seed would be much delayed in sprouting, so that when the chill of winter approached, it would rot in the cold soil rather than take root and grow.

Some villeins not engaged in plowing were gathering wheat stubble from the August harvest to mix with hay as winter fodder for Lord Gilbert's beasts. A few tenants who owed boon work were at this task as well, and would soon be doing the same work upon their own strips. These laborers looked up from their toil as I passed by, and tipped a cap or tugged a forelock in greeting. They needed no advice from me about their work, anymore than I needed their counsel before setting a broken arm.

Darkness was near when I completed my observation of Lord Gilbert's manor, and herders who had been in the forest with their swine, pannaging, were driving the beasts to their sties for the night. I walked to Galen House well content with my lot. I had wed a beautiful lass, and was father to a healthy babe. I owned freehold a house worth ten pounds, and another of like worth in Oxford, part of Kate's dower, a gift of her father when we wed, which brought twenty shillings each year rent. I did have an obligation to seek who murdered John Thrale, but the responsibility did not undermine my spirits on this fine autumn evening as I approached Galen House, Kate, Bessie, and my supper.

I suspected some mischief as I came close to Galen House and saw the front door standing open to the chill evening. I broke into a run, plunged through the door, and found Kate trussed upon the rushes of the floor, her mouth stuffed with a gag made of fabric ripped from Bessie's tiny gown. The rushes were disordered where Kate had thrashed about to free herself, but this she could not do, for her wrists were bound tight together and then to a leg of our table. Our daughter lay beside her mother, unharmed but for the damage to her clothing. As I ran to free Kate I saw, from the corner of my eye, my chest standing open.

I first drew the gag from Kate's mouth, and she immediately shouted that I must make haste and be after them. I made haste, rather, to free her wrists and ankles from their bonds, then asked what had befallen her.

"Two men," she gasped, rubbing chaffed wrists, "came upon me unannounced and asked for you. I told them you were at the castle, upon Lord Gilbert's business."

"They did not leave to seek me?"

"Nay. They exchanged glances, then one seized me and put a hand over my mouth while the other picked Bessie from the floor."

"What then?"

"The man who held Bessie approached the hearth and said I was not to cry out or he would pitch her into the fire." Kate shook as she recalled the moment, and I held her close to calm her quivering.

"My captor then released me, and told me to lie face-down upon the rushes and be silent, else his companion would set Bessie in the fire. I did as he demanded, and from the corner of my eye watched as he moved about the room. He soon saw your chest, opened it, and I heard him tell the other he'd found what they sought."

"The three sacks?"

"Aye. He set them upon the floor before me when he bound me."

"This was how long ago?"

"Not an hour past. They were mounted. I heard them ride off."

I cursed myself that I had not sent Thrale's sacks to the castle when I first learned from the pepperer's wife that I was known to men who sought what I had found in the chapman's house.

"It is nearly dark... too late to follow upon the roads, but I will ask on Church View Street and the High Street if any saw which way they went."

"Do so. Do not fear to leave me. I am not harmed, but

for tender wrists where I was tightly bound."

"Describe the rogues, so I may ask wisely."

"One was tall and slender, the other short and stout. The tall man's beard was trimmed close."

"And he wore a brown cotehardie and a red cap," I added, "while the shorter man wore grey, with a blue cap."

Kate's eyes widened. "Aye... the one who held Bessie to the fire, he wore a blue cap. How did you know?"

"The same men did hamsoken to John Thrale's house in Abingdon. A neighbor described them."

"Are these the men who slew the chapman?"

"So I believe. They tried to learn of the coins and wealth from him, and beat him to make him tell."

"But if the coins were in his house," Kate mused, "why not enter while he was away? Why waylay him on the road and beat him?"

"It was not only the coins he had already found that they sought, I think. The chapman discovered some cache of coins and jewelry in his travels, and each time he did the circuit of villages he renewed his supply."

"What did he do with them?"

"Melted them to ingots in a small iron box, then sold them to a silversmith, I'll wager."

"So these villains knew what you found in the chapman's house, and thought it might be here?"

"Aye. Knew, or guessed. I am a fool. The neighbor's wife told them the bailiff of the manor where John Thrale was found had visited his house. Men who will beat another to death will not so easily give up the pursuit of the loot they seek."

"You think they knew it was you, then, who entered the chapman's house and took away his wealth?"

"Not then, but they knew he died upon Bampton Manor. When they arrived this day the first man they met upon the street could tell them my name and where I was to be found."

"I am glad you were not here," Kate shuddered.

"Why so?"

"You would have tried to do some manly thing when they threatened to harm Bessie. They would not have hesitated to beat you as they did the chapman. I might now be a widow."

I could say nothing, for I suspect Kate spoke true. Fathers do not always behave wisely when wife or children are threatened. There is a field, the Green Ditch, to the north of Holywell Street in Oxford, where a scaffold is raised whenever felons are hanged. I vowed to see the miscreants dangle there. For the murder they did, or for the insult to my house, my wife, my child? I could not say which was the sharper spur.

I left Galen House and found the place on Church View Street where Kate's assailants had tethered their horses. 'Twas near dark, and the evening Angelus Bell rang while I studied the dust where horses had left imprints of their hooves. Close inspection showed that one beast wore a broken shoe, as if the horse had galloped over cobbles and snapped off a small part of a horseshoe. This shoe was not so malformed as to require immediate replacement, but enough to distinguish the animal from any other.

I cast my thoughts back to the discovery of the chapman's cart, and the hoof-prints in the road. I could not recall a mark made there by a broken horseshoe, but other matters concerned me at the time, so I might have seen such a print and taken no notice of it.

I rose from studying the dust and saw Martyn the cobbler peering at me from before his shop. He was surely astonished to see Lord Gilbert's bailiff on hands and knees in the street. I stood, motioned to him to hold his place, and hurried the hundred paces to where he waited.

"Two men on horseback, not of Bampton," I began. "About an hour past. Did you see such men?"

"Aye."

I thought he might, for he has placed his bench before a shutter which, when lifted, provides light and looks out on the street. He sees all who pass on Church View Street.

"Did one wear a red cap, the other blue?"

"Aye."

"When they reached the High Street, which way did they go?"

"East, through the marketplace, toward St. Andrew's Chapel."

I had suspected that, thanked the cobbler for his time, and hastened back to Galen House and my affronted family. Kate awaited me upon a bench by the hearth, nursing Bessie. She looked up expectantly when I entered, but I had little to tell her. The broken horseshoe, which track I intended to follow next day even though it would be Sunday, was my only discovery.

Chapter 4

Kate heard the news without comment. She had not expected, I think, when we wed, that she would be attacked in her house by those whom, in the course of my duties, I had provoked. And this assault was not the first. Would she have accepted my suit had she known what might follow? I sat beside her upon the bench and, in answer to my unspoken question, she rested her head upon my shoulder.

I awoke in the night to the sound of rain upon our bed-chamber window. I was at first pleased to hear this, but as I collected my wits I realized that the shower would obliterate the tracks I hoped to follow come morning. This was no misty drizzle, but a cloudburst, and it was not over and done with quickly. A gentle rain yet fell when Kate and I left our bed at dawn.

I went immediately to our door and walked out into the street, where the evening before I had discovered the track of a broken horseshoe. No trace of the mark remained. There was nothing to follow, no way to discover where the villains had gone once past the marketplace.

I was sure they were of Abingdon, or thereabouts, and was determined to seek them. But not alone. They had proven what villainy they would do. After mass I would seek Arthur at the castle and require him to accompany me.

Arthur had proven himself a useful companion in the matter of Master John Wyclif's stolen books, and always seemed eager when I found it necessary to have his aid. He is a groom to Lord Gilbert, but as he is wed he is not required to travel when Lord Gilbert takes residence at Goodrich or Pembroke. I did not seek a violent confrontation with the miscreants who slew John Thrale and invaded my house, but to apprehend such men might require some compulsion. Arthur is a good man to have at one's side in such a case, thick-set and ready for a brawl.

After mass and a dinner of roasted capon I sought Lord Gilbert, told him of the assault on Kate, and requested permission to take Arthur from his duties at the castle. As is his custom, Lord Gilbert raised one eyebrow as I related the previous day's events. Three years past, when I was new to Bampton, I had tried to emulate him in this. I failed.

My employer was florid with anger when I completed the tale. His brows were now lowered in a scowl, and he seemed ready to leap from his chair to accompany Arthur and me to Abingdon.

"Take Arthur, and any other you may need," he said when I fell silent. "No man will threaten your Kate and Bessie in such a manner and escape, if I can do aught about it."

"Arthur is worth two in a scrap," I said.

"Aye, he is that. And he's no dullard, even so he is low-born."

Arthur, as I suspected, was eager to leave the drudgery of castle labor and set off for Abingdon. I told him to arm himself with a dagger, and be ready to leave next day at dawn. My warning that violence might find us, or we might find violence, did not seem to trouble the man. He raised his head, grinned, and promised to be ready at the appointed time. Men who generally win their fights do not much fear being drawn into another.

I visited the marshalsea and told a page to have Bruce and an old palfrey ready next morn, then set off for Galen House. I was through the gatehouse and crossing the castle forecourt when a disagreeable thought came to me. What if the men I sought learned of my pursuit before I found them? Might they seek vengeance upon me by returning to Bampton, knowing I was in Abingdon, and do harm to Kate and Bessie? I could not leave my wife and daughter alone.

Lord Gilbert was in the solar, with Lady Petronilla,

when I returned to the castle. I explained my worry, and he readily agreed that Kate and Bessie should remove to the castle until I had discovered the men who murdered the chapman and assaulted Kate.

When I was a bachelor I went where I would, when I would. It is difficult to learn a new manner of living, to think of others before making a decision, but after nearly two years since I wed Kate under the porch of the Church of St. Beornwald, I was beginning to consider new obligations before my own plans.

After a supper of bruit of eggs I told Kate she must leave Galen House and lodge with Bessie in the castle, in my old bachelor chamber. She was not pleased with the move, as I knew she would not be, and her lips drew tight across her teeth while I told her what she was to do. But when I pointed out that the men who had attacked her and threatened Bessie might return in my absence, she rubbed her chafed wrists absent-mindedly and reluctantly agreed to my decision.

I told Kate to prepare what she wished to take to the castle, and that next day she should expect a cart from the marshalsea to move her thence. I reminded her to lock the door to Galen House upon leaving, to which admonition she rolled her eyes. Such advice was probably unnecessary, but the longer I am wed, and the more I consider my responsibilities to Kate and Bessie, the more cautious I seem to become.

Next morn I kissed my Kate farewell, and was pleased that her embrace did not betoken so much displeasure as I had feared. At the castle I found Uctred, another of Lord Gilbert's grooms, and told him to take a horse and cart to Galen House, there to load what Kate wished taken to my old chamber off the Bampton Castle great hall. Arthur and I then mounted our horses and set off across Shill Brook.

The journey took us past St. Andrew's Chapel, where I saw John Kellet at work, his robe drawn up and tucked into the cord he used for a belt, mending the tumbled-down wall about the churchyard. He looked up as we approached, sucking upon a thumb as would a babe. Nettles grew in profusion against the wall. I believe the priest had found one as we came into view.

"Good day, Master Hugh," Kellet greeted me amiably, and nodded recognition to Arthur. "A fine day, after the rain."

I agreed that this was so, and asked the priest if he had seen two men ride this way late Saturday.

"Many folk pass by here," he said. "But not so many mounted. There were but two men on horseback toward evening."

"Did one wear a red cap, the other blue?"

Kellet thought for a moment. "Aye... so they did. Passed the chapel twice, first going toward Bampton, then, as I was ready to sound the Angelus Bell, I saw them ride east."

"Did they ride easy, or seem hurried?"

"They seemed in some haste. They'd not spurred their beasts to a gallop, but they did not travel at an easy pace. More like a canter. Fast enough to raise the dust as they passed."

No man would raise dust upon the road this day. I had searched the lane from Bruce's back for any sign of a print made by a broken horseshoe, but between Bampton and St. Andrew's Chapel the only impressions upon the road were the footprints of those who had walked this way since the rain ceased shortly after dawn on Sunday.

I thanked Kellet for this news, bid him good day, and set off for Abingdon. The curate bent again to his labor on the toppled wall, and I marveled once more at the change in the man. The John Kellet I knew two years past would not have troubled himself to repair the churchyard wall of St. Andrew's Chapel even were there no nettles to impede the work.

It was midday when Arthur and I led the horses to the mews behind the New Inn. We found a dinner of pottage of eggs in the public room.

The pepperer's wife had said that John Thrale

had lived in the house on East St. Helen Street since Lammastide. I wondered where he had made his home before, so sought the woman to learn if she knew. Before I set about this task I told Arthur to walk the streets of Abingdon with his eyes fixed to the ground, seeking the track of a horse with a broken shoe. If he found such a mark he was to follow the track, if he could, to see where it led. In the marketplace before the New Inn I drew in the mud a copy of the misshapen horseshoe, then set off for East St. Helen Street while Arthur circled the marketplace before setting off to explore side streets.

The door to the pepperer's shop was open, the owner at work grinding peppercorns and sneezing as a result of his labors. The man's wife was absent, but he was as likely to know where Thrale had lived before Lammastide as his spouse.

"Ock Street," he replied when I asked. "Near to the river, with the tanners."

If John Thrale had lived near tanners it was no wonder he chose to move his residence from the stench of that occupation. I thanked the pepperer for this information, bid him good day, and followed his directions to Ock Street.

Tanners and rope-makers lived along Ock Street – a convenient location, for water was at hand in the river and both trades used large amounts. Near to a place where the river curved close to the street I found a florid-faced tanner fleshing a hide, greeted him, and asked if he knew a chapman named John Thrale.

"Oh, aye… don't live near anymore, though. Bought 'imself a house freehold over on East St. Helen Street."

The tanner shook his head gently as he said this, as if to add to the incredulity in his voice.

"Where did he live before he went to St. Helen Street?"

"Just over there."

The tanner pointed to a hut across the street and two houses closer to the marketplace. There was but one window in the hovel, and a broken shutter hung askew over it. Weeds grew in the dirt before the house, and in several places the thatching of the roof was so thin that the contour of rafters could be seen.

"If you seek 'im, he'll likely be on 'is rounds. Travels about, does John, sellin' stuff to folks as don't have shops or markets in their village. Might be 'ome, but I'd doubt so. Winter comin', 'e'll be at 'is business while roads is firm."

"Have you seen the chapman since he moved from here?"

"Nay. Why'd 'e come by here if 'e didn't have to? Never knew there was such profit in sellin' buckles an' buttons an' such."

"Did he sell the house when he moved away?" I asked. "Looks like no one lives there now."

"Nay. Belongs to the abbey, as does all the 'ouses here on Ock Street. Paid rent, like the rest of us. Abbey wasn't pleased to see 'im go, I'm thinkin'. Empty 'ouses all through the town."

"Most of these the abbey owns?"

"Aye. Good for us who be yet alive, after plague come twice. Rents is supposed to be fixed," the tanner put a finger aside his nose and winked, "but a man – or an abbot – with an empty 'ouse'll do what's needful to find a tenant. Not that abbot Peter" (here the tanner spat upon the ground) "is pleased to do so."

I turned to gaze again at the decrepit house where John Thrale had once lived. Had I lived in such a place, and found a treasure which would permit me to reside elsewhere, I might also have resisted losing the wealth to others, even to the point of death. The tanner turned to follow my gaze, and could hold his curiosity no longer.

"Why do you seek John?"

"I don't. I know where he is."

The tanner was silent for a moment, a puzzled expression upon his face. "You'd know more of John was you to ask 'im, not me."

"Not so. He lies in a churchyard near to Bampton. I helped bury him. He was waylaid upon the road and murdered."

The tanner crossed himself and studied his feet. "Poor John," he said softly. "An' him doin' so well at 'is trade, too. 'Spect that's why some brigands set upon 'im, eh? To seize 'is goods an' money?"

"Aye. As you say. I have heard that he had sisters. Do you know where they might be found? Some of his goods were not taken, and I seek heirs so as to give what remains of Thrale's possessions to them."

The tanner pursed his lips and scratched his head, shoving aside his cap to do so. "'E did speak of kin, but where they may be I cannot tell. Gone often, was John. Would hitch 'is cart to a leather harness 'e made to go over 'is shoulders an' about 'is waist, then off 'e'd go."

"He drew his cart himself?"

"Aye... well, not for some months. 'Bout Whitsuntide 'e bought a new cart, an' a horse to pull it. Had no barn; kept the beast in the house with 'im till 'e went to St. Helen Street."

"The new cart was larger than the old, then?"

"Oh, aye. Wouldn't be pullin' the new cart by hisself. I bought the old one from 'im. Use it to haul hides about. There it sits."

The tanner pointed behind his house to a shed where, at the side, a small cart was parked against a fence. "Gave three pence for it," the tanner added.

John Thrale, near the end of May, had come into money. He bought first a horse and cart, then moved to a larger house in a respectable part of town, for which he paid perhaps as much as ten pounds. The tanner spoke true. An itinerant chapman was not likely to live so well on the profits of his business. And some men more dangerous than the tanner had noticed this also.

I bid the tanner good day and left him to his work. Perhaps a visit to the silversmith on East St. Helen Street should be my next call. The silversmith was not likely to know of Thrale's sisters, but he might be the buyer of the ingots the chapman had made upon his hearth.

He was not, or if he was he did not wish to say so. I asked the silversmith first how he came by the metal which he fashioned into spoons and cups and jewelry. This was a poor beginning. The man was immediately on his guard, which was, perhaps, a clue that some of his supply was acquired in a manner unacceptable to the King.

"From Devon," he said warily, "an' from folks as wish to sell what they may have so to raise funds."

"From mines in Devon?"

"Aye. Cornwall, too."

"And merchants bring bars of silver from the mines to craftsmen such as you?"

"Aye. King's seal stamped on 'em to show taxes paid."

"If a silversmith purchased a silver ingot without the King's seal…"

"He'd pay a fine."

"But if you purchased silver from some man in financial embarrassment, what then?"

"No law against that, so long as the silver was 'is to sell, an' not stolen."

"Have you done so recently?"

The man's eyes narrowed again, and the wary tone returned to his voice. "Not for many months. Next time the King demands taxes to war with France there'll be folk wantin' to sell their plate, but while we're at peace… well, mostly at peace, I'm not offered much."

"Did you know the chapman, John Thrale, who purchased a house a few doors from here at Lammastide?"

"A chapman? On East St. Helen Street?"

"Aye."

"Oh… I've seen a fellow with cart an' horse nearby the house. That him?"

"Aye, probably. Did he offer to sell silver to you?"

"Where would a chapman come by silver? 'Course,

had he any, he might want to sell so's to have coin to buy more stock."

The coin which had fallen from John Thrale's mouth was in my purse. Thieves had the others, but that first coin I had kept with me. I withdrew it from my purse and held it before the silversmith.

"Have you seen such a coin since Whitsuntide?"

The silversmith took the coin and squinted at it, turned it over, then held it at arm's length. He was not a young man. He would soon need to purchase eyeglasses to see work close before his face.

"Nay, never seen such a coin."

More conversation with the silversmith yielded no acknowledgment that the man had ever purchased silver, or any jewel or gold, from John Thrale. I believed him. But what did Thrale do with the ingots he so laboriously made?

Arthur is not a man to miss a meal, so I expected to find him awaiting me at the New Inn. Some things in life are predictable, if others are not. Arthur awaited me before the inn. We made a supper of wheaten bread and cheese, and ale, and sought our beds. Arthur had seen no mark of a broken horseshoe, though he had prowled Abingdon's streets with his head down till dark.

The man who falls to sleep first in an abbey guest house or inn will sleep the best. I lay awake while others, including Arthur, fell to sleep and filled the chamber with their snoring. I did not find rest until some time after the abbey sacrist rang the bell for vigils.

Chapter 5

During a wakeful hour in the night another method of discovering John Thrale's sisters came to me. He had purchased his house on East St. Helen Street from someone. Perhaps the seller knew more of the chapman than his name and the weight of his purse.

Monks do not break their fast, but after lauds set about their work until prime and terce, after which they take their dinner. As the abbey owned the New Inn, the guest master there saw no need to offer a loaf to us who sought lodging there. We could live as monks and be grateful for the well-thatched roof over our heads in the night.

A few paces from the New Inn is an ale house, and across the marketplace a baker has his shop, so we were able to eat and slake our thirst. In a busy town any print of a broken horseshoe upon the street would likely be soon obliterated, but having no better plan, I sent Arthur to roam Abingdon's streets again, and told him to keep to the better sections of the town. No poor man would own a horse, broken shoe or not, and there would be small chance of finding the mark I sought on a street of paupers.

I set off again for East St. Helen Street and the pepperer's shop.

"Good day," the fellow smiled. He could not be certain I would make no purchase some other day, so greeted me pleasantly, as he would any customer.

"Aye, so 'tis," I replied. "And a good day to you, also. John Thrale" – the pepperer crossed himself when he heard his neighbor's name – "lived next door since Lammastide. Who owned the house before him?"

"A widow. Husband died when plague returned six years past. A tailor, was Walter."

"Where does the woman make her home now?"

"Went off to Oxford to live with a son, Thomas. He's a tailor, also. Shop on St. Michael's Street, near to the Northgate, I hear tell. Maud tried to keep Walter's business, she bein' a good seamstress upon a time, but she's the disease of the bones, an' it pained her to ply a needle. Knuckles was all swollen."

"How long was the house empty?"

"Near two years since Maud went to Oxford. There's more'n one house stands empty in the town. She was right pleased to find a buyer, I'm thinkin'. No one to care for the place since Maud left, an' she could do little enough the last few years she was there."

"John Thrale got a good price, then?"

"Oh, aye. Six pounds, four, I heard. Don't know what'll become of the place now. Thatchin' is goin' bad, an' rafters will soon rot, does no one see to it."

The previous owner of Thrale's house would be able to tell me nothing of his kin, being two years gone from Abingdon before the chapman made his purchase, so there was no need to seek her. I left the pepperer with no other scheme in mind to seek either John Thrale's sisters or the felons who slew him. As I stood in the street, pondering what I might do next, my eyes wandered to Thrale's empty house. The shutters, closed, were in need of repair and did not fit tightly against each other. In the crack between the shutters of the left-side window I thought I saw movement, but when I cast my eye back to the fissure all was dark. Perhaps I had imagined a cheek and eye peering out at me?

But perhaps not. Had the chapman's murderers come back to search again Thrale's house? I had no pressing business, so decided to investigate the house. Even if no person was within its walls, perhaps a close examination might reveal some clue I had missed which might lead to sisters or murderers.

I walked quietly and warily to the rear of the house. I did not really believe that some man was in the house, thinking my imagination or some play of light and shadow responsible for the apparition in the opening between shutters.

The window, missing the ripped skin which had closed it, was open to the cool breeze. It was also open to sounds. My cautious steps were silent, but not so the person inside the house. I neared the open window and heard soft sobbing from within the place.

I crept near the window and peered through the opening. The broken window covering and the cracks between closed shutters provided enough light that I could see the chamber and its inhabitant clearly. A woman sat upon the floor, her back to a wall, and wept into her apron. I felt guilty for intruding upon her grief.

Here, I thought, is one of John Thrale's sisters. I was wrong. My error did not trouble me much when I learned of it, as I am become accustomed to the blunders, great and small, I make while investigating felonies upon Lord Gilbert's lands.

The woman seemed to sense that some man looked upon her. She lifted her head abruptly, peered at the window, and drew a startled breath when she saw me gazing down upon her.

The situation required that I speak first. "Pardon me. I did not mean to encroach upon your sorrow," I said through the window.

The woman scrambled to her feet, wiped her eyes again, and asked in a quavering voice, "Who are you?"

The woman who spoke was perhaps near thirty years old, and comely for a woman of her years.

"I am Hugh de Singleton." This announcement would mean nothing to the woman, so I continued, "I am a surgeon, and bailiff to Lord Gilbert Talbot at his manor in Bampton. And you," I added, "must be Edith or Julianna?"

The woman's eyes opened wide. "Nay," she said. "No sister."

She was silent for a moment, as was I, having had my assumption of her identity so demolished. "No sister," she repeated softly. "What does a bailiff from Bampton seek in this house?"

"Thieves and murderers," I replied. This was a blunder, but when speaking to females I seem often to find the wrong thing to say, and say it before considering the consequence. Some men seem not to have this affliction. I envy them.

The consequence in this case was a renewed flood of tears. As I had already spoken unwisely, I thought it prudent to say no more for a time. I held my tongue, and when the woman was able to contain her weeping she again spoke.

"Do you know what has become of John?"

The answer to that question should not be delivered through a window, I thought. "Aye," I said, and went to the door, which had remained unlocked since felons had ransacked the house.

"John Thrale," I continued, when I stood before her in the house, "lies in a grave in a churchyard near to Bampton."

"Dead? John is dead?"

The woman began to sway unsteadily. She seemed likely to swoon, and I made ready to catch her before she toppled to the rushes. But she steadied herself, choked out a great sob, then spoke again.

"What has befallen my John?"

Her John? The pepperer's wife said the chapman was not married.

"Did he take ill upon his rounds? He was well when he set out. Did some sickness strike him down?"

The woman thought of more questions as she spoke. "Why does a bailiff visit his house? And why," she glanced about the room, "is John's house so ruined? Some felons have done hamsoken while John was gone. Do you seek them? Why does a bailiff from Bampton seek villains here, in Abingdon? John is dead?"

The woman fell silent, and then stumbled to the chapman's ruined bed, where she sat and renewed her sobs.

"You spoke of John Thrale as 'My John.' A neighbor said he was not wed."

The woman seized control of her emotions and answered, "The banns was to be read at St. Helen's Church soon as John returned. Said he'd be home today. I came to greet 'im, and found all this ruin, an' no John. Was about to begin to try an' set things right when you came."

"So many tears for a broken table and chest, and torn mattress and pillow? Did you guess some harm had come to him?"

"Nay. Thought he'd be home soon."

"Why, then, such sorrow?"

The woman looked from me to the corner where fragments of the larger chest were mixed with pieces of the small chest and the table leg which had been used to batter it open. "Stolen," she sniffled. "Wealth we was to use to repair the house."

"Ah... you wept for the silver coins and jewelry Thrale had locked in his chest?"

My greatest success in this interview seemed be in regularly causing this woman's eyes to open wide in wonderment, followed by a renewed flow of tears.

"How did you know what was in John's chest?" she sobbed.

I sat on the ripped mattress beside the woman and explained my presence there. I told her of John Thrale's death (leaving out that information which could only cause her more sorrow), my discovery of his cache of coins and jewelry, the attack upon my wife and child, and the theft of the chapman's hoarded wealth.

"You knew of the silver and gold Thrale possessed," I concluded. "Where did he come by it?"

The woman's tears had begun again when I told her of the chapman's death, but by the time I concluded the sad tale she had composed herself again.

"Didn't tell me. I asked. Said as how he knew women like to gossip. If I didn't know where his wealth come from, I couldn't tell another, he said. All I know is, when he come home from makin' rounds to sell goods, he'd have more coins an' such."

"What is your name?"

"Amice... Amice Thatcher."

"You never wed?"

"Nay. I'm a widow. Husband dead three years now, an' two children to feed."

"How do you live?"

"Brew ale. Keeps me an' children alive."

"John Thrale was older than you, was he not?"

"Aye. But a good man is... was John."

"And with the supply of Roman coins he had found, he could ease your life."

"'Tis hard for a widow. You'd not understand."

She spoke true. It is difficult to put one's self into another's place. From what I knew of the chapman, and what I'd seen of his corpse, he was a decade older than Amice Thatcher, perhaps more. Unlikely he would have attracted a comely widow if he yet lived near the tanners on Ock Street and drew his tiny cart about the shire harnessed to it like a beast.

"Did you keep company with John Thrale upon Abingdon's streets?"

Amice frowned at the question, and I explained. "The men who overturned this house, and who threatened my wife and child and stole the coins I took from this place, they will not be content until they know where John found the treasure. They may seek you, and will not be satisfied if you tell them you know not where John discovered the hoard."

"They would deal with me as they did poor John?"

"Aye, and threaten harm to your children if you do not tell."

Amice shuddered, as well she might. "What am I to do? I cannot tell what I do not know. Perhaps these men will not find me."

"Perhaps. But was I you, I would seek safety until the villains are found out."

"Where am I to go? I cannot leave off brewing. I have little enough to feed my children as is."

"I will think on it. Meanwhile I will see you to your house. When I have devised some scheme for your safety I will seek you."

"I live in the bury, with other poor folk... beyond the marketplace."

I had begun to see foes everywhere, so when Amice and I left the house I peered cautiously into the street to see if two men – one slender and wearing a red cap, the other stout, wearing a blue cap – were upon East St. Helen Street. A monk, perhaps the almoner, seeking poor folk, walked the street, followed by two men. Only later did it occur to me that poor folk would not likely be found on East St. Helen Street.

We hurried away to the marketplace and the New Inn, where Arthur awaited. I called to him to join us, and together we escorted Amice Thatcher to her house. I told her to remain there until I returned. She agreed readily, having had time to consider what trouble might come if John Thrale's assailants found her.

There is much poverty on the lanes beyond the marketplace. Little wonder Amice was eager to wed if the sacrament would take her from the bury to East St. Helen Street. Her tears had been for John Thrale, I suppose, but perhaps also for shattered hopes of escape.

Arthur and I returned to the New Inn and between mouthfuls of pottage I related the morning's events to him. While I explained, a way to provide for Amice Thatcher's safety occurred to me.

'Tis but a few paces from the New Inn to St. John's Hospital. I found the hospital porter and asked that he fetch the infirmarer. The man looked down his nose at me, or tried to, but as I stood half a head taller than him, this he found difficult to do. He did make a manful effort. At last he deigned to reply.

"The New Inn, just beyond the gatehouse, serves travelers."

"Aye, and we are lodged there. It is accommodation for another I seek."

The porter made no reply. I believe his instructions were to permit as few folk as possible to enter the hospital. When Amice Thatcher was safely in the hospital, this hostile reception might serve to protect her – if she was first permitted to enter the place.

"I am Hugh de Singleton," I said. "Surgeon, and bailiff to Lord Gilbert Talbot at his manor of Bampton. It is Lord Gilbert's business which brings me here."

"Lord Gilbert wishes lodging in the abbey? I will send for Abbot Peter. He will wish for Lord Gilbert to be his guest. When shall I say Lord Gilbert will arrive?"

The sullen porter was suddenly willing to please. I could fit in no word till he had stopped for breath and had begun to turn from me to send for the abbot.

"Nay, 'tis not Lord Gilbert who wishes lodging in Abingdon."

"You said you are here on Lord Gilbert's business," the porter scowled.

"Indeed. There has been theft and murder done upon Lord Gilbert's lands. One who may know something of the felony needs a place where she may be safe from those who might do her harm so as to silence her and escape my investigation."

"She?"

"Aye. A widow and her two children."

Another silence followed. I would not plead with the porter, and he could think of no reason to deny my request that he seek the hospital infirmarer.

"I will fetch Brother Theodore," he finally said, then turned and slowly entered the hospital.

Arthur and I stood before the porter's chamber, shifting weight from one foot to another, for nearly an hour before the porter reappeared with two elderly monks following. If Lord Gilbert Talbot's name could generate so little haste, it is sure that Master Hugh, surgeon, would have found even less regard in this place. Here was not the first time I had found it convenient to mention my employer's name when I needed something from men who might otherwise be loath to provide for my need.

One of the grizzled monks who followed the porter held a linen cloth over his mouth and nose. When he came close I saw that this fabric was stained with blood and a yellowish effusion.

"Brother Bartholomew," the porter said, "here is... Hugh, bailiff to Lord Gilbert Talbot. Brother Bartholomew," he turned to me, "is infirmarer at the abbey and hospital." The elderly monks bowed slightly, and I returned the greeting.

"You require lodging for a woman, I am told," the infirmarer said. Arthur, who had been standing near, displaying Lord Gilbert's blue-and-black livery to add emphasis to my request, now spoke:

"You've injured yourself?" he said to the other monk. It was impolitic for Arthur to interrupt so, but he is accustomed to speaking his mind, and voiced but what I had thought.

"Nay, no injury. A fistula which will not heal."

"Master Hugh can deal with such as that," Arthur said confidently. "Seen 'im put a man's skull back together after a tree fell on 'im."

"You are a physician?" the monk asked.

"Nay, a surgeon. Is there no brother in the abbey, trained in medicine, who can help you?"

"Brother Bartholomew has prepared salves, but none will cure me. I will go to my grave with this, I think. I have prayed the Lord Christ to ease my affliction, and the saints, also, but as with St. Paul's 'thorn in the flesh,' He has chosen not to do so."

"Some afflictions," the porter said, "serve to bring us to God. As we suffer now, He will requite it of us in purgatory. Brother Theodore's suffering will release him from years of misery to come. And Brother Bartholomew possesses much knowledge and skill. If he cannot deal with Brother Theodore's complaint, 'tis sure no other can."

Arthur rolled his eyes, shrugged, but remained silent. He recognized that the porter was not a man who suffered lightly any contradiction, especially from the commons. The monk, however, saw no need to agree with the porter.

"You made a man's broken head whole again?"

"Aye."

"An' he walks now near as good as ever," Arthur found his voice again.

"Do you have salves which might help me, some ointment Brother Bartholomew does not know of?"

"Nay, no ointment will remedy your hurt."

"See," the porter said, "there is nothing to be done if Brother Bartholomew cannot work a cure."

Brother Theodore turned to me and said, "Is this so?"

"Nay. Such a fistula can be repaired. I saw it done in Paris."

"Paris?"

"Aye," Arthur said. "Master Hugh studied surgery in Paris."

The monk looked from me to the porter, then slowly dropped the linen cloth which had covered his disfigurement.

"Can you deal with this?" he asked.

The fistula was between his nose and his right eye. I believe it had vexed the man for many months, perhaps even years, for it was of great size and oozed constantly a fluid of pus and blood.

I approached close to the sufferer and studied the lesion carefully before I made reply. "Aye, I can. I must tell you, however, that such surgery as I must do to mend you will be painful."

"But after the pain I will have relief?"

"Aye, I believe so. An unsightly scar will remain."

"No more unsightly than this wound I now bear."

"Nay, not so bad as now."

"When can you deal with this affliction?"

"I have no instruments with me. I must return to

Bampton for them. While I do so you and the infirmarer may find a chamber for a woman who needs a place of safety for herself and her children. Felons who have done theft and murder may seek her out to do more villainy."

"I am Brother Theodore," the monk said. "Hosteler to the abbey. Brother Bartholomew and I will see that the woman is safe in the hospital."

I left the abbey pleased that I would be able to help a troubled man, and pleased also that when I did so, I would have a friend inside the abbey walls.

Chapter 6

So it was that the infirmarer of St. John's Hospital, Abingdon, was pleased to find a place for Amice Thatcher and her children. Perhaps the porter, had he some infirmity I might have mended, would also have been willing to see Amice sheltered there. As it was, he showed his displeasure with a scowl and in every way but by words.

Arthur and I left the abbey and returned to the crowded alleys of the bury. Amice Thatcher's door was open for custom, and a bushel was raised upon a pole above her door, to tell all that here was fresh-brewed ale. The narrow lane was swarming with residents, both adult and children. Their numbers would keep Amice safe in the day, but for the dark of night I was well pleased that she would be within St. John's Hospital.

I saw fright in Amice's eyes as my shadow darkened her door. She was, I think, unwilling to shut out customers, but fearful of those who did enter her ale house. I told her of the sanctuary provided her at the hospital and saw her features relax.

"I brewed five gallons of ale fresh yesterday," she said, "and have sold but a gallon this day. It will go stale. Must I remain long at the abbey, you think?"

"Perhaps the hosteler will have need of fresh ale for the guest hall. I will ask it of him."

I was confident that, to retain my good will, Brother Theodore would purchase four gallons of ale. He did, and offered six pence (which price Amice was much pleased to accept), and sent a lay brother following Amice's directions to fetch the cask and bring the ale to the abbey.

When the sacrist rang the abbey church bell for nones Amice Thatcher and her children were safe within

St. John's hospital. So I did believe.

In my travels about Abingdon I had seen several blacksmith's forges. There was yet nearly three hours till dark, so I set out with Arthur to learn if any smith had recently plied his trade upon a horse with a broken shoe. None had, but I left each smith with a promise that, should he do so, and then report the labor to me at the New Inn, he would be rewarded.

Next day Arthur and I, after a dinner of stockfish and wheaten loaves, wandered the town searching the streets for the mark of a broken horseshoe. We saw none.

Thursday morn, after a pint of ale at the ale house across the marketplace from the inn, Arthur and I started for Bampton. There was little more to learn of John Thrale in Abingdon, and the sooner I could apply my skills to the hosteler's fistula the sooner I would have a friend in the abbey.

I must learn to be more observant. We had crossed the Thames at Newbridge, more than halfway to Bampton, before I looked to the muddy road under Bruce's hooves and saw that we followed the track of a horse with a broken shoe. I called to Arthur to bring his palfrey to a halt, dismounted, and squatted in the road to see better if the marks there seemed to be the same as those made by the beast which carried a man who had threatened my Bessie. They were, and Arthur, peering over my shoulder, was able to see clearly now the imprint he had before known only by my description.

"Not likely to forget that," he said after his inspection. "That horse'll soon be lame, I think, does his owner not see to him."

I am not skilled in the care of horses, so I could not judge the accuracy of Arthur's assertion, but it seemed to me I sought some gentleman who suffered from financial misfortune. The fellow had wealth enough that he could own a horse, but not enough to care for the beast properly, and he was willing to beat and murder another to gain what that other man possessed.

My next thought was that the man was headed toward Bampton. Kate and Bessie were safe within the wall of Bampton Castle, so I had no fear for them, but I wondered what other mischief the fellow might be about, or what he sought.

Had we followed the track since leaving Abingdon? Had I been more observant, I might have had answer to that question. The day was yet young. An extra hour or two backtracking to see where the broken-shoed horse had entered the road would not much delay our journey.

The nearer we approached to Abingdon the more folk had been upon the road, and the marks of their passage began to obliterate the track we followed. At one place, where for many paces we saw no mark of a broken horseshoe, Arthur dismounted and led his palfrey, studying the road before us for a resumption of our trail. He found it, briefly, at a place where the tower of the abbey church looked down upon us through an opening in a wood through which the road passed. But a hundred paces beyond, the mark we followed was again obscured by the passage of men and beasts, and this time, search as we would, we could not recover the track.

Before us was a crossroad. We went so far as to examine this lane, where a track would be easy to follow, for fewer travelers went there. We did not find the mark we sought.

I called to Arthur – who had explored the crossing path to the south, while I searched to the north – to give up the hunt. We resumed our interrupted journey to Bampton, followed again the track of a broken horseshoe to Newbridge, and this time searched for where our quarry went, rather than whence he had come.

A mile past Newbridge, nearly to Standlake, Arthur shouted, "Look there!" and drew his palfrey to a halt. He rode to my right, so when the hoof-print we followed broke from the road to a narrow track which led to the right, he saw it first.

Two horses had recently turned into this narrow

lane, one well shod, the other the beast we followed. The path soon became so narrow and overgrown that we were forced to dismount, and at the place we did so the mark of a broken-shoed horse also disappeared. So few travelers had passed this way that grass and fallen leaves had covered the path, and no rider would gallop his horse here to throw clods of turf, where trees grew close over the way and a low limb might unseat him.

We tied Bruce and the palfrey to saplings and made our way afoot into the wood. Where this trail led I could not guess, for the forest soon closed in upon us. Where the mud gave way to turf we had seen the tracks of horses entering this overgrown lane, but there were no marks of any horses leaving it. This was a puzzle. Arthur and I had left our beasts behind, so overgrown was the path. If a man entered this forest track with his horse, he must do so afoot, leading with his beast behind. But where would he go that he would not return the way he came?

The path became so overgrown that I was required to push foliage aside to make a way through. At several places I saw where others had done so also. Twigs and small branches were snapped off, and recently – the breaks showing white and fresh. This was not a silent business, and it occurred to me that the felons I sought might be hidden in the forest, warned of our approach and waiting in ambush. I turned to Arthur, put a finger to my lips, then proceeded with new caution.

There was no need for this vigilance. A hundred or more paces from the road the path entered a clearing in the wood, edged with blackberry thorns. This opening was much like the clearing to the east of St. Andrew's Chapel where I had discovered John Thrale's cart. Was this another place where he had sought solitude for a night's rest? Surely the way from the road to this place was not wide enough for his cart. But when he traveled harnessed to his small cart, might he then have penetrated to this quiet spot?

The forest opening was no more than twenty paces across, and when I studied the opposite side I saw a place where men and horses might have gone. I pointed, motioned to Arthur, and silently he followed me across the clearing to where another overgrown path led into the forest. Where the forest and a tangle of blackthorn met I noticed a strange thing. Several strange things. Spaced little more than one pace apart were hummocks rising from a large depression in the leafy mold. I counted four in one direction, and six in another, so that there were twenty-four of these mounds, identical in size and shape, in an orderly pattern where forest and clearing met.

My curiosity was aroused. I knelt beside one of the mounds, which rose to a height nearly to my knee, and with the point of my dagger prodded the lump to see what might lie in such orderly rows, under the decay of a forest floor. Arthur peered intently over my shoulder as I did so.

Masonry was there. The blade of my dagger struck something hard before I had poked it in the length of my little finger. I did not at first know what I had found, but a few moments with dagger and fingers cleared the moss and overgrowth from the pile enough that a short column of what appeared to be tiles and mortar became visible. These tiles were not a random assembly. They had been cut square and carefully stacked, and there were twenty-three more mounds like the one I had uncovered. What men had done this, and what these short pillars were to do, I could not tell.

I stood and scratched the back of my head in puzzlement. Why would the felons who beat John Thrale to his death seek this place? As the question entered my mind, so did the answer. Here was a place where men had lived long ago. Perhaps those men had buried their wealth somewhere near to conceal it from brigands.

Arthur was as perplexed as I. "What is here?" he finally asked.

"Many years past men built here a house, I think, and these columns supported it. The murdered chapman may have found the place, and somehow discovered a buried hoard. The men who slew him knew he visited this place, and now seek the treasure.

Arthur frowned, looked about him, and placed a hand upon the hilt of his dagger.

"They are not here," I said. "We made noise along that track. They would have heard us coming and fled."

"Fled? Would they not fight for riches?"

"Perhaps, if pressed, but they would sooner flee, so as not to give suspicion that there is anything here worth fighting for. Let's see what may be here… Go about the other side of these hillocks and see what may be found."

Arthur frowned in puzzlement. "What am I to seek?"

"Anything which seems out of place in a forest. Some hole, perhaps, recently dug. Leaves will cover it, so search carefully. I will examine the ground this side of the mounds."

Arthur disappeared into the forest so that all I knew of his progress was the occasional snapping of a twig. Meanwhile I walked the length of the stubby columns but saw no place where any man had made a trench in the earth.

I explored the forest five or six paces beyond the columns and there appeared three declivities in the earth before me. At the moment I saw them I heard Arthur speak through the wood. "Here is a hole… nay, two."

"Stay where you are," I replied, and wound my way through the trees until I saw his blue-and-black livery through the forest. He stood between two leaf-covered depressions, each about three paces across and knee deep.

These holes were fresh. Whoso dug them had piled the dirt nearby, and the mounds and holes had but a thin layer of fallen leaves as cover. I took a broken limb, stepped into one of the holes, and scraped away the leaves. I found nothing.

"There are three hollows much like this over yonder," I said.

"Five holes? Them fellows find that much treasure, you think?"

"Nay. I think they found none."

"None. Why so much labor, then?"

"Aye, why dig in so many places if you knew where you must search? They dug, found nothing, and dug again."

"An' gave up after five holes?"

"Aye."

"What if they found what they sought in the fifth hole?"

"Mayhap," I said. "We must hope they did not."

"An' why dig in these five places? Why choose here?" He pointed to the excavation before us. "Why not over there?" He pointed to an untouched opening between two great beech trees to our left.

"I cannot tell," I shrugged. "There may have been some sign which the felons thought might tell of riches below the ground. Perhaps their digging obliterated it? When we find them I will ask it of them.

"For now, let's follow the track beyond the clearing and see where it leads. There may be other ruins nearby, and other holes."

There were not. The overgrown trail began to bend to the left, and perhaps a quarter of a mile beyond the five holes the path rejoined the road. To the right was Standlake, a half-mile distant. To the left, no more than two hundred paces off, was the place where we had left the road, following the track of a broken horseshoe.

I looked down at the road where I stood, and saw there the mark of the ill-shod horse we had followed into the forest. We had trailed the beast back to the road. Arthur followed my eyes and studied the mud at our feet.

"Them fellows didn't return the way they come," he said.

"Nay. Had they found treasure in the forest, they would return home, but the track leads on toward Standlake... unless that is near their home. We'll retrieve the horses and see where these men may lead us."

Past Standlake the roads diverge, one way leading north, to Witney, the other west, to Bampton. I considered as we passed through Standlake what I should do if the trail led north.

I was spared the decision. The mark of a broken horseshoe traveled toward Bampton.

We followed, watching closely for any place where the horse had left the road.

Through Aston and Cote we saw no such trail, and at Cote rain began to fall, soaking us thoroughly and slowly obliterating the track we followed.

The deluge had nearly blotted out the trace of a broken horseshoe when we came to the place near to St. Andrew's Chapel where John Thrale had been beaten to his death. Here the horse we followed again departed the road, and went along the same path which led to the clearing where I had found the chapman's horse and cart.

I turned Bruce from the road, and Arthur followed. We were already soaked through, wet and cold. What matter if we became colder and wetter?

It was not necessary to dismount to follow this path. I knew the way, and I thought I knew where it would lead. I discovered soon enough that my knowledge was incomplete.

We came to the clearing where John Kellet and I had found Thrale's horse and cart, and here I dismounted to inspect the surrounding forest for cavities made by those who sought the chapman's hoard. No such digging was visible, but two wicked men had recently come to this place for some reason. It was not to enjoy the solitude of a peaceful autumn wood.

I told Arthur to circle about the clearing to the right, and I would do the same to the left. No more than ten paces from the clearing I found a duplicate of the ruins we found near Standlake. Here there were twenty leaf-and-mold-covered columns, four across and five in length, standing in a shallow declivity, as in the first discovery. Here was a place where ancient men had once lived, but a half-mile from Bampton, yet so far as I knew, no man of Bampton knew of the place. Perhaps some swineherd had passed by, or men seeking downed limbs for winter firewood, but if they saw the lumps in the forest they thought little of them. I was sure I would find holes dug into the earth nearby, and soon did so; four of them.

I called softly to Arthur and a moment later he appeared, stepping silently through the sodden forest.

Here the layer of fallen leaves covering the holes and the accompanying piles of dirt was thinner than at Standlake. Rain had surely loosened some this day, so whoever dug these pits had done so recently, perhaps this very morn. I held a finger to my lips to silence Arthur, though in truth he made no sound as he stepped near, and glanced about to see if any men might at that moment be seen observing us from behind an oak. Arthur caught my intent, and did likewise. We stood thus for some time, silent in the dripping wood, but neither saw nor heard any other man.

"'Tis sure the villains who delved here found no riches at Standlake," said Arthur.

"Aye, they would not trouble themselves here had they done so. Nor did they find silver or gold here, I think."

"Four holes, rather than one?"

"Aye, unless the fourth pit rewarded their labor."

Arthur peered about, water dripping from his cap and eyebrows, and shivered. This was unlike him, for he bore discomfort as well as any man. I knew this from having spent some hours with him bound uncomfortably in a cold swineherd's hut a year and more past.

"We have missed our dinner," I said. "But mayhap cook will have a morsel remaining, and I am wet through and need dry clothes. Let us be off."

Once or twice as we neared, then passed St. Andrew's Chapel, I thought I saw in the road the mark of a broken horseshoe, but the pelting rain had so eroded all impressions in the mud that I could not be sure the felons had entered the town. And I was so wet and chilled, I no longer cared much where the fellows had gone. My mind, as we approached Bampton Castle, was fixed on warm, dry clothes, and a warm, dry wife. I found both readily.

Chapter 7

Rain continued all the next day. I sought Arthur and told him we would not return to Abingdon until the morrow, when the deluge, I hoped, would have passed. I spent the day in my old bachelor quarters, playing with Bessie and enjoying conversation with Kate.

Saturday dawned clear but cold. After a loaf and a cup of ale, Arthur and I were off again for Abingdon, with a sack of my instruments and herbs slung across Bruce's rump. I had spent so much of the journey on Thursday watching the road pass beneath me that I could not refrain from doing so this day as well. If the men I sought had found no treasure yet, perhaps they might be again upon the roads. They were not.

We left our horses in the mews behind the New Inn, consumed a dinner of stockfish and pease pottage, then set off for St. Nicholas's Church and the abbey gatehouse.

The porter was not present, perhaps at his dinner, but the lay brother who served in his place trotted off willingly to seek the hosteler. Brother Theodore appeared soon after, the stained linen cloth pressed to his cheek. The monk did not seem comforted to see me.

I carried over my shoulder the sack of instruments and herbs I would use to mend Brother Theodore's fistula. His eyes went to the sack as he approached and I saw him sigh.

"I have brought all things needed to deal with your hurt," I said.

"I am sorry for your inconvenience," the monk replied.

"You have changed your mind? You no longer wish me to treat your fistula?"

"Nay. I wish it heartily, but m'lord abbot forbids it."

As we spoke the porter appeared, returning to his post. He overheard Brother Theodore and explained.

"Saturn is in the house of Aries, as any competent leech or surgeon should know, and will remain for a fortnight. No surgery upon a man's head or face will succeed at such a time. Brother abbot has forbidden it."

I knew the tradition that Saturn, that malignant planet, might bring medical and surgical care to naught, was the physician or surgeon so bold as to try his skill when Saturn was opposed.

But I also knew of Henri de Mondeville's experience in mending men after battle. He once extracted an arrow which pierced a man's cheeks, through from one side of his face to the other, no matter the position of planets or the moon in the zodiac. What good to a man wounded in battle to wait a fortnight, or even a day, to minister to his injury?

De Mondeville wrote of his cures that recovery from wounds seemed dependent more upon the skill of the surgeon than the position of the stars and planets. So after reading *Surgery*, which book set me upon my chosen work, I paid scant attention when learned doctors at the university in Paris required of us students that we become expert in the zodiac and the influence of the stars and planets over our work.

And while a student at Baliol College I read *The Confessions of St. Augustine*. He wrote that astrology strikes at the root of human responsibility. To men it says, "What has happened is not my fault, it was decided by the stars. Venus or Mars or Saturn did this, not my foolishness or sin." God, creator of the stars and planets, is to be blamed for whatever mistakes we make or evil we do.

But if the abbot forbid me dealing this day with Brother Theodore's fistula, so be it. An abbot may not be contradicted within the walls of his demesne. Brother Theodore had lived with his malaise for some years. He would need to endure a fortnight longer.

"How does Amice Thatcher?" I asked.

"Brother Anselm sent her away this morn," the hosteler finally said.

"Away? Why so? She may be in danger. The infirmarer knew this. What cause did he give?"

"Said the children were too noisy, disturbed those who were ill."

The hosteler seemed skeptical. Had it not been so, I would not have prodded the monk further.

"Did you hear of others who complained?"

Again the hosteler hesitated. "Nay... well, not much. My chamber is in the guest hall, so as to be near my charges. I'd not have heard even were the children troublesome."

I believe he did not wish to seem disloyal to a friend, but wished to speak the truth. This is often a trying thing for an honest man, whether he serves abbot, bishop, or King.

"Did Mistress Thatcher annoy the infirmarer? Had she some distasteful habit, or did she demand more than proper of a guest?"

"Nay, not so far as I could see. But somehow she vexed him. He was in a choler when I saw him this morn, before matins."

"Did she return to her home?"

The hosteler shrugged. "Brother Anselm didn't say."

"How long past was it she left the hospital?"

"She was gone well before terce."

"I must find some other haven for the woman. There are men about who may believe that she knows of treasure, and would threaten harm to her and her children if she does not tell them where it is hidden."

"Treasure? The woman knows of treasure?"

"Nay. But there are men who may think she does."

"I could not think so poor a widow could possess knowledge of treasure," said the hosteler.

"Let us hope the felons who seek the loot agree with you."

"You know where the wealth is to be found?" Brother Theodore asked.

"Nay. But those who seek it have murdered a man already to have it, and I fear for Amice Thatcher if they believe she can lead them to the treasure."

All this time the hosteler had held his stained linen cloth before the ugly fistula which lay aside his nose, high on his cheek. He looked down at the befouled·fabric, then spoke again.

"'Twill be many days before Abbot Peter will permit you to deal with my wound. You are sure you can heal me?"

"Few things in life or surgery are sure. But I know how to repair the fistula so that God, does He will it, may complete the cure."

"There is another matter," the hosteler hesitated. "I own nothing, nor does any monk. If you are paid for the skills you apply to my face, it must be from abbey funds. What is your fee for such surgery?"

I thought for a moment of the wealth accumulated in the abbeys of England, then replied, "Three shillings."

The monk's eyes widened at this, and well they might, for I would serve a poor man who suffered so for three pence, which I believe the hosteler knew. But he voiced no complaint; he merely said, "A fortnight, then, when Saturn leaves the house of Aries."

"Indeed," I said, and was about to turn and seek Amice Thatcher in the bury when three monks appeared between the guest hall and the abbot's kitchen, striding purposefully toward the porter's lodge and the gatehouse. This path took them straight toward me, Arthur, and Brother Theodore. The hosteler saw my attention diverted and turned to see what had caught my eye.

"Oh, Lord," he said softly.

Since none of the three who approached seemed to resemble the Lord Christ, I took his remark to be a malediction.

Two of the approaching monks were of normal size and appearance, but the third, who walked, or rather waddled, between the others, was nearly as wide as he was tall. His tonsured head thickened where it sat upon a neck which disappeared into multiple chins and rolls of fat. The monk's robe billowed before him as if some great gust of wind had filled it like a sail, but 'twas his belly. An ornate cross hung from a golden chain about the monk's fleshy neck.

Brother Theodore said nothing more as the three approached. I noticed that his eyes were cast down.

The three monks stopped before us and waited for Brother Theodore to speak. He did so, and introduced me to the cellarer, the prior, and the rotund abbot, Peter of Hanney. The abbot peered at me through the fleshy slits in his face, and said, "So you're the surgeon who would treat Brother Theodore when the heavens declare any cure at such a time must fail."

"The heavens," I said, "declare the glory of God, but say nothing of a surgeon's skill."

"No skillful surgeon," the prior growled, "would defy the stars and planets. Saturn must not be trifled with. 'Twas when Saturn conjoined with Jupiter and Mars that the Great Pestilence, with its choler and noxious vapors, struck down so many souls."

"So it was said."

Behind the three monks smoke arose from a chimney of the abbot's kitchen. I wondered if he followed the Benedictine Rule as ardently as an abbot should. His girth said not. Abingdon is on the way between Oxford and Winchester and an abbot has an obligation to serve high-born guests at his table. Rule or not, I suspect that Abbot Peter partakes often of the beef and pork and lamb served to his visitors.

Abbot Peter dismissed me with a wave of his fleshy hand and turned toward the abbey church. The prior looked back briefly, then followed his superior. His glance said much: a message of dismissal and disdain. The cellarer continued toward the porter's lodge.

"By heavens," Arthur said when the abbot was a safe distance away, "I'd like to graze in 'is meadow."

God will forgive a man his sins, if he asks, but his body may not. What other of the seven deadly sins Peter of Hanney may be guilty of I know not, but he is surely guilty of gluttony.

I was about to bid Brother Theodore good day, when four men stepped from the porter's lodge at the cellarer's approach. The cellarer did not break his stride, but passed through the gatehouse into the marketplace. The four men followed. They were not monks, and I saw that each man had a sword slung from his belt.

Brother Theodore followed the direction of my gaze and explained. "Four years past the town hired a lawyer, up from London, to plead against the monastery's claims upon the town and market. M'lord abbot bribed the jurors, and the judges dismissed the case. There is much bad blood," the hosteler sighed, "between abbey and town, so that monks cannot walk the streets unless they are defended."

Arthur and I followed the cellarer to Burford Street, and watched as he walked toward St. Helen's Church. A few men doffed their caps and bowed as the monk passed, but as many, when his back was to them, spat in the street behind him before continuing on their way. No cowl is so holy but that the devil can get his head under it.

Arthur and I sought the alley where Amice Thatcher dwelt and I soon stood before her door. No bushel topped the pole set there. The woman had no ale fresh this day, but as there was no sign of her or her children, I assumed she was at work brewing a fresh batch, her children perhaps joining in the labor.

I rapped upon the door, but received only silence in response. I thumped again, louder, so that the fragile assembly of planks seemed ready to collapse, but yet there was no sound from Amice Thatcher's house.

The pounding had attracted the attention of a crone who dwelt across the street. "Ain't 'ome," she said. "Come 'ome, then went off again."

"Amice returned here this morn?"

"Aye. Didn't stay. Two fellas come by an' she went off

81

with 'em. Her an' the children."

Two men? Were these the same who had slain John Thrale? If so, how did they discover she was no longer under the protection of abbey walls?

"Was one of these men tall, wearing a red cap, and the other fat, with a blue cap?"

The old woman pressed a finger to her cheek, thought for a moment, then spoke. "B'lieve so. Didn't pay 'em much mind. Folks often seek Amice's ale... she don't water it as some do."

I looked to Arthur. He read my mind and said, "Too many folks about. If one of them rides a horse with a broken shoe, the track would be well covered."

The crone heard him and said, "No man comes to the bury mounted. Streets be too narrow, an' men hereabout don't think much of gentlefolk."

"When Amice departed with these men, which way did she go?"

The old woman pointed a bony finger to the declining sun, where the narrow lane curved around toward the south.

"Toward Ock Street," she said.

Arthur and I elbowed our way through the crowded lane. Or, more truly, Arthur pushed through the mob and I followed. Arthur is well able to clear a path through a throng, and I trailed like a rowing boat drawn behind a great ship.

Where the narrow path entered Ock Street the crowd thinned, but yet the mud of the street was too trampled for a horseshoe, broken or whole, to be identified. Amice Thatcher was gone, likely now in the hands of men who sought silver and gold, and who thought she knew where it might be had. She did not, or so she had said. Did she speak true to me? If not, would she tell where John Thrale had found his treasure in order to save herself and her children? If she did not know where Thrale found the cache, what would wicked men do to her or her children to force from her that which she could not give?

The sun was low in the west and the evening was

chill and threatened rain. There was nothing more to be done this day. I told Arthur we would seek the New Inn and a bowl of pottage, and renew our work next morn.

Sleep did not come readily that night. I thought of what I might have done to safeguard Amice Thatcher. Was not a monastery hospital as secure as any place where she might have found refuge? There was nothing to be gained by questioning now the decision I had made four days past to place Amice in St. John's Hospital, but I did so anyway, thus forcing sleep from my troubled mind.

I thought also of the coin, and John Thrale's dying words: "They didn't get me coin." Why had he but one coin, and that hid in his mouth? If he had visited his find earlier on his tour of villages and customers, would he not have had more of his treasure with him, hid somewhere on his person or in his cart? Perhaps he did, and his attackers found it. But he said not. And if the felons had discovered his treasure, why did they yet seek it? No, John Thrale had not visited the covert place where ancient coins and jewelry were hid before he was attacked in the forest near St. Andrew's Chapel.

But if the cache was yet to be visited when Thrale made his rounds, why had he one coin hid in his cheek? The answer to that question drove sleep even farther from me. The chapman had one coin because it was there, in the wood to the east of St. Andrew's Chapel, that he had found the hoard. If he had already visited the cache, he would have had more loot in his possession. Buried somewhere in that wood was the treasure Amice Thatcher's captors sought. Perhaps John Thrale had been surprised as he uncovered the hidden wealth, and managed to hide it, but for one coin, before his assailants came upon him. If the treasure was at some place farther along his route, he would have had no coin with him.

I had more questions than answers, and slept little that night for considering these matters over and over again.

Chapter 8

Arthur and I left the New Inn early next morn, attended mass at St. Nicholas's Church, sought the baker so as to break our fast with a loaf, then set out for the crooked lanes of the bury. I had some forlorn hope that Amice Thatcher might have returned to her home, or would do so early this day. If not, she would not know about or resent me entering her house to see if there was anything in it which might tell me of her abduction, if that was truly what occurred when she went off with the men who had slain John Thrale.

The hour was yet early, but the lane before Amice Thatcher's hut was aswarm with those who lived or labored in that place. It would not do to break down her door, flimsy as it was and easily breached. Inhabitants of such lane look out for each other, and I saw several sideways glances of suspicion as we stood before Amice's door.

I rapped my knuckles smartly upon the decaying planks of the door. There was no response, not even from the crone who lived across the way. She was about some work of her own, no doubt, which was good. Busy with her own tasks, she would not see as Arthur and I left the street and sought the rear of Amice's house.

The passages between Amice's home and those on either side were narrow. But if she earned a living as an ale wife there must be a toft behind her hut where she had vats and tubs for brewing. And if so, there must be a door opening to the toft from the rear of the dwelling. Such a door would not, I thought, be stronger than the door which opened to the street, so might be more easily forced, with the added advantage that doing so would be unobserved by a neighbor.

The space behind Amice Thatcher's house was as I

expected. The tubs and kettles necessary to her trade were there, and a door did indeed open from the house to this work space. It would be impolite to burst in upon the woman if she was within, so I rapped upon the door as I had earlier at the front of the house. There was, again, no response.

Oddly enough, this rear door was more stoutly constructed than its fellow at the front. Perhaps Amice believed that if some intruder sought uninvited entry he would be more likely to do so from the privacy of the toft than the street, where his deed might be observed. If so she thought, she was correct.

No fences separated Amice's toft from those of her neighbors. I studied both spaces before turning to Arthur and making known my intent. There was no latch or lock upon this rear door – iron is too dear for such folk. The door was simply barred inside. A thin blade, slipped between door and jamb, might raise the bar and gain us entry. With my dagger, while Arthur kept watch, I hacked away at the doorframe until I could slide the dagger between door and jamb. The bar lifted readily.

Someone had been here before us. Amice Thatcher's few belongings were strewn about the single room. Even the hearthstone in the middle of the chamber was overturned, and some man had dug up the soil beneath it. Arthur and I stood silently and gazed at the mess. After a moment I walked to the front door and tested it. It opened readily. It was not locked. Either Amice had failed to lock it when she and her children were taken off, or men had come in the night with a key. I chided myself that I had not tried the door the day before.

Little sunlight penetrated the single window of oiled skin, for the day was cloudy and a light drizzle had begun to fall. But there was enough light that the shambles which was Amice Thatcher's home was plain.

"Didn't tell 'em where the chapman found 'is coins," Arthur said.

"Aye. Doesn't know, or wouldn't tell, else they would not have overturned this place seeking loot."

"Did they come in the night, I wonder, or did this happen yesterday?" Arthur swept his hand and his gaze about the ruin.

"We might learn from the old woman who lives across the way. She strikes me as the sort who allows little to escape her notice."

Arthur grinned agreement, and followed as I pushed through the front door and crossed the narrow lane to the crone's hut. Vigorous thumping upon the woman's door brought no response.

In the silence after my pounding Arthur heard something which had escaped me. The gentle mist softened other sounds, so when the old woman groaned a response to my knocking Arthur barely heard her and I heard nothing at all. And at the moment he was unsure of what he had heard.

I saw Arthur raise a finger and frown, then cock his head attentively toward the door.

"What is it?" I asked.

"Dunno… someone in there's in trouble, I think. Heard a moan, like, just now."

I tried the latch and the door swung open. If someone was within they had not troubled themselves to bar the door. They had not done so, I soon discovered, because they could not.

Rusty hinges squealed when I pushed the door open. When they quieted I heard from within the house a groan, frantic in nature, as if the soul who voiced it feared she would not be heard or discovered.

The interior of the house was dark, my vision obscured, but when I sought the source of the moaning I saw, propped against a wall, the shape of the old woman who had told me of Amice Thatcher's departure the day before.

Rushes were thin upon the floor, and had not, I think, been changed for many months. So when I knelt beside the woman my knees rested upon dirt. She looked up to me and seized my arm with bony fingers when I bent close.

Her bed lay nearby, and I wondered why, if she was ill, she had not sought it rather than the uncomfortable place where she lay, her head pillowed by the wall of her house. I soon discovered the reason.

"Kicked me, the knave," she whispered.

"Who?"

"Them as was pryin' about Amice's house last night."

The effort to report this to me sapped the woman's strength. She had raised herself upon an elbow when she spoke, but fell back against the wall, exhausted, when she finished.

Arthur peered over my shoulder. I told him to take the old woman's shoulders, and I would lift her feet. Together we would lay her upon the bed. Then, when she was more comfortable, perhaps I might learn more of who had kicked her and why they had been prowling about Amice Thatcher's house. I thought I knew the answer to both questions.

The crone gasped when Arthur and I lifted her from the floor, but sighed gratefully when we set her gently upon her bed. I placed her pillow beneath her head, and when I did, she spoke again. "Ale," she whispered.

Arthur heard, and crossed the small house to a crude table where rested an equally crude ewer. I watched as he lifted it, then turned it upside down.

"Empty," he said. "Seen another ale house down toward the marketplace. Be back shortly."

"Who was it did you this injury?" I asked when Arthur disappeared through the door.

"Dunno," she mumbled. "Heard voices. Opened the door to see who was about so late, an' saw a light in Amice's house."

The woman fell silent for a moment, as if to renew her strength, then continued. "Thought Amice was come home, so went 'cross the street to see was it so. Wasn't."

Again she hesitated, longer this time, and did not resume until Arthur entered with the ewer filled.

"Two men was searchin' her place. Overturned all, they did."

"You surprised them?"

"Aye."

Arthur poured ale into a cup, gave it to me, and I lifted the woman's head from her pillow so she could drink. The liquid seemed to invigorate her. She continued her tale with a stronger voice.

"I heard thrashin' about, an' seen they was up to no good, so left 'em an' sought me own door, but one of 'em saw me an' caught me up before I could get home. Knocked me down, 'e did, then kicked me in the ribs. Kicked me again, in the head. I must 'ave swooned, 'cause next I remember is the two of 'em draggin' me inside. One said, 'We can't leave her on the street. Someone will find her, mayhap before we can finish the search.'

"They thought I was dead, see, or near so. The other said, 'Don't worry. Folk'll not trouble themselves over some old woman found dead in her house.' They left me where you found me."

"Were these the same fellows who took Amice Thatcher away?"

"Dunno. Too dark, an' they had but one cresset lit in Amice's house."

"Where did the fellow kick you?"

She drew a hand to her ribs. "Just here," she said.

I touched the place through her threadbare cotehardie and the woman gasped under the light pressure of my fingertips. "Ow," she rasped. "Hurts, that does."

I touched another rib, above the tender place, and received no response. But when I moved my fingers lower, the crone caught her breath again. I found two cracked ribs where some villain had delivered a kick to the old woman's side as she lay upon the street.

"You say he kicked you in the head, also?"

"Aye."

"Let's have your cap off and see what injury may be there."

"Who are you, an' why are you seekin' out my wounds?"

"I am Hugh de Singleton, bailiff to Lord Gilbert Talbot on his manor at Bampton, and also a surgeon."

"Master Hugh can fix you up proper, like," Arthur said.

"Ah, well, then, I thank you. Most folk don't care much what befalls an old woman."

Under the woman's cap I found a small laceration in her scalp. The cap and her braided hair had cushioned the blow. The wound required no stitches, and although there was caked blood in her hair, a scab now stopped any further flow.

"Them rogues break her ribs?" Arthur asked.

"Aye. Two, I think."

"What'll be done with her? Can she care for herself with two broke ribs?"

"Nay. She must be bound tight, and have care for many weeks. Return to St. John's Hospital. Seek the infirmarer and tell him of what has happened here. Ask for two lay brothers to come for... what is your name?"

"Amabel. Amabel Maunder."

"Have them bring a pallet. Amabel is too abused to walk, even with aid."

Arthur departed for the hospital while I remained with my patient. I considered leaving her for a short while and seeking the New Inn, where I had left my instruments, but thought better of it. Nothing I had brought from Bampton would help Amabel Maunder, and the infirmarer at St. John's Hospital would have linen, which could be wound tight about the old woman's ribs to ease her pain while the bones knit, and herbs to dull the ache.

'Tis but a few paces from St. John's Hospital to the bury, so Arthur returned with the lay brothers and a pallet in a short time. I saw Amabel received at the hospital, and made provision with the infirmarer and a sister to have her ribs bound, and for ale laced with the ground seeds of hemp to be provided her twice each day. There was nothing else to be done for Amabel, but I did promise the woman that I would return to her house, tell her neighbors of her plight, and ask them to keep watch over her house and scant possessions.

So it was that Arthur and I returned to the bury and met John Mashon. As we approached Amabel's hut I heard from the toft next door a rhythmic thumping. I rapped upon the door of this house, but there was no response. The pounding in the toft covered the sound of my fist against the planks.

Arthur followed as I walked around the house to the toft. There I found a man flailing away upon a length of wet flax. He was preparing to make thread. The fellow was absorbed in his work, so did not notice our approach until we were nearly upon him. He stepped back in alarm when he did see us, and raised his flail before him as if to defend himself. Perhaps in the bury such readiness is needful.

"Amabel Maunder, your neighbor, was attacked last night," I said quickly, and stopped in my place so to cause the man no further worry. "Did you see or hear anything?"

"Amabel? She's got naught worth stealin', and does no man harm."

"She was not assailed for either of those reasons. She saw men lurking about Amice Thatcher's house, and when they knew she saw, they knocked her down and kicked her. She has two broken ribs and a lump upon her head. I have taken her to St. John's Hospital."

"You have? Who are you?"

"A friend to Amice and Amabel. What do you know of last night and Amabel's attackers?"

The man shook his head. "Heard somethin' in the street, but it's not healthful to meddle in other folk's business."

"Especially in the dark of night," I agreed. "Did you hear any words which might tell who did this thing?"

The thread-maker hesitated. Perhaps he feared retribution. I assured him that I would hold his information secret. His furrowed brow did not relax. I think he set little store by my pledge, but after warring with himself, and considering what had befallen his inoffensive neighbor, he finally spoke.

"All was silent, see, else I wouldn't 'ave heard."

"Silent?"

"After the ruckus. 'Eard a screech, and voices, then all went still."

"Amabel yelped when kicked," I offered.

"Aye. They kicked 'er head, too?"

"They did. Then put her in her house, thinking she was dead, or near so."

"Wasn't right away after, but before I could fall to sleep I 'eard men speak, quiet like. Me wife slept through all, and the children, too. 'We best be off,' one said, 'else we'll not get back to East Hanney before day.'"

"Men love darkness rather than light," holy writ says, "because their deeds are evil."

Whoso had ransacked Amice Thatcher's house, and dealt so perfidiously with Amabel Maunder, did not want anyone to know they had been upon Abingdon's streets, so chose the night to work their malice. But where, I wondered, was East Hanney?

I had heard of the place before. The abbot was Peter of Hanney. The village must be near, for men to come from there to Abingdon and return in one night.

Arthur and I returned to the New Inn for our dinner, and while I consumed a meal of stewed capon I considered what I must do next. John Thrale's find of coins and jewelry seemed to me likely to be hid in the forest where was found his cart and horse. Would his assailants come to the same conclusion?

Perhaps not, for they did not know of the coin Thrale had kept hidden in his cheek while they beat him. Without knowledge of the coin the men who sought his cache might look elsewhere for it, and the coins and jewels might remain where they had been hidden and safe for a thousand years.

But Amice Thatcher was not safe. I could not be sure

where she was taken, but if the men who overturned her house and abused Amabel Maunder were of East Hanney, it seemed likely they had taken her and her children there. I must find the place and free the woman before some harm might come to her. If harm had not already come.

I am from Lancashire, having come to Oxford as a student at Balliol College. I know little of Oxfordshire, but I thought Arthur might know of East Hanney. He did not.

The abbey hosteler would know of the place. His abbot came from there, and, if asked, might keep my inquiry to himself. If foul deeds occurred at East Hanney, it would be well that those who did such wickedness did not know of my interest in the place.

Arthur and I hastened to the abbey after our dinner, and the porter's assistant, when asked, went in search of Brother Theodore. The monk soon appeared with his linen bandage pressed close to his cheek, a questioning look to his features. I would not yet be permitted to deal with his fistula. He, no doubt, wondered what other business I wished with him.

"Good day, brother," I greeted him. "Your abbot is called Peter of Hanney, is this not so?"

"Aye."

"Where is Hanney? Is it near?"

"Aye, not far. Four miles… perhaps five."

"Can you direct me to the place?"

"Aye. Go west on Ock Street, pass through Marcham, then take a road to the left. But if you seek the abbot, he will be here. He seldom returns to Hanney."

"'Tis not him I seek, but two others."

Brother Theodore's brow furrowed. He did not ask, but I guessed his thoughts.

"I do not seek them as surgeon, but as bailiff. The woman I brought here three days past… she is missing. Two men of East Hanney, so I believe, have carried her and her children off."

"Are these the thieves you spoke of, who did murder and were a threat to the woman?"

"Aye, the same."

"There are two Hanneys, East and West."

"From which does your abbot come?"

"West."

"No matter. An abbot is not likely to have dealings with such men as took Amice Thatcher."

At the New Inn Arthur and I made ready Bruce and the old palfrey, and shortly after the sixth hour we set off down Ock Street toward Marcham. The misty morning had become a cloudy afternoon, but dry. Wet or not, men were busy in the fields and forest as we passed by. Beechnuts and acorns littered the forest floor, and swineherds watched as their pigs sought the nuts. Final plowing of fallow fields was completed, and these fields were now being planted to wheat and rye. Small boys ranged through these newly sown fields, heaving clods at birds who would have the seed before it could be covered.

Past Marcham we found the road leading south to Hanney, and a short while later a squat church tower appeared, barely lifting above the trees. Less than a mile from the village the road entered a wood. I had considered how best to investigate the village, and the forest provided an answer.

At a place where the forest undergrowth was not so dense I signaled Arthur to stop, dismounted, and led Bruce from the road into the forest. Arthur followed. A hundred paces into the wood I stopped, led Bruce to a small oak, and motioned to Arthur to do the same with his palfrey. All this time neither of us spoke, as if we thought we might be overheard, distant yet as the village was.

We pushed through the wet forest, becoming thoroughly damp, until we reached its southern limit. A field lay before us, encircled by a low stone wall, where grain had been cut some months before. Now sheep wandered across it, munching upon the stubble and manuring the ground for next year's crop of peas or beans. A hundred paces across this field was a manor: a large house, several barns, and some smaller outbuildings. Many of these needed repair, as did the manor house. The thatching was old and decayed, and I could see a place where a chunk of daub had peeled away from the wattles. The lord of this manor was either uncaring or too poor to keep up his property. I wondered if he was too impoverished to see to his horse's broken shoe.

Arthur stood beside me, gazing at the distant manor. Beyond it was the village, and in the distance, above the rooftops of the houses, I saw the low tower of the village church and another, larger house, of two stories. This village had two manors; was the second as poor as the first? This seemed unlikely, for the larger house had a slate roof.

I returned my gaze to the closer manor, and saw a man appear from behind a ramshackled outbuilding. This structure appeared at a distance to be much like a hencoop, but if it was, Reynard would not be long in devising some means of entry. The man was unkempt, shaggy and meanly clothed.

I pointed silently to the fellow, and Arthur whispered, "I see 'im." There was no need to speak softly. At that distance even a normal conversation would go undetected. But at the verge of the wood, where we stood, we might be seen. I took Arthur's arm and drew him a few steps deeper into the forest.

"What's 'e doin'?" Arthur asked.

"Nothing. Look there... he turned and walked behind that shed."

Indeed, the man had disappeared, resuming the place he had occupied when we first saw the manor.

"Let's watch and see if the fellow reappears."

He did. A few minutes later he again sauntered into view, then seemed to bend toward the shed and peer in. Perhaps there was a door there, or a chink in the wattles.

"'E's sayin' somethin'," said Arthur.

We could not hear his words, but even from one hundred paces it was possible to see that the fellow spoke. Folk do not speak to decrepit hencoops unless they are addled. Someone was inside the shed.

"You thinkin' what I'm thinkin'?" Arthur asked.

"Aye. Look there, he's moved from the shed, but does not walk far away."

"Somebody's in there... unless 'e talks to chickens."

"And he's laughing, I think."

"Did someone inside that shed make a jest?"

"I doubt so," I replied. "I think the man laughs because of the state someone is in... which he finds amusing."

"I'd like to know who, or what, is in there."

"You shall. We will wait here behind this wall till dark, then approach from behind that barn you see to the right of the coop. If the fellow is yet guarding the place, and it's my opinion that's what he's doing, we can be upon him in a few steps when he turns in his pacing."

"What if there's no one in that shed?"

"The fellow is behaving strangely if that is so. And we'll deal carefully with him. Find a fallen limb here in the wood which will put him to sleep when laid across his skull, but not so large as to give him more than a headache tomorrow."

"Aye," Arthur smiled. "I'd best be about it while there's light an' enough to see."

The day had been cloudy and drear since dawn, and so now, at the tenth hour, it was already growing dark. I heard Arthur searching the forest while I kept watch on the guard and the shed. I was convinced that Amice Thatcher and her children were held there, and if I acted wisely and boldly I could free them. But sometimes wise acts are not bold, and bold acts are unwise.

Arthur soon returned carrying a downed oak limb nearly the size of his arm.

"Don't swing that too hard, or the fellow will not awaken till next week."

"Was all I could find," Arthur said, glancing down at his cudgel. "I'll be kind. The fellow'll not feel nothin'."

"Till he awakes," I laughed.

"Aye. By then we'll have done what's needed an' be gone."

Just before the twelfth hour, when the forest was dark and the field between us and the manor near so, a second figure approached the shed. The two faced each other for a moment, and perhaps spoke, but 'twas too dark to see. Then the first man departed and the newcomer took his place. I dimly saw the fellow bend toward the shed, but if he spoke or not I could not tell.

"Changed the guard over who's in the hencoop," Arthur said. "Must be someone important. Whoso put 'em in there don't want 'em to get away."

"Amice Thatcher is in the shed, I think."

"My guess, too," Arthur agreed. "Think it's dark enough?"

"Not yet. We've waited three hours. Another half-hour will not do us harm."

When it was so dark that I could no longer see the shed or the man who stood beside it, I whispered to Arthur, "Let's be off," and together we climbed the stone wall and crossed the field. Nettles grew in the stones of the wall, and when I pulled myself over the top my hands found them. This was not an auspicious beginning to the business. Arthur must have found the nettles also. I heard him mutter a curse as we dropped to the other side of the wall.

The wheat stubble was wet and pliant under our feet. We made no sound crossing the field, and even the sheep, huddled together for the night near the center of the enclosure, paid us no attention.

When we first came upon the field I had seen that near the shed was a gate. I had decided to avoid it and its squealing hinges, and vault the wall, as we had done leaving the forest. But the thought of another encounter with nettles persuaded me to try the gate.

It was a crude affair, made of coppiced poles and fastened together with lengths of hempen cord. Such cords also formed rough hinges and, unlike iron, offered no protest when used to swing the gate open. I pushed against the gate, and Arthur followed through the opening and across an open space until a barn hid us from the shed and the manor house.

The house was perhaps twenty paces from where we stood. I could hear voices from within, and candlelight flickered from two of the windows, which were of glass. If the man standing beside the shed was allowed to raise an alarm, those in the house would surely hear. Whatever we did must be silent.

Perhaps a change of plans was in order. If I circled behind the second barn I could approach the shed and its guard from the direction of the house. If I made no effort to be silent or conceal my appearance the guard would turn his attention to me. Perhaps he would think his lord was making a last inspection of the prisoner in the hencoop before taking to his bed. While I approached Arthur might sneak up behind the guard, and seize him with a hand across his mouth. Then, with Arthur's dagger at his throat, he might be persuaded to keep silence while I opened the shed to free Amice Thatcher and her children. If the fellow seemed unwilling to cooperate there would always be Arthur's club to fall back on. If we could keep the fellow conscious he might be persuaded to answer some questions after I released Amice and the children.

I whispered the scheme to Arthur and he nodded agreement. The clouds had begun to clear, although there was no moon, and so by starlight I could faintly see Arthur glance regretfully at his cudgel. It might yet be put to use.

The toft was muddy from the day's drizzle and I feared the guard might hear the ooze sucking at my feet while I crept around the second barn so as to approach him from the house.

I reached the house unnoticed and was halfway from the manor house to the shed when I saw the guard stand erect from where he had been leaning against the hencoop.

"That you, m'lord?" he said.

"Aye," I lied. May the Lord Christ forgive me.

"Come to see all's well with the maid?" the guard asked.

"The maid"? His words startled me. Amice Thatcher, attractive as the widow was, was no maiden, and was furnished with two children to prove it so.

There was little time, however, to consider the man's words. I saw Arthur's dark shadow creep from behind the barn as I approached the guard. I worried that there might be enough light that the guard would see that I was not the man he expected, so slowed my pace to be sure that Arthur would clap hands about the fellow's throat and mouth before he might take alarm.

The guard was a small man, short and slight of form, and Arthur well suited for the task given him. He seized the fellow with one arm about his neck, a hand over his mouth, and lifted him, kicking wildly, into the air. I leaped forward, and together we flung the fellow face-first into the mud. I heard his muffled splutter through the muck and Arthur's thick hand.

Chapter 9

"Silence!" I hissed. "Be silent and no harm will come to you." Well, no harm but for a faceful of mud.

The guard did not immediately cease his struggle, but neither did he cry out, which, even with Arthur's hand over his mouth, he might have done. When he lay still, or nearly so, I motioned to Arthur to turn his face from the mud, drew my dagger, and held it before his eyes.

"Remain silent and I will not use this against you," I said.

The starlight was dim, there in the mud between the shed and barn, but what light there was gleamed from my blade. I knew the fellow could see it.

"You understand? Blink your eyes twice if you agree."

The man blinked twice, and I told Arthur to free the guard's mouth, yet otherwise keep him tightly restrained.

"You thought I was your lord," I said. "Who is that?"

The guard made no reply, so I thrust my dagger before his eyes again and repeated the question.

"I'm not to say. Not where the lass can 'ear. She's not to know who has her, nor where she is."

I raised my dagger to his eyes again and tried to appear resolute.

"Rede," he finally said. "Sir Philip Rede."

"Who is in the hencoop? Who do you guard?"

"Dunno."

I frowned and held forth my blade again. The fellow may not have seen my scowl, but he saw the dagger.

"Some maid is there," he mumbled. "Dunno her name."

"And you are to be sure she does not escape in the night?"

"Aye."

"Hold your dagger to this knave's throat while I see who is imprisoned here," I directed Arthur. He drew his dagger from his belt and laid it across the guard's neck. I saw the man wince, and his eyes widened as he felt the touch of the blade.

The shed door was fixed shut with a wooden plank dropped into slots on either side. It was a simple matter to lift the bar, set it aside, and swing the door open. The interior was as black as Sir Simon Trillowe's heart. If a woman was there I could not see her.

"Come out," I whispered. Had I known who was to emerge, I might have dropped the plank across the door and fled.

"Who is there?" a feminine voice whispered.

"'Tis Master Hugh."

Silence followed, but after a few heartbeats the voice said, "Who?"

Amice Thatcher was not in this shed. Some other woman was imprisoned here. "I am Hugh de Singleton… come to release you. Make haste. We may soon be discovered."

Who it was who was held in the shed I did not know, but no lass should be used so. I felt, rather than saw, the approach of the hencoop's inhabitant. The door was low, and I backed away from it as a slender form bent to pass through the opening.

"Has my father sent you?" the lass asked.

"Nay. Who are you? Who is your father?"

"I am Sybil. Sybil Montagu. My father is Sir Henry. If my father has not sent you to free me, who did so?"

"Here is no place for conversation. We must be away before we are discovered. This fellow," I pointed to the guard who yet lay in the mud, Arthur close upon him, "may soon be relieved by some other."

"What'll we do with 'im?" Arthur whispered.

"You may as well slay me," the man whispered. "If you do not, Sir Philip will when he finds the maid gone."

"What? For your incompetence you will die?"

"Aye. Just slit me throat with that dagger. I'll not cry out."

Arthur, his muscular forearm yet about the man's neck, gazed at me with open mouth, to hear a man plead for death.

"Sir Philip'll hang me, or have 'is lads beat me till I'd be better off dead."

I thought on his words. I had no wish to cause a man's death at the hands of a cruel lord.

"He'll come with us, for now," I said.

I had come to this manor seeking Amice Thatcher and found Sybil Montagu. I had not before heard of her or her father, and was loath to interrupt searching for Amice while I dealt with this new entanglement.

Sybil followed me to the gate, Arthur and the guard behind. We had no cord to bind him, so Arthur kept his left arm about the man's neck, and with his right hand held his dagger against the fellow's throat. He offered no resistance as we crossed the field of wet stubble, but not so the maid.

"Ow. Where do you lead?" she protested. "This field is wet. My feet are cold."

"You would prefer to be dry in yon hencoop?"

When we reached the wall opposite the manor I considered the nettles, and felt tenderly along the stones until I found a place which seemed free of the stinging foliage.

It was not. I lifted Sybil to the top of the wall. She reached a hand to steady herself and found nettles I had missed. She yelped, cursed me for a dolt, and fell in a heap over the wall. I heard the guard chuckle.

"What yer laughin' about?" Arthur demanded.

"Sir Philip got more than 'e wished for when 'e seized that one."

"Help me up," the lass commanded from over the wall. I clambered over, finding the nettle patch again, and assisted the maid to her feet.

The forest was dark and wet, and I wished to be

gone from the place, but I also wished to know who Sybil Montagu was, and why Sir Philip Rede had seized her and confined her in a dilapidated hencoop.

"What means this," she fumed, "tossing me over the wall?"

"I ask your pardon. 'Twas not my intent."

"Now I am wet and cold," she complained.

"As we all are," Arthur said. "An' muddy, also." He had pushed the guard over the wall behind me, then scrambled over himself. I heard no curses from either man. They must have escaped the nettles.

"Why did Sir Philip Rede shut you in that hencoop?" I asked.

Sybil did not immediately reply, but the guard did. "'Cause 'e couldn't stomach 'er in the house no longer."

"You were a guest of Sir Philip's?"

"Nay," Sybil said. "Didn't know his name till now, nor where I was. The scoundrel took me from my father's manor and demands a ransom."

"Ah... how much does he demand?"

"Fifty pounds."

"Wouldn't pay," the guard said. "Sir Philip sent armed messengers to demand the ransom. Sir Henry told 'em he had two sons left, an' the hammer an' anvil to make more daughters."

"They threatened to slay me if my father would not pay," Sybil sniffed.

"Her tongue be so sharp, Sir Philip couldn't abide 'er in the house no longer. Put 'er in the hencoop till 'e could decide what to do with 'er."

"How long," I asked, "have you been in the hencoop?"

"Three days. Now you must take me to my father."

"Reckon 'e don't want 'er either." The guard was a voluble fellow when he thought himself free of his lord's wrath, even so he yet had a dagger at his throat.

"You mind your tongue, knave!" Sybil snapped.

"Where is your father's manor?"

"South Marston."

When I did not respond Arthur said, "I know the place. 'Tis but a few miles from Swindon. Went there with Lord Gilbert once."

"We'll not travel that way this night. And 'tis no time for a maid to be upon the roads if it can be avoided. You'll come with us to Abingdon and we'll see tomorrow about returning you to your father."

"I wish to go home now!" Sybil stamped her foot, but the effect was lost on the damp, leafy mold of the forest floor.

I was becoming vexed with this petulant damsel, and began to feel some sympathy for Sir Philip. She was a nuisance to him, and now to me.

"You will go where I tell you. I did not come to this place to free you from your captor. I had other business, which is now put out of joint because I must deal with you."

"What'll we do with this fellow?" Arthur asked. Arthur yet held his dagger close to the guard's neck, and clasped the man's right shoulder with his other hand. "If we release 'im he'll likely raise the alarm to save himself from 'is lord's wrath, an' them as are in the manor house'll be upon us before we're halfway back to Abingdon."

Similar thoughts had troubled me. "Sir Philip will be furious with you for allowing us to overcome you and make off with the lass?" I asked the guard.

"Aye, he will that," he replied, and unconsciously rubbed his neck near where Arthur pressed the flat of his dagger.

"So if we release you, you will hasten to tell him what has happened so to deflect his rage, will you not?"

"Sir Philip's ire don't pass so easy as all that. Likely he'll hang me."

"So what is to be done with you?"

"I left the club back at the shed," Arthur said. "I could find another, an' swat 'im 'cross the head, gentle-like, just so's to raise a welt. Then 'e could go back when 'e woke up an' tell 'is lord 'twas the club next the shed what felled 'im. By the time 'e awoke an' returned to the house we could be on the horses an' near Abingdon."

Arthur is ever willing to be helpful, but I did not think our captive would approve the plan.

"You are a tenant of the manor?" I asked the fellow.

"Nay... villein."

"Is Sir Philip in other ways a good lord?"

"Nay. A hard man, is Sir Philip, an' that's when 'e's sober. When 'e's in 'is cups a man had best stay clear."

"Was he drinking this night?"

"Aye, as every night."

"So his rage will be great?"

"Aye. He'll have me whipped first, then 'e'll hang me, twice, most likely."

"Twice?"

"Aye. Cut me down when I'm near gone, toss a bucket of water on me, an' when I've come to me senses, hang me again."

"He has done such a thing?"

"Aye, him an' Sir Simon."

"Sir Simon Trillowe?"

"The very man. Sir Philip caught a villein stealin' eggs from 'is hencoop two years past."

"And Sir Simon helped him hang the thief?"

"Aye, hanged 'im twice, so I heard. Didn't see for meself. A villein stealin' from 'is lord is treason, so Sir Philip said."

"Is that how he regularly deals with villeins who displease him?"

"Aye. Had a few strokes when I was a lad."

"Have you never thought of leaving? Have you a wife and children?"

"Think on it near every day. Got no family to suffer for me runnin' off, but where would I go? A lad fled the manor last year. Sir Philip an' his men found 'im in Banbury. Didn't hang 'im 'cause 'e was little more than a child, but beat 'im so 'e can't stand straight now."

I had taken an unaccountable liking to this guard, who seemed an honest fellow caught up in an impossible situation. I decided to try him with another question.

"Has Sir Philip any other captive who might bring him gain?"

The guard scratched the back of his head before he replied.

"Sir Philip don't say much with the commons about to hear 'im. All I know is what 'is valet overhears an' gossips about. He's needy, is all I know."

"But you know of no other he's taken because they might enrich him?"

"Nay."

"If I return you to Sir Philip, he will slay you – so you believe. So then, do you wish to accompany us and be away from this place?"

"Aye. I've nowhere to go, but when I get to somewhere new I'll not be whipped and sent to a gibbet... 'less Sir Philip finds me."

"If I am to help you escape your manor, I should know your name."

"I am Osbert – Osbert Hanney."

We stumbled through the forest, becoming thoroughly wet, until by the light of stars through bare branches we found the horses. Sybil complained the entire time; her feet were cold; her cotehardie had become snagged on a twig and ripped; she stubbed a toe against a root; I should take her to South Marston this very night, and if I did not her father would hear of my neglect of her. I was nearly ready to do her will so I would no longer hear her grievances.

Sybil rode the palfrey, I was upon Bruce, and Arthur and Osbert walked before. Stars gave enough light that the road lay faintly visible before us, and no brigands accosted us. We reached Abingdon well before dawn, and I was required to pound upon the abbey gate for some time before the porter's assistant heard me and opened to us. I told the fellow I had with me a high-born maid for whom I sought provision for the remainder of the night, and when Sybil was safe in the abbey guest house I led Arthur and Osbert to the New Inn. It was nearly time for the Angelus Bell before my head rested upon a pillow. I had accomplished nothing toward finding Amice Thatcher, or the murderers, or the location of the lost treasure, and had succeeded only in enlarging my own responsibilities.

No matter how choleric Sybil Montagu was, it was my obligation to see she was reunited with her father. And I, a bailiff, was now assisting a villein to flee from his manor and lord. These thoughts troubled my slumber so that when dawn roused the other sleepers in the New Inn's upper room, I was awake before them.

What to do with Sybil Montagu? After several days the hosteler would surely wish to be rid of the maid. He would turn her over to the abbot. I could imagine Sybil complaining loudly to Peter of Hanney, and his response. The vision brought a smile to my lips. The abbot would find some quick way to return the lass to South Marston.

And there was Osbert to consider. He and Sybil were by now discovered missing, for he had told me he was to be relieved at dawn. Sir Philip or his minions would prowl the streets of nearby towns seeking the man. It would be best if he was away from Abingdon. But where? Perhaps South Marston.

I could send Osbert to tell Sir Henry that his daughter was safe in the abbey, and to come and retrieve her. This would remove Osbert from the easy reach of Sir Philip Rede, and solve the problem of what was to be done with Sybil, assuming her father would come to reclaim her, or send servants to do so.

I told Arthur and Osbert of my plan while we broke our fast with loaves from the baker. But before I sent Osbert on his way I had a question. I thought I knew already the answer.

"Beyond Sir Philip's manor at East Hanney I saw another great house, just beyond the church. Who's manor is there?"

"Sir John Trillowe," he replied.

"Does his son, Sir Simon, reside there?"

"Aye. Him an' Sir Philip is cronies. Was lads together."

"Has Sir Philip other close friends?"

"Nay, not many."

"I have reason to believe him and some other guilty of a felony."

"You mean takin' the lass?"

"Nay. Murder."

Osbert was silent for a moment. "Sir Philip's a bad-tempered sort, him an' his brother."

"Sir Philip has a brother? Does he reside on the manor?"

"Aye."

"Describe these brothers."

Osbert did so, and I was convinced that these were the men who had slain John Thrale, threatened my Bessie, and seized Amice Thatcher.

Arthur knew of South Marston, and told Osbert how best to travel there, avoiding East Hanney. He was to take the road to Faringdon, and thence to Swindon. He would come to South Marston a few miles short of Swindon. I gave the fellow two pence to see him on his way; enough to feed himself at some inn in Faringdon going and coming, but not so much as to give him thoughts of absconding with my coin without performing his duty.

"When you return," I said, "we will find some place for you where you will not be ill used. If you do not find us here, ask the way to Standlake and Bampton. You will find me in Bampton."

I hoped this was so, for if I had returned to my home it would mean that I had found two murderers and Amice Thatcher. I could not leave Abingdon with these obligations unfulfilled.

I was eager to return to East Hanney, convinced that Amice Thatcher lay somewhere in the village, but this desire was tempered now with the knowledge that Sir Simon Trillowe, a man who harbored much ill will against me, might be encountered there. Rather than Amice Thatcher, I might find much trouble in the village.

Never again will I set out upon some venture which might prove hazardous with but an hour of sleep in the previous night. And Bruce seemed resentful of being pulled from the mews and saddled. Perhaps he had more wit than I.

By the third hour Arthur and I, Bruce and the palfrey, were again upon the road to East Hanney. For the first two miles, till Marcham, we followed the way Osbert would have taken, and I thought we might catch him. But not so; the man was a fast walker.

After Marcham we turned our beasts south, to East Hanney, and again dismounted before we reached the village and led the horses into the same forest they had visited a day before.

From the same nettle-covered wall we peered out at Sir Philip Rede's manor. All was quiet. Perhaps too quiet. None of the normal autumn labor was in view. No men were planting wheat and rye in new-ploughed fields. I had been worried that swineherds might drive their hogs into the wood, pannaging for beechnuts and acorns, and discover us there, but none were about. Tenants and villeins should also be gathering downed wood for winter fires at this season, and, indeed, I saw suitable fallen boughs in the forest behind me, but no man was collecting them.

Arthur voiced my unease. "Awful quiet," he said.

I was tempted to walk brazenly through the village to see what was there, and learn why no men were about, nor women, either. But Sir Simon Trillowe knows me well, and should I come upon him Kate might soon be a widow. I could not ride Bruce into the village, for a stranger on horseback is noticed where the same fellow afoot might draw little attention.

Sir Simon had seen Arthur a time or two, but I doubted he would have taken much notice of him. Nobles rarely pay much heed to the commons, and aside from the thickness of his chest and arms there is little about Arthur to cause a knight to take a second glance his way.

"Something is amiss in that village," I said.

"Aye," Arthur nodded.

"No man of East Hanney knows you, I think. Walk through the village purposefully, as a man determined to reach some place before nightfall, and see what folk there are about. When you have passed through the place circle about through the fields and rejoin me. Do not return through the village, or some man will be suspicious of who you are and why you travel the streets in two directions."

Arthur nodded and set off. From behind the wall I watched his head and shoulders – all I could see of him from behind the wall which divided field from road – until he disappeared behind a house.

I stood behind the wall, leaning upon the stones and careful to avoid the nettles, while I awaited Arthur's return. Occasionally I looked to the west, to see if I might catch sight of him returning by the way I had advised, although I did not expect to glimpse him so soon. When he did reappear it was not in the manner or place I had suggested.

Arthur appeared from behind the house where I had last seen him. His head and shoulders bobbed rapidly behind the wall. He was running. This was an exercise Arthur avoided, and did not perform well when it was required. Something was wrong in East Hanney, and Arthur hurried to tell me of it.

I moved from my place, sought the road, and met Arthur as he plunged from the road into the forest. I said nothing, asked no question, for I was sure Arthur would explain as soon as he could. He gasped several times, and bent at the waist, hands upon his knees, to catch his breath, then hurriedly spoke.

"Hangin' 'im," he said finally.

"Who?"

"Osbert." After another deep breath he continued, "Floggin' 'im now. Whole village is watchin'."

Here was the reason no man of East Hanney was at his work this day.

"Got 'im tied to a post, whippin' 'im. Some men is raisin' a gibbet before 'is eyes while the others beat 'im."

These sentences Arthur blurted between gasps, then bent again, hands upon knees, to suck more air into his lungs. Whether Sir Philip intended to hang Osbert once or twice I did not know, but I had put him in this place and I must now do what I could to draw him from it. Arthur thought the same.

"What we gonna do?" he said.

Perhaps more sleep might have given me more wit this day. I could think of nothing but a straightforward plunge upon Bruce and the palfrey, into the village.

"To the horses," I said, and ran stumbling through the forest. Arthur wheezed along behind. During this dash it occurred to me that we must have some sort of plan. When we reached the clearing where the horses were tied I turned to Arthur and told him of my purpose. He made no other suggestion, nor did he roll his eyes at the foolishness of my intent.

The forest was too thick to mount our beasts there. We led them to the road, scrambled into our saddles, and poked heels into the horses' ribs. The animals obliged by careening into a thunderous gallop which made up in momentum what it lacked in speed. I had ridden Bruce at a gallop once before, and vowed I would never do so again. I was airborne as much as in the saddle. Whether Arthur fared better I cannot say, but palfreys are known for a smooth gait. He could not have been more jolted than me. How Lord Gilbert, clad in armor, stayed upright upon Bruce in the charge at Poitiers I will never know.

I had no sword, but the men I wished to surprise would likely have but daggers on their belts. I had told Arthur to go to Osbert, slash him free from the pole where he was bound, or cut him down from the gibbet if he was already raised there, and toss him over my saddle before me. I would drive men from the place with Bruce's plunging hooves while Arthur did so. Then, with Osbert over Bruce's neck, we would flee the village. Our beasts were not speedy, but by the time Sir Philip and his men could saddle horses and be after us we might reach Marcham. What safety that village might provide I could not say, but if we were to be caught up it seemed to me better to be overtaken in some public place than on a road in some barren forest.

The street curved as it entered the village, so the throng about the whipping-post and gibbet heard us approach before we were seen. All eyes were turned to us as we galloped into the village and plunged into the crowd. Those who were laying stripes across Osbert's bloody back ceased and stared open-mouthed at our rumbling approach. Across the sea of faces I thought I recognized Sir Philip Rede, but I was too much involved with other matters to introduce myself.

Bruce drove into the mob, impelled by my heels poking at his tender flanks. When we neared the whipping-post I goaded the poor animal again with a sharp kick in his ribs, then yanked back on the reins. The insulted beast reared upon his hind legs, his massive forefeet thrashing the air. Those closest to the post scrambled away, including one of the two who had been assigned to flog poor Osbert. This man, in his haste to be away, dropped his bloody lash as he ran. The other stood his ground, sensing what I was about, and swung his whip toward Bruce.

The lash caught Bruce across his muzzle. This so terrified the animal that he reared upon his hind legs again. His flailing forehooves caught the fellow as he was drawing back his lash for another blow. One ponderous hoof struck the man full in the face. I saw his countenance disappear in a red bloom, then he dropped below my sight, into the crowd of frantic onlookers.

I remember wondering at that moment how I had managed to get myself into such a predicament, but I was too busy to ponder causes just then.

From the corner of my eye I saw Arthur leap from the palfrey and attack Osbert's bindings with his dagger. Above the din I heard a voice cry, "Stop them!" but no one seemed eager to interfere with a brawny man armed with a dagger and another mounted upon a beast which had flattened a man's face while they watched.

I kicked Bruce again in his ribs and set the horse to spinning about the post, where Arthur had completed slashing the cords which fastened Osbert. When he was free Osbert slumped to the ground, senseless from the flogging. Arthur shoved his dagger into its sheath, lifted Osbert's crumpled, bloody form, and when Bruce passed by threw the fellow – Osbert, you will remember, is not a large man – across the pommel in front of me. To a conscious man this would have been painful, but Osbert did not so much as grunt in discomfort.

I again kicked Bruce in the ribs and sent him through the same opening we had made when we entered the crowd. So quickly had events occurred that the mob had not filled in the breach. Once again I heard a man shout, "Stop them!"

This was reassuring. Arthur was behind me now, on his own. Had he been subdued, the fellow would have cried out, "Stop him," not "Stop them." So the mind works at such times.

Bruce lurched into a gallop and when I had him pointed toward the street which curved north out of the village, I turned to see if Arthur followed. He did, and I saw no other horseman, as the bend in the street hid the stunned crowd.

Bruce slowed his gallop. To save the beast for later exertions which I might require of him, and to allow Arthur to catch up, I permitted the frightened horse to slacken his pace. This may have been a mistake.

Chapter 10

All summer, upon a Sunday afternoon, it was my duty as Lord Gilbert Talbot's bailiff to organize archery practice and competition. By the King's edict such contests occur throughout the realm. Men of Bampton are surely no more skilled with a bow and arrows than residents of other villages, and the worst of Bampton's archers can put ten of a dozen shafts into the butts at a hundred paces.

Arthur, upon the palfrey, had just drawn even with Bruce when I felt a terrible pain high on my left side. I thought for a moment that Bruce's jouncing gallop had cracked a rib or caused some other part of my body to come out of joint.

But not so. I looked down and saw, protruding from my cotehardie, the iron point of an arrow. Some bowman had taken his lord's request to heart and loosed an arrow at me. Blood flowed freely from the rent in my cotehardie and dripped onto Osbert's already bloody back. I could not guess how serious my wound was, but if the shaft had pierced my lung I was a dead man.

Without my heels in his flanks Bruce continued to slow his pace, so Arthur and the palfrey drew ahead. Arthur turned to learn why I did not keep pace, saw my bloodied cotehardie, and reined his beast to a halt.

"What has happened?" he shouted.

"An arrow… some archer has pierced me."

"What am I to do?"

I was beginning to find it difficult to stay upright in the saddle. The arrow had entered high on the left side of my back, just under my shoulder, and I felt my left arm lose grip of Bruce's reins.

"Take the reins," I said, "and lead us to Marcham as

quickly as may be. Take me to the church there, and I will tell you what must then be done."

I tried to lift my left arm to give the reins to Arthur, but could not extend it. Arthur leaned from his saddle to grasp them, and as he did so another arrow hissed past and embedded itself in the road ten paces beyond. Arthur needed no more encouragement to make haste.

When we were again on our way I raised the right sleeve of my cotehardie to my lips. When I drew it away I saw no blood upon the wool and was relieved. Perhaps the shaft had missed my lung, and I might live.

The saddle became wet beneath me, and slippery with blood. Arthur urged the horses to a canter, and even at that pace I found it hard to remain upright. I glanced down and saw blood dripping from the stirrup. Where the arrow entered my back I must be bleeding copiously, although I could not turn to see the place.

To make sure of my seat I thought to lean forward upon Bruce's neck, but this I could not do. The movement twisted the arrow where it passed under my arm, and brought greater pain. And when I bent forward the iron point of the arrow pushed into Osbert's already bloody back. I must stay upright.

A fog seemed to settle before my eyes, and the road before us seemed to tilt, first one way, then the other. Through the haze I saw Arthur turn, and heard him shout, "We're nearly there. Hang on!" He saw that I grew weak.

I must not fall. If I did, before Arthur could get me back upon Bruce, pursuers from East Hanney would likely be upon us. We must seek the church at Marcham, and sanctuary.

I recognized the corner where the road to Faringdon and the west met the road to East Hanney. Arthur slowed our pace as he guided the horses to the right, and above the rooftops of the village, less than a mile to the east, I saw the square tower of All Saints' Church in Marcham.

Through the fog which obscured my vision I kept my eyes upon the church tower. It seemed to me that, so long as I kept my gaze fixed upon the tower, it would remain an attainable goal, but if I lost sight of it I would be lost as well.

The remaining distance to the church passed in a blur. Indeed, of what I now write I have little remembrance. Arthur told me later of events I could not recall.

Arthur brought the horses to a halt before the lychgate, tied them there, then assisted me from my bloodied saddle. I remember the shocking pain of dismounting, although Arthur was as gentle as he could be.

I could not recline, not with an arrow protruding from my back, nor could I sit, resting against the church wall. I gripped the lychgate with both hands, directed Arthur to take Osbert to the church, then slid to my knees as dizziness overcame me.

Arthur was loath to deal with Osbert while I yet held a shaft through my body, and protested, but I told him I would need his full attention to deal with my wound, and it would be best to lay Osbert out where he would be safe while the arrow was dealt with.

Arthur grimaced agreement, hoisted Osbert to a shoulder, and set off for the church porch at a trot. Osbert remained unconscious, but I could do nothing for him, pierced as I was.

I did not notice Arthur's return, but suddenly he was standing above me. "What am I to do?" he asked.

"Help me to the church. Then you must find wine and remove the arrow."

I threw my good right arm over Arthur's neck and together we stumbled through the churchyard to the porch. Arthur had left the church door open, and I saw Osbert flat upon the stones of the floor as we entered.

"How am I to remove the arrow?" Arthur asked.

"Take first your dagger and cut through the arrow near where it enters my back. Try not to shift it much."

Arthur drew his dagger from his belt and I winced as he grasped the shaft and began to whittle through it. The pain sent me to my knees and the fog before my eyes appeared again. Then I heard the arrow snap and fall to the flags, and Arthur said, "Done."

When I could catch my breath I told Arthur I must lie down, or I would collapse when he drew the arrow. I lay on my right side, told Arthur to be certain there were no splinters where he had hewn the shaft in two, then told him to grasp the point and pull the arrow through.

He did so, and all went black before my eyes, but I heard him say, as from some distance beyond the lychgate, "There... 'tis out."

A deep, overwhelming ache replaced the sharp agony of Arthur's pulling the arrow through my chest. The blackness before my eyes began to clear. I saw the stones of the floor, and my wits began to return.

"You must seek wine, to bathe my wounds and Osbert's," I said.

"Where am I to find wine in such a place? Perhaps..."

Arthur's hesitation caught my attention. He had been kneeling at my side, but scrambled to his feet as a distant voice spoke.

"Who is here?" a man said. "Is that blood I see spotting the porch?"

With the removal of the arrow, blood again flowed from my side. I tried to call out, but Arthur saw and clapped his hand over my mouth. He thought, he said later, that men from East Hanney had followed us.

The day was cloudy, and the windows of the old church were few and narrow, so the man spoke again before he saw us. "What man is in my church?"

It was the village priest who spoke. As he did so he saw Osbert; then Arthur, standing, caught his attention.

"What has happened to this man?" he asked Arthur. "Does he live, or is he dead?"

"Dunno," Arthur replied. "Been too busy with Master Hugh to notice."

"Master Hugh? The fellow at your feet? What affliction is here? This man," he said, glancing to Osbert, "is all bloodied." The priest's eyes were becoming accustomed to the dim church interior. "Is this your work?"

"Nay," Arthur replied. "That is Osbert. His lord has flogged him near to death, an' would've had his neck in a noose had we not freed him. Then, as we fled the village, an archer put an arrow into Master Hugh's back, an' he lays here, near dead also. He's asked for wine, to bathe 'is wounds, an' Osbert's. Have you any?"

"Wine? Oh, yes... and some for Extreme Unction. Have these men received Extreme Unction?"

"Nay," I managed to whisper. "Nor will I be this day."

After receiving last rites the Church considers a man as good as dead, even should he mend. I had no desire to recover from my wound but to fast perpetually, go barefoot at all seasons, and never again lie with Kate.

The flags were cold. I began to shiver, and Arthur saw.

"We must take Master Hugh and Osbert someplace where they may be warmed," he said to the priest, "and remove Master Hugh's bloody kirtle and cotehardie."

But that was not yet to be. Before the priest could reply, I heard the hooves of several horses. The priest had left open the door to the porch. The horses were reined to a halt at the church wall, near the lychgate, where Bruce and the palfrey were tied, and I then heard men's voices, one shouting louder than the others, although I could not hear clearly his words. I did not need to. I was certain we had been pursued from East Hanney, and Sir Philip Rede now stood at the lychgate with his men, ready to finish his work with Osbert, and me also.

Arthur understood this as well, and looked open-mouthed from me to the church door, awaiting some command.

Before I could summon my wits the priest turned and hastened to the porch to see who had arrived so noisily. I saw him glance through the open door and heard him mutter some indistinct oath. Then he did a surprising thing. He slammed the church door closed and slid the bolt to fix it shut in the face of Sir Philip – if indeed it were he who a moment later pounded upon the door and demanded admittance.

"Why did you not say 'twas Sir Philip Rede you had fled?" the priest asked Arthur.

"You didn't ask," he replied. "You know the man?"

"Aye. A blackguard, was ever one born of woman. He was to hang this one, you say?"

"Aye. An' he comes through that door he'll do it, an' finish off Master Hugh, as well."

"He'll not do so," said the priest. He looked down upon me, where I shivered upon the stones. "Do you claim sanctuary?" he asked.

"Aye," I managed to whisper between rattling teeth. "I do."

If Sir Philip had been a powerful lord he might scorn violating sanctuary and the threat of excommunication. But a poverty-stricken minor knight will think twice before hauling a man from a church before the allotted forty days have passed.

Sharp pounding again reverberated through the heavy oaken church door. Sir Philip hammered upon it with some hard object, perhaps the pommel of his dagger. At the same time he shouted a demand that the door be opened. This continued for some time, but none of us in the church made reply.

When Sir Philip grew weary of beating upon the door, the priest called out to him.

"Who do you seek?"

"My villein," came the reply, "and the men who stole him from me."

"They claim sanctuary," the priest shouted.

To this there was no immediate answer. Sir Philip was unprepared for this announcement. I imagined what he was thinking. For forty days he would need to station guards at the church door to see we did not escape.

Osbert moaned. While unconscious he had been free from pain. If he regained his senses this would no longer be so. My sack of instruments and herbs was in Abingdon, at the New Inn. The church provided sanctuary, but was also a jail from which I could not escape to seek help for Osbert or myself.

I heard voices once more beyond the church door, and saw the priest turn his attention there again. I could not hear what was said, for the words spoken were not from voices raised in anger.

The priest said a few words through the closed door, then opened it a crack and another robed figure slipped through. As soon as this man entered the church the priest shoved the door closed again.

This newcomer and the priest exchanged a few muttered words, then the fellow walked off toward the tower. A few moments later I heard the church bell ring for the noon Angelus. The new man was the priest's clerk.

I called out to the priest when the bell was silent. I needed a pallet for Osbert, and wine, to cleanse his wounds and my own. The clerk could come and go freely and could bring these things. And another scheme was forming in my mind. I had no wish to stay forty days in All Saints' Church, my whereabouts unknown to any who could help to extricate me and Arthur from this confinement.

The priest, I learned, was Father Maurice. He listened while I told him of our needs, and agreed to send his clerk for the items. I asked for three pallets, if they could be had, wine, and a pouch of whatever herbs he might possess. The priest had lettuce seed and a vial of the juice of St. James's Wort. The pounded lettuce seed, in a cup of ale, would help Osbert sleep, and the juice of St. James's Wort would, along with the wine, prevent his stripes from festering.

Next I asked for a thing which caused the priest to raise his eyebrows. I requested a length of sturdy rope as long as the church tower was high. This tower was not so tall as might have been in a larger village.

The clerk was sent on his way with instructions to return with the needed items, and also loaves and ale. Father Maurice announced that he would remain, as he did not trust Sir Philip to respect the sanctity of his church was he away.

'Twas near the ninth hour when the clerk, accompanied by a young assistant, returned. He brought three straw-filled pallets, three blankets, the pounded lettuce seeds and the vial of the juice of St. James's Wort, a ewer of wine, another of ale, three loaves, and a roasted capon. His delay, he said, was due to trouble finding a rope. This he had failed to locate.

I was so weak and sore from my own wound that I was not able to help myself or Osbert. I instructed the priest to bathe Osbert's lacerated back with wine, then coat the area with the juice of St. James's Wort and wrap him in a blanket, and with Arthur's help lay him upon the thickest pallet. Osbert cried out as the wine touched his wounds, but I urged Father Maurice to pay no heed and continue the work. When he was done Arthur offered bread to Osbert, but he would have none. Arthur did manage to raise Osbert so that he could take some ale into which Father Maurice had poured a good measure of pounded lettuce seeds. Osbert moaned when Arthur and the priest placed him face-down upon the pallet, and was then silent.

I asked Arthur's aid in removing my cotehardie and kirtle, for my left shoulder was stiffened and to move my left arm caused much pain. I was no more hungry than Osbert, but knew I would heal best if I ate, so after Father Maurice had bathed my wounds with the remaining wine I ate some bread and a bit of the capon. Some of the pounded lettuce seed remained, so I asked the priest to pour it into a cup of ale and drank the mixture down.

Arthur helped me to wrap myself in another of the blankets and I lay, aching and exhausted, bleeding upon a pallet. My plan to escape All Saints' Church depended upon a length of sturdy rope, and I had none.

While I lay wrapped in the blanket the clerk rang the evening Angelus Bell, and I was yet alert enough that the bell rope suddenly dangled in my clouded thoughts.

I called Arthur and Father Maurice to me and explained my plan. Someone must travel to Bampton and tell Lord Gilbert of my plight. If the priest or his clerk attempted to leave Marcham I feared Sir Philip might find them upon the way and stop them. I wished no more men to suffer on my behalf.

Arthur is not so tall as me, but weighs nearly fourteen stone. A rope which can support his bulk must be well made. No frail cord would do. I asked Father Maurice about his bell rope.

"Nearly new," he replied. "Got it last year from a rope-maker in Oxford."

"If it was loosed from the bell, and fastened from the top of the tower, would it bear Arthur, you think?"

The priest cast an apprehensive eye at Arthur, measuring his bulk. His frown gradually faded, a smile replacing it.

"Ah, I see. Aye, I believe it would."

"Sir Philip will have men placed at the doors," I said, "but 'tis near dark, and I think he will pay no attention to the tower."

"You want me to escape by rope down the tower?" Arthur asked.

"Aye. Get to Bampton as quickly as you can. Tell Lord Gilbert where I am, and why, and ask if he will send Lady Petronilla's wagon to take me and Osbert to Bampton. Sir Philip must be driven off, so a half-dozen or more grooms should accompany the wagon."

"An' what am I to tell Kate?"

"That I am wounded, but 'tis not grievous."

I did not wish for Kate to suffer unnecessary worry, and, indeed, I did not believe my wound so perilous as when I first looked down and saw an arrowhead protruding from under my arm. I had coughed up no blood, so was convinced that the shaft had missed my lung.

There was yet part of a loaf remaining from the meal the clerk had brought. I told Arthur to eat it, so as to maintain his strength for the night's journey. It was dark when he finished the loaf, licked his fingers and said, "I'm off, then."

Father Maurice had lit a candle, and in its dim light I saw Arthur and the clerk disappear into the dark in the direction of the tower. As he set off I warned Arthur to be careful in untying the rope. It would not do to have the bell sound.

Much time passed before the clerk returned, so that I worried that some misfortune had befallen Arthur. But eventually the man appeared from the dark at the base of the tower and announced softly that Arthur had gone safely over the top of the tower, and the bell rope was now again fixed to the bell frame.

Father Maurice sent the clerk and his young companion to the vicarage, then informed me that he would spend the night in the church.

"If Sir Philip sees me leave, he'll find some excuse to enter and carry you off. If I protest to the bishop he'll claim you were seized trying to escape, and he'll have put you to death, so you'll not be able to dispute him. I know Sir Philip."

Father Maurice wrapped himself in a blanket and settled upon the remaining pallet. He was soon snoring softly. Osbert also slept, although he occasionally shifted upon his pallet and moaned when he did so. The lettuce seed was more effective for Osbert than for me. I lay alert well into the night.

How had I come to such a plight? Perhaps if William of Garstang had not given his books to me, six years past, when he was near to death from plague, I would not be here, wounded, upon the floor of Marcham Church. One of William's three books was *Surgery*, by Henri de Mondeville. I read it, and changed my vocation.

Had I not spent a year of study in Paris, I could not have stitched up the lacerated leg of Lord Gilbert Talbot when a horse kicked him upon Oxford High Street. Then I would not have been offered a post as Lord Gilbert's bailiff at Bampton, and was I not given such authority in that place I would not have known of John Thrale's death or his coin, and would not now lay pierced upon the cold flags of All Saints' Church.

But it was my skill as a surgeon which led me to meet Kate Caxton and claim her for my bride. I might wish the flow of my life had followed some other course, so to avoid the sorrow which occasionally afflicts me, as with all men, but had it done so I would never have known the joy of life with Kate. I would not have bounced Bessie upon my knee and heard her squeal with delight.

Why should I wish my way had been altered so as to avoid this place and this moment? Some other sorrows would surely have come to me had I chosen to walk other paths, and the bliss I found with Kate, the pleasure of life among the folk of Bampton, the satisfaction of my work as surgeon and for Lord Gilbert, all this I would have lost.

I turned upon my pallet to seek a more comfortable position, adjusted the blanket, and finally fell to sleep, content with my lot. I did awaken often through the night, and when I did I breathed a prayer that the Lord Christ would take pity upon me and send me, whole and recovered, back to Kate's arms. I resolved never again to question His direction for my life, or lament the sorrows which come my way, for then I must also repent of the delights He has allowed me.

When dawn gave enough light to see, Father Maurice opened the door to the porch. He glanced through the opening, then closed the door and walked my way.

"Four men," he said. "Didn't see Sir Philip among 'em. Probably sought his bed and left others to do his work. No doubt there are more watching the other doors."

There had been no shouting or commotion the night before, when Arthur let himself down from the tower. I was sure he was safely away. Had he been discovered there would have been tumult. Arthur would not be easily taken, even by half a dozen men.

From Marcham to Bampton is nearly ten miles. Even if Arthur was cautious upon the road he would have roused

Wilfred, the porter of Bampton Castle, by midnight. Would he seek Lord Gilbert straight away, or allow his lord to sleep the night in peace before he gave him my message? I had supplied no instruction on the matter.

I had convinced myself that Arthur had awaited the new day to seek Lord Gilbert when I heard hoof-beats in the distance. The priest heard also, and turned to me with concern in his eyes. He believed, I think, that Sir Philip had returned with reinforcements. When I saw the concern upon his face I felt also some anxiety, but this soon faded. Had Sir Philip wished to violate sanctuary, he had had enough men with him last night to do so, and carry me, Osbert, and Arthur off to East Hanney.

"'Tis Lord Gilbert's men," I said, and was shocked at how weak my voice had become.

The thunder of many hooves reached a crescendo, then came to a clattering halt. There was a momentary stillness, soon followed by the shouts of many agitated men.

While the bellowing continued there came several firm blows against the church door, and we heard a shout over the din: "'Tis me, Arthur, with Lord Gilbert an' men of Bampton!"

Father Maurice leaped to the door, and from the corner of my eye I saw Osbert attempt to lift himself upon an elbow to see what clamor had roused him from his sleep. The priest drew the bolt, swung open the door, and fell back as Lord Gilbert and Arthur charged through the opening. From beyond the porch, with the door now open, I could hear angry words, but they seemed to diminish in volume rapidly.

Arthur had stood aside to allow Lord Gilbert to enter the church first. "You are Father Maurice?" he asked. The priest bowed in reply.

"My man has told me of your good service. This church will see my gratitude. Where is Master Hugh?"

The morn was clouded, but brighter than the dim church, so Lord Gilbert cast his eyes about as he spoke, and they did not find me till Father Maurice pointed silently in my direction.

I tried to rise, and got as far as one knee, when I toppled to the flags. I was dizzy, I suspect, from loss of blood. Although de Mondeville did not address the phenomenon in his book, I believe it to be a consequence of a wound which bleeds much.

"Nay, Hugh, lay yourself down. No need to rise. Arthur has told me all. Lady Petronilla's wagon follows, and your Kate is in it. She would not be prevented when she heard of your wound."

"Bessie?" I said.

"Nurse is caring for her along with our own babe."

The church door filled with the shadows of many men, and Lord Gilbert turned to see the reason for the deeper gloom.

"Gone," a voice said. "All of 'em. Was two at other doors, but they fled when they saw t'others ride off."

"Very well," Lord Gilbert said. Then, to Father Maurice, "Is there a baker in Marcham? I would break my fast."

"Aye, m'lord. He should be drawing loaves from his oven as we speak."

Lord Gilbert handed coins to Arthur, told him to take another groom with him, and fetch loaves and ale. He then squatted by my pallet and spoke.

"I would hear more of this, when you are stronger. Arthur said there is a woman and children missing, and the woman may know something of the dead chapman."

"Aye." I did not intend to whisper, but that was all the response I could make.

"What of that fellow?" Lord Gilbert asked, pointing to Osbert. "Arthur said he fled his manor."

"Aye. Did Arthur tell why?"

"He was hurried. 'Tis all a muddle. Something about the fellow guarding a maid Sir Philip Rede had seized."

I raised myself to one elbow and intended to explain all to Lord Gilbert, but my strength failed. "The lass was stolen from her father and held for ransom," I said, but then fell back to my pallet.

Lord Gilbert saw my weakness and did not press me further. I slept fitfully again, awakened often throughout the morning by the murmur of low voices. Shortly after the noon Angelus Bell I awoke to loud voices, and one of these feminine. A moment later Kate knelt by my pallet, cradled my dazed head in her arms, and pressed her wet cheek against mine. I began to feel better.

Lord Gilbert announced that, if we were to return to Bampton before nightfall, we must leave Marcham immediately. I called to Arthur and asked him to assist me to my feet. With his sturdy shoulder to lean upon I tottered across the churchyard, through the lychgate, to the privy behind the vicarage. I was much relieved! Here is no jest. I saw no blood in my discharge.

Chapter 11

My thoughts were troubled and my body pained as Lady Petronilla's wagon bore me, Osbert, and Kate to Bampton. I had thought that riding an old dexter like Bruce was a jolting experience, especially if the beast was spurred to a gallop, but enduring a dozen miles atop Bruce was nothing compared to the jarring I felt through the straw pallet which Kate had arranged upon the wagon's planks.

Osbert suffered also, but after a mile or two he gave up groaning each time a wheel encountered a rut and bore the experience silently. Or perhaps the pain caused him to fall insensible again.

Kate would not be content until I told her all. Relating the tale helped me to concentrate my mind on the matter of John Thrale and his coin, and disregard the rutted road.

When we crossed the Thames at Newbridge there was yet enough light to see the bare branches of trees reflecting darkly from the river, but all was darkness at Standlake. We heard the bell of the village church ring the Angelus as we passed.

Kate took my head and rested it in her lap, told me I must say no more, but rest, then stroked my hair until I was nearly fallen to sleep. Shortly before the ninth hour I heard the voices of our escort speak of Bampton. I was home.

I remember being lifted, upon my pallet, from the wagon and taken to our chamber off the Bampton Castle hall. Kate then offered a loaf, from which I managed a few mouthfuls, but I remember nothing more till I awoke next day well after dawn. Kate sat in a shaft of bright sunlight, and when she heard me shift upon our bed she rose from her bench and was at my side.

I asked of Osbert. Kate was unaware of his condition, but promised she would seek John Chamberlain and learn where he'd been placed and how he fared. While she did so she required of me that I eat from a fresh loaf of wheaten bread and drink from a cup of ale she left beside the bed. As Kate put her hand to the door I asked that she also seek Arthur. I had a task for the man.

Arthur and Kate returned together. I sent Arthur to Abingdon to retrieve my sack of instruments and herbs from the New Inn, and to inquire of the abbey hosteler of Sybil Montagu. The maid weighed upon my conscience. Sharp as her tongue was, she was alone and defenseless in Abingdon.

Osbert, Arthur said, was put to bed in his chamber in the lodgings range, where Cicily, Arthur's wife, could attend him. I bid Arthur take two grooms with him to Abingdon, for he might be recognized and need assistance should he meet Sir Philip Rede or his men in Abingdon or upon the road. The fellow was not eager to leave Bampton again so soon, but grooms learn early to do as they are bid.

In my pharmacy I had a vial of the juice of adder's tongue. Early each summer I walk the hedgerows and along the banks of Shill Brook seeking this fern. The oil from its leaves and roots makes a soothing and healing salve. When Arthur was on his way I asked Kate to seek the vial. When she found it I told her to mix a small portion of its contents with clean water from Shill Brook to the proportion of three parts water to one part oil of adder's tongue, then take the ointment to Arthur's wife and direct her to apply it to the wounds upon Osbert's back.

I explained that the oil of adder's tongue, thus applied, would cleanse and speed the healing of Osbert's lacerations. Kate nodded, took a clean bowl from our cupboard, and promised to return with water from Shill Brook.

When she returned she mixed the two liquids in a flask, then approached our bed.

"This will aid poor Osbert?" she asked, holding the flask before her.

"Aye."

"Then I will apply some to your wounds also."

I tried to explain that adder's tongue was most useful when employed to bathe ulcerated wounds which resist healing. I had kept my own injury under close inspection and was pleased to see that scabs had formed where the arrow entered my back, and where the point had protruded from the muscle under my arm. Some small drops of blood yet oozed from these wounds, but little pus, for which I was much relieved. Most physicians and surgeons hold that thick, white pus issued from a wound is a good thing, and thin, watery pus is to be feared. But I hold with de Mondeville that no pus at all from a wound is to be preferred.

Adder's tongue is not so helpful when applied to a wound which is scabbed over, but if there was any use to its application to my wounds, Kate would hear of no reason to abstain from dosing me, back and front. Being an apt scholar, I had learned soon after we wed that when Kate was set upon her course I had best keep silent if I disagreed. Oddly enough, her determination in such matters often proved correct. I ceased my objection and allowed her to pull down the blanket and coat both entrance and exit wounds with the thin ointment.

When Kate returned from the lodging range she reported that Osbert was alert but in much pain. I bade her return to Cicily with a pouch of pounded hemp and lettuce seeds to add to ale. This mix was a favorite of mine for reducing pain and bringing sleep, and when Kate learned of it she demanded I drink some of the mixture myself. She did not need to argue this time.

I slept through dinner, which, when I awoke, surprised me, for the hall is just the other side of the door to my chamber, and dinner in Bampton Castle is not generally a quiet affair.

Another surprise, and a pleasant one, was that I awoke hungry. The wounds were yet painful, and when I breathed deeply or tried to turn in my bed I was reminded of them anew. But I have observed that when an injured man recovers his appetite he is likely to regain his health.

I did not wish to rise from my bed and eat supper in the hall, so Kate brought my meal upon a tray. The first remove was farced capon, a dish I dearly love, and apples in compost. Perhaps I ate too much of these, for when Kate returned with the second remove upon her tray, a game pie and cabbage with marrow and cyueles, a few bites of game pie was all I could manage. I saw concern in Kate's eyes, for she knows I am rarely so discomfited that I cannot consume my share and more of a meal. Of the third remove I know nothing, for I begged to be excused from any more nourishment from Lord Gilbert's table, asked only for another cup of ale with crushed hemp and lettuce seeds, and under the influence of these herbs and a too-full stomach soon fell to sleep again. The last I remember of the day is Kate drawing her stool close beside the bed to watch over me. I was unhappy that I was the cause of Kate's distress, but reflected that I would be even more melancholy if there was no one to sit with me and mourn my infirmity.

Next day I felt well enough to rise from my bed. After a loaf and cheese I went, with Kate nervously attending every step, to the lodgings range to see how Osbert fared. He did not fare well.

His lesions were many and much pus and blood yet drained from them. The fellow was alert, no longer insensible from the thrashing he had endured, which is not' to say he no longer suffered.

I asked Osbert how he fell into Sir Philip's hands.

"Men come on me when I was past Frilford. They was afoot. I'd've made for a hedgerow if I'd heard horses comin'. I was enjoyin' the walk, wool-gatherin', like, an' they come into the road before me afore I could take notice an' hide. When I seen 'em begin to run I knew whose men they must be, though they was too far away to recognize faces. 'Twas John, Adam, an' Martyn. Thought they was my friends. I ran into the fields, but Martyn cut me off. Fleet of foot, is Martyn. Sir Philip promised three pence to any man who could take me."

Osbert lay upon his belly, an arm drawn up upon which he pillowed his head. It caused me some discomfort to bend over him to inspect his lacerated back, and this he noticed.

"'Ow'd you get me free?" he asked. "Last I remember, they'd tied me to a post an' was layin' on with the lash."

"I will tell you all when you are recovered. Your back needs attention, else it will not heal properly."

I told Osbert and Cicily that I would return shortly with instruments and salves, then with Kate ever at my elbow lest I grow faint, I returned to our chamber.

Some of my instruments I had taken to Abingdon, but what I needed to deal with Osbert's back I had in the castle. From my supply of herbs I took a flask of ointment I had made by boiling leaves of moneywort in the juice of wild pears. This salve is of my own devising, as moneywort serves well for old wounds, and pear juice is useful for new. I decided a year past to try the two combined. Osbert provided my first opportunity to see how the two might serve when mixed together, for under most circumstances I apply no ointment to any wound.

Flayed skin lay in tattered ribbons upon Osbert's back. I drew down the blanket covering him and hardly knew where to begin. I must first cleanse the lacerations of caked blood and pus, so sent Cicily to the buttery for half a ewer of wine. While she was away I used tweezers and a tiny scalpel to tease away detached skin. This did not trouble Osbert much, for the skin had been peeled from his back and was no longer sensitive. But when my scalpel touched living flesh he gasped and the muscles of his back quivered. I prepared another draught of ale with a strong dose of crushed hemp seeds for the fellow to drink. The work I must do would cause him some pain.

It caused me some discomfort also, to bend over Osbert as I must. Kate had accompanied me again, being unwilling to believe my protest that my strength was much increased. She saw me wince as I bent to the work, and dragged a stool to the bed so I might sit closer to my task and have less reason to bend to it.

Cicily soon returned with the wine and I gently flushed coagulated blood, shredded fragments of skin, and layers of pus from Osbert's wounds. The flesh of his back convulsed as he felt the sting of the wine, but he bore the pain without crying out.

When I had cleaned his back as well as could be I stitched two of the lacerations which were deeper and wider than the others, then dipped a clean fragment of linen cloth into the ointment of pears and moneywort and daubed it thickly upon Osbert's wounds.

De Mondeville taught that wounds heal more readily when left open to the air, rather than wrapped tight in bandages. Since my year of study in Paris I have practiced this method of his, and found good success. Most folk find this new procedure suspect, and when I told Cicily that she must leave Osbert's back exposed till the ointment was dry, then cover him lightly only with a blanket to keep him warm, she frowned at the instruction.

I took dinner in the hall, and when the meal was done was about to seek our chamber and rest when John Chamberlain approached. Lord Gilbert, he said, would see me in the solar.

My wounds pained me, and where the arrow had pierced my back I felt a renewed flow of blood. Bending over Osbert had broken open the puncture. Kate would not be pleased to see another kirtle stained. But when a great lord calls, a man must answer, especially so if the lord is his employer and has given him a house in the town freehold.

Kate appeared with Bessie in her arms. I had not seen the child for many days, and felt a pang that I had neglected her. I vowed that when Lord Gilbert was done with me I would atone for my negligence.

I found Lord Gilbert in the solar, enjoying a blaze in the fireplace which warmed his back. He bade me sit, and asked of my health.

"My wound troubles me some," I said, "but I am likely to survive."

"Good. The villein that you attend, when will his wounds be healed so that he may be returned?"

"Returned? To the lord who abused him so?"

"Abuse or not, Sir Philip is his lord and he must be sent back. Since plague far too many of his station have fled their manors. Such must be stopped."

"If he is sent to Sir Philip it will mean his certain death."

"A lord has such warrant over disobedient villeins."

"What crime did the man commit worthy of death?" I asked.

"He fled his lord and manor," Lord Gilbert frowned.

"Because of me. If he is sent back to East Hanney and to his death, you make me complicit."

"Why so?"

"He was assigned to guard a maid who had been stolen from her father and held for ransom. Arthur and I approached Sir Philip's manor after dark, seeking another woman we thought might be held there, and released the lass. Osbert feared Sir Philip would deal severely with him for being surprised in the night and allowing the maid to be freed."

"So you carried him away as well as the lass?"

"What was I to do? Leave him to die at the hands of a wicked lord?"

"Wicked Sir Philip may be, but he was the man's lord."

"May be? He took a knight's daughter and kept her for ransom. Because Osbert failed to assist this felony, he must now die?"

"Perhaps Sir Philip would not have destroyed the fellow."

"He was doing so when Arthur and I freed him."

"Ah, but that was for running away, not for failing to properly guard his prisoner."

"You believe Sir Philip would have dealt more

leniently with Osbert for allowing his captive, for whom he was demanding fifty pounds, to escape?"

"Whether Sir Philip is lenient or not is his business, not yours... or mine. The man was his villein and his to command."

"He commanded him to aid him in a felony. Must a man obey his lord and violate the laws of God and the King?"

"It is for his lord to decide obedience to the King, and a priest to determine what is due God."

"If you send Osbert back to Sir Philip, he will slay the man, and if the past days are a measure, he'll seek some ghastly way to do it."

"I cannot control what another knight does upon his own manor. I must do what law requires and send the fellow back. The man must be returned to Sir Philip as soon as he is recovered from his wounds."

"When he will receive fresh ones. You may as well pack him upon a cart and send him back now."

Lord Gilbert grimaced involuntarily, for he had seen the bloody flesh of Osbert's back. He pounded a fist upon his table to punctuate his next words. "I will not permit my bailiff to aid a villein who would flee his lord, and there's an end to the matter. When the fellow is strong enough he will be returned. See to it."

"I cannot," I said.

"You what?" Lord Gilbert stood, as then did I.

"I can no longer serve you, m'lord. If Osbert is to be returned to Sir Philip and his death, I must resign my post."

"Bah... you think a surgeon in Bampton can find custom enough to feed his family?"

"Probably not. I will take Kate and Bessie to Oxford. I have treated men's wounds and injuries there, and have some small reputation."

"Then go to Oxford! Go where you wish. I care not. But my bailiff will not tell me where my duty lies. I took you into my service to ease my burdens. Now you seek to increase them. Of what use are you to me?"

The conversation was clearly at an end. I bowed stiffly, because I was stiff, and because my attitude toward my employer was rigid. I stalked from the solar, descended to the hall, and banged open the door to our chamber, causing Kate to start and Bessie to whimper.

"We are to return to Galen House," I said.

Kate brightened. She had never enjoyed being required to live in my old chamber in the castle. Then I told her why we would return to Galen House and her countenance fell.

"You have displeased Lord Gilbert."

"Aye. I wish it was not so, but I could see no other way."

"What will become of Osbert?"

"I have a plan. It will require your help if I am to save him from Sir Philip's vengeance."

"You shall have it. Is there no way to compromise with Lord Gilbert?"

"None. Osbert must either be set free of his obligation to Sir Philip, or be returned to certain death. There is no middle way."

"And you," Kate smiled gently as she spoke, "are a stubborn man."

"Principled," I corrected

"And Lord Gilbert is stubborn?"

"He is also principled, but not all principled men serve the proper principles."

"They may be costly, these principles of yours."

"Aye. We may be required to leave Bampton."

"I would be sorry to do so."

"And I, also. I built Galen House to be our home. We will remain within it if we can."

"What of your plan for Osbert?"

"We will take him from the castle lodgings range to Galen House. If Lord Gilbert learns of it and asks why, I will tell him that Osbert requires constant care, which is no lie, and 'tis inconvenient for me to visit the castle several times each day to see to his wounds."

"Can he recover?"

"I believe so, but his back will be badly scarred. He may never again bend to touch his toes."

"What will you do when he is healed?"

"I will tell the man he must flee in the night, and leave Oxfordshire far behind him. If Lord Gilbert asks of his healing I will tell him it goes slowly, so he will not, I hope, require Osbert to be sent back to East Hanney before he can safely escape Bampton."

"You would lie to Lord Gilbert?"

"To save a life? Aye, I would. But I will not lie to him… I will not tell him the whole truth, that is all."

"What will Lord Gilbert do when he learns the man has fled? Must you then resign your post?"

"He may require it of me. So be it. I am content, whatever befall."

"What of the dead chapman and his coin?"

"So long as I am bailiff to Lord Gilbert I will serve him in the matter, and any other. And it may be because of me that Amice Thatcher and her children were taken."

"You will return to Abingdon to seek them?"

"I must… when my wounds are better healed."

Before nightfall of that melancholy day I had assigned three grooms to move Kate and me and our goods from the castle to Galen House, and Osbert was placed upon a cart and taken there also. Kate laid a fire upon the cold hearth, and set a kettle of pottage to simmering for our supper. I went to our bed that night strangely content, for a man who had displeased his employer, was in danger of losing part of his income, and had been recently pierced by an arrow.

We had no bed for Osbert, so laid his pallet upon the floor, close to the fire. Even though he slept there upon the ground floor, and Kate, Bessie, and I were in our chamber up the stairs, I heard him groan in his sleep when he shifted upon the pallet and his wounds caused him pain.

Osbert's appetite was returning, so next morn he

ate readily a portion of maslin loaf and cheese, and drank from a cup of ale into which I poured more crushed hemp seeds. He asked why he had been taken from the castle to this place, and I told him where he now was, and why. His face fell as he learned of his peril.

"Sir Philip will send me to my grave," he said when I had finished.

"So I told Lord Gilbert, but he would not be moved."

"How long before I am well enough that you will send me back?"

"If all goes as I hope, that day will never come."

Osbert looked up to me, questions in his eyes. "You think I will not recover from the beating?"

"I believe you will regain your health, though 'tis likely the scars upon your back will always be with you, and will prevent you bending as a man otherwise could do."

"Then I do not understand. How is it the day I must be sent back to East Hanney may never come?"

"I have a plan. I intend for you to escape this place, when you are well enough to travel."

"Where am I to go?"

"I will tell you more later, when I have thought more about it. For now, you must regain your health. We will worry about where you are to go when the time approaches for you to flee."

Truth to tell, I had already in mind a plan for Osbert's escape, of which I thought he would approve, but I wished to think more on it before I told him, so that, had he questions or objections, I would have answers for him.

Shortly after we broke our fast and I had told Osbert of his danger, there came a loud thumping upon Galen House door. I opened to Arthur's smiling face, and saw in his hand my sack of instruments and herbs. I bid him enter and tell me of Abingdon. There was much to learn.

"The maid Sybil has returned to her father, who sent men for her. So the abbey hosteler said," he began.

Here was reassuring news. I had enough to worry about with Osbert and Amice Thatcher and the death of John Thrale weighing upon me. I did not need more worries about the welfare of an irksome maid. I dismissed Sybil Montagu from my mind and asked Arthur of Brother Theodore.

"Told 'im of your hurt, an' told 'im you'd return to deal with his wound when you could. He said 'e'd pray for your quick healing, as well 'e might. Must be a great trial to 'ave an' oozin' sore like that on yer face."

Arthur looked past me and saw Osbert upon his pallet. I saw the question in his eyes, and hastened to explain why he was here, rather than under Cicily's care. But I did not tell him all. I did speak of Lord Gilbert's demand that Osbert be returned to Sir Philip when he was well enough to travel, but I did not tell him of my plan to have the villein escape. The fewer who know a secret the less likely it will be discovered.

Arthur did not respond well to this announcement. He served Lord Gilbert well, and, I think, held his lord in some esteem. But the thought of returning Osbert to a punishment so severe as we had already seen, and from which we had risked life and limb to rescue the man, brought a heavy scowl down upon Arthur's face. I wished to tell him of my scheme to prevent the carrying out of Lord Gilbert's wishes, but held my tongue. Arthur would continue to serve Lord Gilbert, I thought, but perhaps not so readily as in the past.

I told Arthur to be ready to return to Abingdon in three days, All Saints' Day, when I thought I would be enough recovered from my wounds that I might renew the search for Amice Thatcher and John Thrale's assailants. Kate thought otherwise, but I persuaded her that I should be about the tasks. The sooner I completed them the sooner I would be able to resume a peaceful life as husband, father, and sometime surgeon.

Kate prepared an egg leech for our dinner and I was pleased to see Osbert consume a fair portion. I put another handful of ground hemp seeds into his ale, and when he had downed the mixture I sought to question him more of Sir Philip Rede and his manor at East Hanney.

Somewhere in the village Amice Thatcher was confined, of this I was certain.

Osbert, as he had told me some days past, knew of no other person Sir Philip had taken and detained, but I thought he might know of some places on the manor where a woman and her children might be confined without the fact being known to most who lived in the village; a loft in a barn, for example.

"Stores oats an' hay in the loft, does Sir Philip," Osbert said. "Though 'is horses get their fill of oats, 'e does keep hay for winter fodder."

"His horses get their fill of oats? I thought you said he was in some financial plight."

"'E is, but spends 'is coin on wine an' horses as if 'e had plenty."

"Wine and horses… these are Sir Philip's interests?"

"Aye. Well, an' a pert maid."

"How many horses does Sir Philip own?"

"There's seven in the barn, includin' two what belong to 'is brother."

"Are these beasts treated well?"

"Oh, aye. Better'n we who labor for Sir Philip."

"Does he employ a farrier to care for the horses?"

"Nay. Can't afford that. Uses Sir John Trillowe's man when 'is horses need shoein'."

"Have you known Sir Philip to allow a horse to go about with a broken horseshoe?"

"Broken bad enough to maybe injure the beast?"

"Aye."

"Never. Don't care whether them who labor for 'im has shoes or not, but 'is horses is always well shod."

"You never saw the print of a horse with a broken shoe in the mud before the barn?"

"Nay. Sir Philip wouldn't tolerate that from the lads what serve in 'is stable. Minute they knew of such they'd have the beast to Sir John's farrier, or Sir Philip would set 'em to work in the fields or herdin' swine."

Chapter 12

My theory was shattered. Sir Philip Rede, an impoverished knight, so poor that he captured another knight's daughter and kept her for ransom, had seemed likely to me to be a man who would beat to death another in an attempt to make him tell of a treasure. And a poor knight might ignore the needs of his horse. So I thought.

But Osbert said this was not so. Was it Sir Philip who took Amice Thatcher, or some knight unknown to me who rode a horse with a broken shoe? Was there another impoverished manor in East Hanney?

Perhaps Amice was held in some other place. The wretches who ransacked her hut spoke of returning to East Hanney, but mayhap they confined her somewhere else. Were these scoundrels not the same men who beat John Thrale, or rode a horse with a broken shoe? How could I discover answers to these questions?

I spent the next days nursing Osbert's wounds and my own, thinking how I might find Amice Thatcher, and pondering a remove to Oxford. The last day of October, a Sunday, was All Hallows' Eve. Kate had occupied herself for two days baking soul cakes for the children and poor men and women who would beg the cakes before our door on All Saints' Day and All Souls' Day.

Mornings were worst. When I crawled from our bed it seemed as if the arrow Arthur had drawn from my back was yet there. After an hour or so of cautious movement the aggrieved flesh flexed more readily, so that by the time mass was done on All Saints' Day I felt tolerably able to mount Bruce and make for Abingdon. As Saturn would soon leave Aries, I took along the sack of herbs and instruments which had already made the journey once.

Osbert could not stay in Galen House while I was away and only Kate resided there with him. Sunday afternoon I had visited the castle and sought Alice atte Bridge. The lass worked in the scullery, a position I had found for her some years past, after the death of her father. She was willing, as who would not be, to leave her duties at the castle and occupy a room at Galen House, there to assist Kate in treating Osbert's wounds and dissolve any gossip which would surely surface if Kate was left alone to nurse my patient.

I instructed Kate and Alice in the use of salves, and told Kate to continue to dose Osbert's ale with crushed seeds of hemp and lettuce also at nightfall. I advised Kate that, if Lord Gilbert sent a man to question her of Osbert's recovery, she was to tell him that many weeks would pass before he could leave his bed. Then I set out for Abingdon, assured that matters in Bampton were in hand.

'Twas near dark when we stabled our horses in the mews behind the New Inn and sought some supper. I was concerned about leaving my sack of instruments with the innkeeper. When Arthur returned the sack four days earlier I noticed that my finest scalpel had a nick in the blade. The innkeeper had used it, I think, to bone a chicken for his stew pot. It was my intent to leave the sack with Brother Theodore, but the day was too far gone to seek him. Tomorrow, after I had concluded some other business, I would find the hosteler and make provision for my instruments. Tonight I would keep the sack near.

While we rode to Abingdon that day I had told Arthur of Osbert's claim that Sir Philip Rede cared well for his horses, and would not permit one to go lame because of a broken shoe. I did not doubt Osbert, but wished to be sure of the assertion before I sought some other man. That night, as we prepared for bed, I told Arthur that we must rise early, before dawn, and once more travel the road to East Hanney.

All Souls' Day mass is also obligatory. It was my plan to ignore this requirement, travel to East Hanney, and again approach Sir Philip's manor through the wood. When the church bell had called all the village to mass we could cross the meadow, enter the stable, and inspect the right rear hooves of the horses kept there.

So when the bell of the abbey church rang for matins I elbowed Arthur awake and together we stumbled down the dark stairs, across the yard, and into the mews.

The stable boy had left a cresset lighted upon a stand, as is common, so he might see to deal with any beast which needed attention in the night. By its flame we saddled Bruce and the palfrey. I tossed my sack of instruments across Bruce's rump, being unwilling to leave the sack with the innkeeper for even one day, and we set off down Ock Street guided by the light of a quarter moon.

The eastern sky was growing light when we approached the wood north of East Hanney. The path into the forest was yet dark, but we had traveled that way often enough that it was no trouble to find the clearing where we had before left the horses, then make our way to the nettle-crusted stone wall. I was heartily weary of the journey and this place, and breathed a prayer to the Lord Christ that I could soon put East Hanney forever behind me.

By the time we arrived at the wall the new day had grown light enough that we could see Sir Philip's manor, its house and outbuildings, quite clearly. I was astonished at what else I saw.

Two shadowy figures stood beside the decaying hen coop where we had found Sybil Montagu. Someone was once again imprisoned in that shed. Was Sybil there again? If so, the men who were to take her to her father had rather come from Sir Philip. But how would he have known that she could be found at the abbey guest house?

Perhaps another prisoner was in the shed. Amice Thatcher? That seemed unlikely. Or perhaps Sir Philip, his scheme for ransoming Sybil Montagu a failure, had seized some other nobleman's child, or the heir of some wealthy burgher.

The morn was cold, and my wounds, stiffened in the

night, ached as we peered over the wall.

"Two men now," Arthur said. "Sir Philip ain't gonna chance 'is prisoner escapin' again. But who could he have there now? Suppose it's Sybil Montagu?"

"Mayhap."

"We gonna free 'er again, then?"

"I have other concerns. If Sir Philip has retaken Sybil Montagu, he can keep her for a time. Serve him right."

"Aye," Arthur chuckled.

Only those with good reason may absent themselves from mass on All Saints' Day and All Souls' Day. Would an assignment to keep vigil over Sir Philip's prisoner be considered good reason?

It was. Less than an hour after Arthur and I took station behind the wall, the church bell called East Hanney's residents to the church, where on this day would be said prayers for those dead but not yet released from purgatory. If such souls there be, prayers can do them no harm, and if no purgatory exists, prayer is generally a good thing anyway.

We heard the pealing of the bell and watched to see if the guards left their post. They did not.

"Reckon Sir Philip's got the lass back in that shed?" Arthur asked.

"Or some other prisoner has been taken and is now held there. If it is Sybil in the shed, somehow Sir Philip learned that she was at the abbey guest hall."

As I spoke the words I guessed how Sir Philip might have discovered Sybil. The abbot was Peter of Hanney. Was he a friend to Sir Philip Rede, and had he learned who was sheltered in his guest hall? This could be, but I would not concern myself now with the possibility. If Sybil was once again held in the shed, the experience could do her little harm. She might even learn humility, which discovery would greatly improve her disposition. When I could, I would send word to her father of where she might be found.

"How we gonna spy out them horses with men

standin' so near to the stable?" Arthur asked.

I had been considering the same problem, and thought I had an answer. The guards stationed at the shed were in stature much like Arthur: sturdy and squarely built, short-legged and made for strength, not speed. I could easily outrun Arthur, and even but a week removed from being pierced by an arrow I felt recovered enough that I could successfully flee the two men I saw across the meadow.

"If I distract one of those fellows," I said, "can you take the other?"

"Believe so," he grinned.

"Here is my plan. All others are at the church. We'll have but those two to deal with. Walk with me on the road to the village. We'll not cross the field. They'll see us coming and be ready for mischief. No honest men would approach them through a wood and across a meadow rather than by the road.

"If they see us approach the village they will likely take us for two simple travelers, unconcerned about who might see them enter the village. We will be too far away to be recognized, I think, if they were among those who witnessed Osbert's beating and our rescue.

"After we pass behind the first houses, you hold back. I will turn from the road just past the third house, and enter the gate to Sir Philip's manor. I'll try to get the guards to chase me. Few men can outrun me – surely not those fellows.

"If they both follow, you open the door to the shed and see who is there. Then go to the stable and inspect the right-rear hooves of the beasts there. You know what to look for."

"If 'tis Sybil in the hencoop," Arthur grimaced, "what am I to do with her?"

"Nothing. Tell her, or whoever is there, to flee to the church, and after the mass seek the priest and tell him of her plight. I wish to be done with her."

"And if both them fellows don't chase after you, what then?"

"You must overcome the one who remains behind. When you have done so, toss him in the shed in place of whoso may be there now. I'll allow the one who pursues me to keep close, so he may believe he can catch me, until you have had time to inspect the stable. We will meet here in an hour or so, after I have shaken loose from pursuit."

The events which followed went nearly according to my plan, which, later, when I thought back on the day, surprised me. Generally when I construe some design for catching felons, or seeking the truth of a matter, some unforeseen complication unhinges the scheme.

The gate before Sir Philip's manor was constructed of rotting wood and rusting iron. He needed to spend more upon his manor and less upon French wine. But even though the hinges squealed, the guards did not know of my approach and so looked up, startled, as I strode around the corner of the house and approached them.

"Who're you?" One of the guards found his tongue and challenged me.

"I come from Sir Henry Montagu, of South Marston. He has sent me to demand the return of his daughter. Where is Sir Philip? At mass, no doubt. You are left here to see that the lass does not escape? Must be in that hencoop, eh?"

"Dunno what yer talkin' 'bout," one said. "Sir Philip don't like folk creepin' about 'is manor."

I would not have described my approach as "creeping," but thought the moment inopportune for a discussion of word definitions. The guard who clarified Sir Philip's likes and dislikes was reaching for his belt, where an unornamented but serviceable dagger was sheathed.

"Tell Sybil that her father knows of her capture, and if she is not released to me immediately, he will return with a dozen of his men to tear this manor to pieces!"

This I said loudly enough that Sybil, were she in the shed, might hear and would not need to be told again. I would have advised the guards to say the same to Sir Philip, but the more irascible of the two had by this time drawn his dagger and begun to approach me. Sir Philip would learn of my words soon enough even if I did not instruct the guards to repeat them to him.

I took to my heels, feigning fear of the approaching dagger. Actually, I did fear the blade. As I hoped, the guard lumbered after me, waving his dagger over his head and demanding that I halt. I had hoped that both would follow, but so long as one came after I was confident that Arthur could deal with the man left behind.

The guard was faster than I expected, or I was slower than before my wound. I had thought I would need to keep my pace to a trot so as not to leave the fellow so far behind that he gave up and returned to the manor. I did stay comfortably ahead of the fellow, but 'twas not so easy to do so as I had thought 'twould be. I resolved to seek no more foot-races until I had recovered fully from my wound.

I leaped a wall and turned to see if my pursuer followed. What resulted could not properly be called a leap, but he did get over the wall, dropping in a heap at its base and cursing loudly. Nettles again, no doubt.

The sight of my pursuer toppling over the wall caused me to seek other obstacles. I was careful to stay but a dozen or so paces in front of the fellow, whose breath soon came in such noisy gasps that I thought him closer behind than he was.

We went over two more walls before he balked at the fourth heap of stones, cursed me for a knave, and shook his dagger at me. Arthur had by this time probably completed his tasks at the manor, but I could see no reason not to extend the chase, to be sure of Arthur's success.

From across the fourth wall I grimaced at my wheezing pursuer and shouted imprecations at him. I loudly questioned his birth and parentage, and suggested that he possessed little appeal to the fair sex.

The man was so incensed that his lips drew back from his teeth like an alaunt after a stag. He charged the wall and went over it head first, so wrathful had he become.

I took to my heels, pleased that the guard had been

foolish enough to continue the chase. I had run another fifty paces or so when I turned to see why I did not hear the fellow panting and stumbling behind.

He lay in a heap at the base of the wall, unmoving. My curiosity got the better of me and I did then what might have been a foolish thing. Perhaps my training as a surgeon was to blame – leading me to aid even an enemy in distress.

I retraced my steps cautiously, a hand upon my dagger, until I stood over the supine guard. The field had been sown to oats, and I saw his dagger in the stubble four or five paces from where he lay.

He was not dead. His chest rose and fell rapidly. But he was unconscious and the reason was clear. A stone had fallen from the wall, and when, in his rage, the fellow dived over the wall he landed head first upon this rock. A red stain had appeared, soaking through his cap.

I put a finger aside his throat and felt his heart beat, strong and rapid. I drew the cap from his head to inspect his wound. 'Twas a deep gouge, and bled much, but he would not go to his grave from it. I felt the skull about the laceration and found it whole. When the fellow awoke he would have a frightful headache, but he would awaken in this world rather than the next. I had not drawn the man to his death, and for this I was relieved. He did but his lord's bidding.

There was now little need to circle around the town, but I did so anyway, in case the village priest concluded the mass early and folk might be about the streets.

Arthur had returned to our meeting place before me, and he was not alone. Sybil Montagu was with him. He saw the look of dismay upon my face, rolled his eyes, and said, "She followed me. Wouldn't seek the priest. What was I to do?"

I thought of a suggestion, but bit my tongue.

"My father sent a man for me," Sybil said. "I heard him tell Sir Philip's men what would befall them if I was not released. We must find him."

I sighed. "'Twas me who spoke. No man has come from your father."

"Then you must take me home. Had you done so before, Sir Philip would not have seized me again."

"How did he do so?"

"Don't know. A lay brother set a meal before me at the guest-hall refectory. While I ate I heard voices in low conversation in another chamber, and a man spoke my name. After I ate I went to the cell I was assigned. I felt in need of a nap. When I awoke I was in the hencoop again. But now I know who it is has seized me, and this time he does not ask ransom of my father. I heard the guards speak of Sir Philip selling me as servant to Italian wool-buyers, so to keep my father from learning who took me."

Arthur and I exchanged glances. She had been dosed with some herb, likely mixed with ale, which put her to sleep. There are many plants which will cause slumber. Pounded lettuce seed is a favorite of mine when a patient is in need of sleep. But lettuce will not send a person into such deep repose that carrying them from Abingdon to East Hanney would not awaken them. Something stronger was used to so stupefy Sybil Montagu that she did not know she was being transported. I could not believe the hosteler was in league with Sir Philip Rede, but perhaps a lay brother was.

"You will take me now to my father!"

Sybil did not say this as a question. It was a command.

"I would like very much to throw you upon your father's care, but I cannot."

The lass spluttered in anger, but I ignored her. "The stables," I said to Arthur. "Did you inspect the horses there?"

"Aye. 'Twas as Osbert said. All are well shod."

"Speaking of horses," I said, "we should mount and be off. Mass will be done soon, if 'tis not already, and Sir Philip will find his captive gone again."

"'Less you send 'er back."

The thought was tempting.

We returned that day to Bampton, arriving after dark. Arthur took the beasts to the marshalsea and I sent Sybil through the door of Galen House before me. In the light of a candle I saw Kate's surprise at this visitor, and understood that my explanation for her presence had best be good.

I had told Kate of Sybil Montagu, and her character, so my spouse was not much surprised when Sybil stamped her foot in anger when I told her she would share a pallet that night with Alice atte Bridge.

"I demand a bed. My father is a gentleman. I'll not sleep upon the floor with a scullery maid!"

Arthur had made the mistake, while we traveled home to Bampton, of speaking of Alice atte Bridge and her duties at the castle. Sybil rode the palfrey behind him, and heard.

"I have no other bed," I replied, "nor have I another pallet. You may sleep upon the floor, or sit, with your back against the wall. I care not."

"Set that fellow upon the floor," Sybil demanded, pointing to Osbert. "He's one who kept me confined."

"He is injured, and will remain as he is."

"My father will hear of this."

"Soon, I hope. There is much your father needs to hear. Tomorrow, early, I will take you to the castle. Lord Gilbert Talbot will make a place for you until your father can be summoned."

I might have taken Sybil to the castle this night, roused Wilfred the porter, and turned the lass over to John Chamberlain. He would have found an unoccupied chamber for her. But her behavior was so repulsive that I decided I would trouble no man to meet her wishes.

Sybil fumed, but when she saw 'twas to no avail, she thumped down upon the pallet beside Alice.

"I am sorry," I apologized to Alice, "for this imposition. Sybil will trouble you for but one night."

That I begged pardon of Alice rather than her for the

sleeping accommodations infuriated Sybil even more. Her eyes flashed anger but I cared little for her rage.

Kate, Alice, and Osbert had already eaten supper, and there was little remaining, so I made a meal of maslin loaf and cheese. I offered some to Sybil, but she snarled a rejection and turned her face to the wall. Alice peered at me with raised eyebrows, left the pallet, and spread her cloak upon the reeds across the room from Sybil. She would rather sleep upon the floor herself than share a straw pallet with such a shrewish companion. Someday, possibly, Sybil Montagu will wed. I wonder how many nights her husband will sleep upon the floor?

While I chewed upon the maslin loaf I spoke to Osbert, who had already consumed his evening cup of ale laced with ground lettuce seeds. Kate must have provided a strong dose, for 'twas all I could do to keep the man awake and lucid.

I described the men who had entered Galen House, threatened Kate and Bessie, and made off with the coins and jewelry I had found in John Thrale's house. The two, Osbert answered, might be mistaken for Sir Philip Rede and Piers, his younger brother, who was not tall, and was given to indulging his appetite. But this could not be so, for no horse with a broken shoe was found on their manor. I asked if other men matching the description could be found in East Hanney.

"Many gentlemen about who be tall an' spare, or short an' stout," he said.

"Aye, but the tall fellow commonly wears a red cap, and the short man wears a blue cap. And they may often be seen together."

Osbert was silent, thinking. I feared he had fallen to sleep while he considered my words, and this was nearly so, for his speech was slurred when he replied.

"Sir John's got squires. Might be two of them you seek. Folk like me don't see much of gentlefolk from another manor, but I seen 'em a time or two when they was with Piers. The three of 'em is friendly, like."

"Sir John Trillowe?"

"Aye," Osbert finally replied. I saw that I was losing him to Morpheus and decided further questions could wait for the morning. In the other room Alice slept upon her cloak, and Sybil breathed heavily upon the pallet. I lifted the candle and with it lighted my way up the stairs to Kate, Bessie, and my bed. I had ridden Bruce far that day, and my wounds ached.

I awoke next morn to the sound of movement below. The east window of our bedchamber allowed enough light from the grey dawn that I could see my way down the stairs, where I found Alice tending the coals upon the hearth, fanning them to flames under fresh wood she had placed there. Osbert was awake, observing the procedure. Sybil lay upon her pallet, watching from under a scowl.

I turned to Osbert and was pleased to see him rise to an elbow, take a deep breath, then push himself to a sitting position upon his pallet.

"Dreadful stiff," he said, "an' hurts some. But I'm weary of layin' here on me belly. Won't spill so much ale if I can sit up."

We broke our fast with what remained of yesterday's maslin loaves. I ate rapidly, so as to be rid of Sybil Montagu the sooner. She was eager to go to the castle, assuming that there she would be amongst folk of her own quality, and be assigned a feather mattress upon which to sleep.

Wilfred had the portcullis up and the gate already open, so I did not have to rouse him to admit us to the castle. I found John Chamberlain, told him briefly of Sybil Montagu and the reason she now stood pouting beside me, and asked him to relay the tale to Lord Gilbert. Men must be sent to South Marston, I concluded, so as to inform Sybil's father of where he might collect her. I should probably have taken Sybil to Lord Gilbert myself, but I had little desire to stand in my lord's presence.

Somewhere in East Hanney Amice Thatcher and her children were held, and likely in conditions designed to persuade her to tell her captors where John Thrale had found his loot.

She did not know, so she said, and I believed her. But would those who took her agree? If they finally did so, would they release her, or do murder so as to cover one felony with another? And if they thought she did know the place where the chapman found coins and jewels, what hurt would they inflict upon her and her children to compel her to tell? Whether Amice Thatcher knew of the cache or not, I must find her and set her free. If I could not, harm would come to her, no matter her knowledge or ignorance. And when I found Amice I would also find the men who murdered John Thrale.

Osbert was prone upon his pallet when I returned to Galen House. "Got dizzy," he said in explanation. This was good to know. If Lord Gilbert asked of his recovery I could honestly tell of his infirmity.

When I sat before him upon a stool to learn more of East Hanney he rose again from the pallet, catching his breath once as pain stabbed him.

"Do you know much of Sir John Trillowe's manor?" I began.

"Nay. Never been inside the gate."

I feared as much. "You would not know, then, if there was some place – an unused hut, perhaps – where two squires might keep a hostage unknown to Sir John?"

"Nay. Might be such a place. Most villages 'ave abandoned 'ouses now, since plague."

"Are there many such in East Hanney?"

"Aye. Two on Sir Philip's lands. Don't know how many on Sir John's manor, but I heard tell there was some."

"Sir Philip's lands lie to the north of the village?"

"Aye."

"Whereabouts are Sir John's lands?"

"Most of the village is Sir John's, an' to the south an' west. His lands is greater than Sir Philip's."

"Do you know of Sir Simon?"

"Him of the ear what's skewed out aside 'is head?"

"Aye."

"Some years past 'e spent 'is time in Oxford, mostly, but a year or so ago 'e come back to East Hanney. Returned to help see to 'is father's lands, folks do say."

I did not tell Osbert why Sir Simon left Oxford, nor why he had a misshapen ear. Perhaps another time I shall do so.

I wished to prowl the lanes of East Hanney to learn what I could of the village, abandoned houses there, and sheds and huts which might be found adjoining Sir John Trillowe's manor house. And while I explored the place I would study the mud of the street to see if the mark of a broken horseshoe was there.

But I was known in East Hanney. I could not set foot in the place without some villager recognizing me as the fellow mounted upon the crazed dexter who helped free the villein who, according to Sir Philip's design, was providing entertainment for the village nine days past.

As I considered this my hand went absent-mindedly to my beard, which I had not trimmed for many days, and a solution to the problem came to me. A few days past I had examined myself in Kate's mirror and saw white whiskers amongst the brown. Each month there seemed to be more. I complained of it once, and Kate replied that the graying of my beard made me appear distinguished and mature. Kate can be tactful. What she meant was that I am beginning to appear old. If I powdered my beard and hair with wheaten flour from Kate's bin, I might appear older than my years.

From one of Lord Gilbert's ploughmen I could get an old, tattered cotehardie and surcoat, and a pair of worn shoes. Garbed in such a manner, with hoary beard, I might pass unrecognized through East Hanney. When I told Kate of my plan she gazed at me as if I'd been dropped upon my head as an infant, the result only now becoming plain.

I took a sheet of parchment from my chest and asked Osbert to sketch upon it a map of East Hanney. With my hand under an elbow he stood and walked unsteadily to a stool I had set before our table. The man could not read or write, but was a competent artist. When he was done I knew the location of Sir John's manor, the village well, the blacksmith's forge, the baker, St. James' Chapel, and where Sir Philip's manor stood in relation to the village.

After a dinner of pease pottage and wheaten bread I set out for the castle to seek Arthur. I intended him to accompany me as far as the forest north of East Hanney, there to wait for me to complete a survey of the village. When I told him of my scheme he also studied me as if I'd lost my wits. Perhaps I had, but if I could not do something for Amice Thatcher, and soon, there was a fair chance the woman would lose her life.

From the castle I went to the house of Alfred, a ploughman. Some years past, when I was new come to Bampton, I had surgically removed a stone from his bladder. Alfred surely wondered why I asked the loan of his oldest cotehardie and surcoat, but when a lord's bailiff makes a request, most men will answer as needed. And Alfred remembered the relief I had brought him.

He had but one pair of shoes, but I found a shabby pair in the castle, belonging to Uctred, another of Lord Gilbert's grooms. Thus equipped, I was ready to set out again for East Hanney early next day, and instructed the castle marshalsea to have Bruce and the palfrey ready when the Angelus Bell sounded from the tower of the Church of St. Beornwald.

A man wearing such frayed clothing, yet riding a great horse, would attract unwanted attention. So when Arthur and I set out from Bampton next morn I carried Alfred's and Uctred's contributions in a sack slung over the pommel of my saddle. In the sack also was a length of stout hempen rope. If we found Amice, and she was guarded, it might be necessary to bind the man.

'Tis eleven miles or thereabouts from Bampton to East Hanney. Arthur and I arrived well before noon, having met few travelers on the way, and none since Marcham. Again we entered the convenient forest at the north edge of the village, and there I donned my shabby disguise and powdered my beard and hair with the flour.

I had brought with us a bag containing two maslin loaves and a small cheese. We shared one of the loaves and a bit of cheese, and so fortified I set out for the village.

According to Osbert's map Sir John's manor lay to the west of the village, and to find it I must turn to the right when I reached a chapel dedicated to St. James. As I walked I affected a limp, hoping to further convince any observer that I was poor and harmless and not worthy of their interest. This seemed effective. Although I was a stranger passing through a small village, where folk knew one another, few bothered to give me a second glance when I passed.

Sir John Trillowe's house was indeed fine. He had done well, I think, pocketing fines when he served as Sheriff of Oxford, which post he lost when King Edward tired of complaints from Oxford burghers and replaced him.

There had been little rain for several days, but a muddy road does not soon dry in November. As I limped past the manor I turned my face from the house, partly because I feared that, even in disguise, Sir Simon, if he looked from a window at an awkward moment, might recognize me, and partly because I sought the mark of a broken horseshoe. Sir Simon did not see me, but I found the mark.

This print of a broken horseshoe had not been recently made, but it was clear enough that I had no doubt it was the print I had followed on other roads in days past. And the beast which made it turned from the road at the gate which led to Sir John's manor. Somewhere beyond that gate was Amice Thatcher. I was sure of it. And also there were two men who had beaten another man to death and threatened my wife and child. It might be easier, I thought, to find and free Amice than prove the guilt of John Thrale's assailants.

I continued my limping progress past the manor house, and as I did I considered some course of action. Would a King's Sheriff, even one replaced in some disgrace, hold an ale wife hostage in his house, or allow a squire to do so? I could not think it of the man, venal as I knew him to be.

Sir Simon was a different matter. From what I knew of him, he would take coins from a beggar.

If Sir John's squires were the men I sought, it seemed unlikely that they could hide Amice and two children in the manor house. Sir John would soon know of his guests. Amice would be held someplace Sir John was unlikely to visit.

If Amice and her children yet lived, they must be fed. I continued past the manor for a distance of two hundred paces, then, at a place where the wall which bordered the road was joined to another which ran perpendicular to the road, I glanced around to see that no one was about, then scrambled from the road to follow the second wall.

This wall divided a fallow field from another which had been planted to grain, now harvested. I followed this wall to another, intersecting wall, fifty paces or so from the road. Behind this wall was a forest, a part of the same wood where, at its eastern end, Arthur awaited my return. Beyond the wood, visible now through leafless trees, flowed a small stream.

Unless some villager prowled the forest seeking fallen branches for fuel, I was not likely to be seen if I squatted behind this wall. From the wall I could see the enclosure behind Sir John's manor house – the barns, coops, stables, sties – all was visible. I could watch to see if any man took a bundle which might contain food from the house to some other building.

No man did. I had set before myself a fool's errand. Perhaps, even if Amice and her children were held, like Sybil Montagu, in some outbuilding, they were fed but once each day, in the morning. I would not crouch here behind a wall for a day to see was it so. And my wounds began to ache, bent over as I was. Alfred's cotehardie and surcoat were threadbare, and a cold wind cut through the thin fabric.

Osbert spoke true. Plague had emptied many houses in East Hanney. Might Amice be held in one of these? I could not enter them in daylight without a chance of being seen. That an impoverished vagrant might seek shelter in an abandoned house would surprise no one, but if I was seen entering one of the decaying huts Sir John's bailiff or reeve or the village beadle might be told of it, and I would be run from the village at the point of a dagger. I could not then re-enter the place, disguise or not.

I retraced my steps to the road, having wasted an hour behind the wall. I limped back past the manor house, through the village, paying special attention to the vacant houses. I saw four near to Sir John's manor. It seemed to me that if Amice's captors had imprisoned her in an abandoned house they would choose one close by the manor.

Pretending an injured leg meant that I could pass slowly by the empty houses and study them without causing interest in those who might see me. Two of the houses lay close by other, occupied dwellings. Soon or late, two children would make noise neighbors would hear. A squire might demand silence of the neighbors if they discovered Amice, but I know tenants and villeins well enough to know that gossip would soon fill the village with news of the woman and children held against their will. Osbert had heard no such rumor. I crossed the two houses from my mental list.

Another house was so decayed that its roof was partly collapsed. If I were a felon who wished to hide a captive, would I choose such a place? No other house was near, and I might not care if rain fell upon my prisoner. The discomfort of such a dilapidated house might bring her to tell what I wished to learn, so as to escape the cold and wet. But a roof open to the sky would let out the cry of an infant as well as allow rain to enter.

The nearest neighbor was forty paces from the place, but living the past year with Bessie has taught me that an aggrieved babe can make her displeasure known beyond forty paces. And one shutter hung askew, so that anyone confined, unless they were bound, could peer through the opening, which had lost its skin, their face visible to those who passed by. I dismissed this house, also.

Beyond the chapel, on a narrow path which led south, was another unoccupied dwelling. It was a hundred paces from the chapel, the only house built along the little-traveled lane. The priest who served this chapel lived in a small chamber built away from the porch. This placed the chapel between his quarters and the distant house. If a squalling infant was hid in the house he'd not be likely to hear it, or if he did, might assume the racket came from some house nearer the chapel in the opposite direction.

This house was not so decayed as the one with a fallen roof, but it was missing chunks of daub, the thatching was rotting and no doubt inhabited by legions of mice, and one of the gable vents was nearly plugged where a rafter pole had given way and allowed thatch to cover the opening.

I hobbled past the house and saw in the mud a curious thing. Fresh footprints turned from the path to disappear in the overgrown toft. The house had surely been uninhabited for many years, I think. All around it was grown up in weeds and thistles. These obscured the footprints a few paces from the path so I could not follow them to see if they led to the door.

I glanced to the house, turned back to the path, then looked to the house again. Across the door, fastened to the jambs, rested an iron bar. This bar was not designed to keep folk out of the house, for it was held in place on one side by an iron lock large as my hand. This bar was in place to keep someone in the house, and other folk out. The bar, hasp, and lock were worth more than what might be left in an empty plague house.

No man was near me on the path, nor woman, either. The closest soul was a housewife more than a hundred paces to the north who sat upon a bench before her door, enjoying a watery sun while she mended some article of clothing. She would not hear what I said.

In a loud whisper, without breaking my limping gait, I said, "Amice, if you are in this house, knock upon the door."

I slowed my already slack pace to give the woman time to reply, was she in the house. I was past the toft, near to a broken-down fence, when I heard the soft reply.

I sat heavily upon a pile of coppiced poles which had once, perhaps, been an enclosure in which sheep were folded. With my head bent to the ground so no man might see my moving lips, I said, "'Tis Master Hugh. Knock again if you hear."

This time the answering tap came immediately.

"If you are alone, knock once. If your children are there also, knock twice."

Two gentle raps sounded upon the door. I was surprised that children could remain so silent.

"Are you well? Can you travel this night? Knock once if yes, twice if no."

A single soft blow rattled the door upon its rusting hinges. I turned my face again to the ground and said, "An hour after night falls I will come for you. Be ready. Knock once if you understand."

The answering knock was immediate, and straight after I heard her whisper through the door, "Men come in the night. I hear them walk about, sometimes rattling the door."

I was warned. Releasing Amice Thatcher, now that I had found her, might prove troublesome.

Chapter 13

I did not wish to raise suspicion by retracing my steps through the town. Poor men may often be seen upon the roads, but they generally do not change their destination and return to some starting-place. I continued west, toward another village, West Hanney, until I came to a place where the road crossed a small stream. No man was about to see me, so I abandoned both the road and my limp and plunged through the forest northward, until I guessed I was beyond Sir Philip's meadow. I turned then to the east, found the stone wall which edged the meadow, and soon came upon Arthur. He had heard my approach, and hid himself behind a large beech tree till he was sure who came his way.

I told him of my discovery, and we sat with our backs to the wall and plotted how we might free Amice Thatcher.

"No guards in the day?" Arthur asked.

"I saw none."

"Sure of their prisoner."

"Amice warned that a watchman is assigned in the night. We must approach the house with caution. The men who seized her in Abingdon must have known that Sir Philip held Sybil Montagu in his derelict hencoop. It gave them the notion to capture Amice and hold her in much the same way, for a kind of ransom."

"Ransom bein' she must tell 'em where the chapman found 'is loot?"

"Aye."

We sat with our backs to the wall and consumed a cold supper of bread and cheese, waiting for darkness. Before the forest was obscured I told Arthur to join me in searching out some sturdy fallen tree limbs. Such were few, for villagers had recently scoured this wood seeking downed boughs for winter fuel.

"What we need these for?" Arthur asked, when we had found what we sought. "We got daggers."

"They are not for a beadle, or a guard. If we see such fellows, we'll try to avoid them."

A nearly full moon would rise this night a short time after darkness came. I wished to have Amice Thatcher safely out of the village before its light would make our flight visible to an alert watcher. When we were well away from East Hanney, moonlight would be welcome.

Small as East Hanney was, it might have a beadle assigned to watch and warn, or we might run afoul of a man sent to patrol the path and toft around Amice's jail. We must be cautious, or risk joining the woman and her children as captives.

We passed Bruce and the old palfrey as through the dark forest we sought the road. They whinnied softly, no doubt hungry and thirsty and curious as to why they were so often tethered in this place.

Occasional clouds obscured the stars, so we were able to enter the village in such darkness that, was there a beadle prowling the streets, he could not have seen us unless he was nearly upon us. He would have been more likely to hear us, so I urged Arthur to silence as we crept past the chapel and entered the path to the house where Amice Thatcher awaited us.

As we entered this narrow, overgrown lane, the cloud which had covered the village drifted on, and the rising moon to the east provided increased visibility. I motioned to Arthur to follow, and we hugged the chapel wall till we reached the western end of the structure. From that place to the house there was no cover.

I strained to see if any watchman was near, but such effort was useless. If a man was near, he probably sat with his back to a wall or a tree, hidden in the shadows. Unless he moved or coughed we would never know of his presence.

We stood silently against the chapel wall, and in the

stillness of the night I heard a sound which should not have been there. Arthur heard also, and plucked at my sleeve. A man snored softly somewhere near. A nearby house, with a torn window, might account for such a low rumble, but there was no house close, yawning window or not. A guard, asleep and failing his duty, was somewhere near.

So long as we heard him snoring we could be sure we were undiscovered, unless two men were posted here, and one remained alert while the other dozed. That was a risk we must take. Soon the moon would lift above bare branches and the door to Amice's prison would be illuminated as if with a torch. We must act or flee.

If we reached the house undetected the barred door would become our next obstacle. That was why I wanted branches from the forest floor. I hoped that the wood of the jamb was decayed enough that, when two poles were used together, we might lever the bolts from the wood.

"Don't see nuthin'," Arthur whispered after we had spent several minutes staring into darkness toward the abandoned house. "Where do you suppose that fellow is?"

"See the tree across the lane from the house?"

Arthur nodded.

"He sleeps propped against its roots, I think."

I whispered to Arthur my plan to use the downed branches to pry the bar and hasp from the door jamb.

"What if it don't work?"

"The house is much decayed. A plague house, from many years past, I believe. Daub has broken away from the wattles in many places. If we cannot force the door we will go to the rear of the house, find some place where wattles are open, and pull them away. If need be, we can cut through with our daggers."

I touched Arthur upon his arm and we crept from the protection of the chapel's shadow. I expected with each step to hear a loud challenge from an alerted watchman.

We reached the door unobserved and unheard. In the silence of the night I heard the watchman's steady snores. I whispered through the door to Amice that we had arrived.

"We are ready," came the reply.

I sent Arthur to the path to watch and be ready should our business awaken the sleeping sentry. Then I held one pole against the door just below the iron bar and near the hasp. The other limb I fitted over the first pole and under the bar, which was just far enough out from the door that the branch would slide beneath it.

The house was surely untenanted for many years, but the jamb was not so decayed as I had hoped. I pried so forcefully against the iron bar that the branch I used for the purpose cracked under the strain. It was more rotted than the jamb.

The sound of the pry-bar snapping seemed loud as a thunderclap. I stopped all movement and listened to hear if the watchman would awaken. He spluttered, and seemed to shift his position, but a few heartbeats later his regular breathing resumed. The breaking branch had not awakened him. Yet.

I dropped the useless pole as Arthur appeared at my elbow. "What was that?" he whispered.

I told him, bid him follow, and together we hastened to the gable end of the house and sat low against the wall, watching and listening, to learn if the sentry might awaken.

The moon was now risen nearly above the bare topmost branches of the trees. We could no longer work at opening the door. Any man who stood there in the moonlight would be seen from a hundred paces away.

I motioned again to Arthur, stood, and crept to the rear of the house. I whispered to Arthur that he should remain at the corner of the house, watching for the guard, who might yet awaken, while I sought some place on this western, shadowed side of the house where daub might have fallen from the wattles.

There was a door here, also, but if the front door was barred, surely the rear would be, so I had given little thought to breaching the opening. I went to the door first, however, and saw there two planks nailed across the door.

No man would silently pry them from the opening.

There were several places at the rear of the house where over the years rain, lashed by a west wind, had caused daub to crumble and fall free of the house. I selected one of the larger of these perforations, inserted my dagger at one end, and began quietly to cut through the wattles. It was but a matter of a few minutes and I had cut through a length of wattles nearly as high as my arm is long. The thin twigs were decayed from contact with rain, and pulled free of the interior daub more readily than I had expected.

This work I did as silently as possible, but Amice heard me, of course, and when I had drawn the wattles free of the gap and pushed the daub inside the house away, she whispered a warning from within the hole.

"'Tis you, Master Hugh? Be on guard. I heard a man circle the house not an hour past."

Amice had no sooner spoken than Arthur was at my elbow. "That guard woke up," he whispered.

If the fellow approached the house and inspected the door closely he would see the poles, one broken, which I had used in a failed attempt to force the door. If he walked behind the house he might see the hole I had punctured in the wall.

I thought briefly we might crawl into the house and hide there, hoping this sentinel would see neither the poles nor the opening in the wall. This notion I quickly abandoned. If he saw either the poles or the hole and raised the alarm, we would be trapped in the house with Amice and her children.

Five or six paces behind the house was a thicket where perhaps a tenant had at one time built a hutch. This had collapsed over time, and a clump of bushes had grown up amid the ruins. This vegetation was the only shelter I could see in the toft. I grasped Arthur's arm and ran toward it. We were briefly visible in the moonlight as we ducked from the shadow of the house to the thicket. If the approaching watchman was alert he might see us, and as we hid in the foliage I expected him to cry out. He did not.

We waited and watched and soon heard the fellow talking to himself as he circled the house. He appeared around the corner of the dwelling, clutching the broken pole. His words were indistinct, but what I could hear seemed to question the discovery of the broken branch and how it came to be at the door of the house.

A few more steps and the fellow would be aside the break I had carved in the wall. I waited to see what he would do if he found it, having no way to prevent the discovery.

When he came to the breach he fell silent for a moment, laid the pole aside, and knelt to peer into the black interior of the house.

"What's 'ere?" he said, speaking again to himself. Then louder, "You, in there... you there?"

He did not wait for an answer, but crawled into the hole. He was halfway through when I heard a muffled thud and saw the fellow cease moving and lie flat.

"Come," I said to Arthur, and ran for the house.

The watchman lay still and silent in the hole. I grasped his heels and pulled him from the opening. He was as peaceful as a corpse, and stank, and I wondered what had befallen him. I learned soon enough.

"Master Hugh?" Amice whispered.

"Aye. Send your children out, quickly, then follow."

The two children crawled from the house and Amice followed. "What happened to him?" I asked, looking to the watchman.

Amice stood and whispered an explanation. "They left an iron pot in the house, for want of a privy. I hit 'im with it."

The watchman began to stir. Even a stroke across the head from an iron pot will not put a man to sleep forever. Well, it might if Arthur delivered the blow, but not if a frail woman did so.

The man must be prevented from giving alarm. Arthur carried the hempen cord. I bound the guard's wrists tight behind him, and his ankles I tied to his wrists. Alfred's surcoat was threadbare and easily torn. I ripped a sleeve from the garment, stuffed a fragment into the guard's mouth, then tied the remainder tightly about his mouth. I told Arthur to take the man's shoulders while I grasped his knees, then I bid Amice and her children follow.

We carried the sentry to the chapel. I hoped the door would be unbarred, and so it was. We deposited the man upon the flags, shut the door behind us, and fled the town. If the fellow was not soon able to free himself from his bonds, or shout for help with a mouth full of tattered wool, we would be able to escape at least as far as Marcham, where the church might again become a refuge.

The sleeping watchman was not a slender fellow. Carrying him had caused my wounds to ache, but there was no time to seek relief.

The moon illuminated the forest where Bruce and the palfrey awaited. Arthur lifted the children to the palfrey, one before him and one clinging to his back, and I drew Amice up to Bruce's rump, there to cling to me behind the saddle. Her perch was precarious and I breathed a prayer that I would not need to spur Bruce to a gallop. The woman could never retain her seat if I did so.

A mile north of East Hanney the road crosses a brook upon a narrow stone bridge. As we approached Bruce sensed the water and I realized that our beasts were thirsty. We dismounted, led them from the road to a place where the bank sloped gently to the water, and allowed them to drink their fill. They were surely hungry, as well, but I could do nothing about that.

We remounted and rode on toward Marcham. As we did I learned from Amice what had happened to her since she and her children were taken.

"Infirmarer said the children was makin' too much noise, disturbin' them as was ill… that's why we was thrown out of the hospital," she said. "But they wasn't troublesome. I made sure we was no bother to anyone. He said as how someone complained to the abbot, an' the abbot told 'im we must go."

"When you were taken from your house, what then?"

"'Twas as you said. Them as took us wanted to know where John found coins an' jewels an' such. Told 'em I knew not. Didn't believe me."

"You've been in that plague house since?"

"Aye, most of the time. Told me we'd be set free when I named the place where the treasure was hid. How could I do that? I don't know. Second night we was held, little Tom begun to weep, an' the watchman heard. Spoke through the door for me to quiet 'im. I tried, but 'e was right fearful... place was so dark at night, an' we was hungry. Next day them what took us come again, asked if I was ready to tell 'em where John's treasure was. I couldn't, so one stayed with the children while the other took me across a field and into a wood. Feared what 'e was about, but I went. Feared what would 'appen to Tom an' Randal did I not. We come to a pit dug in the forest, covered over with branches. The man said we'd be put there if I couldn't keep the children quiet. Told 'im I could do that was they not so hungry."

"But you were not harmed?"

"Nay. I told the children what would become of us if they were not silent. They're old enough to understand bein' put in a pit is worse'n bein' prisoner in a house... even an old house what leaks when it rains."

The moon lighted our way to Marcham, and when we entered the village I considered once again seeking shelter in the church. But Arthur and I had done so already, so pursuers might seek us there, even if it was squires to Sir John Trillowe and not Sir Philip Rede who followed this time. And I did not relish sleeping again upon a cold stone floor.

We instead drew the horses to a halt before the vicarage. Father Maurice had expressed disdain for Sir Philip. Perhaps he held similar views of Sir John. So I hoped.

'Twas near midnight, so I was required to pound vigorously upon the vicarage door for some time before the clerk opened to us. He was in a foul mood, as I might be if awakened and drawn from my bed on a cold autumn night.

"Who is there? What is it you wish?"

"I am Hugh de Singleton. Do you remember a week and more past I sought refuge in the church?"

"Aye," he yawned. "What now?"

"We seek Father Maurice's help again. May we enter?"

I believe that the clerk assumed that when I said "we," I meant myself and Arthur. He stood aside to permit our entry and I saw, even in the dim light of the clerk's candle, his eyes blink and widen as Amice and her children passed him by.

A moment later the priest came down the stairs from his chamber in the upper story, wondering about the muted conversation he heard below. The candle provided enough light that the priest recognized me.

"Hugh... again in Marcham in the middle of the night? And seeking aid again, I'll warrant."

I told the priest he was correct, introduced Amice Thatcher, told him of her plight, and asked refuge for the night.

"You shall have it," he replied. Then, peering out the door, which was yet open to the night, he said, "We must stable your beasts. If Sir John or his squires followed they will see them and know you are here."

To his clerk he said, "Take the horses to William Burghill's stable. He'll not mind waking to extra animals in his stalls."

When the clerk returned his warm bed was taken. Father Maurice had sent Amice and the children to rest there. Arthur, I, and the clerk made our bed of cloaks laid upon rushes piled in a heap. I have rarely slept better.

William Burghill is of that class of prosperous yeomen who are not gentlemen, but possess land enough that some knights – Sir Philip Rede may be among them – envy their wealth. Burghill, Father Maurice said in the morning, cultivated three yardlands, and had married his oldest daughter to a knight of Wantage.

Burghill was not only prosperous, he was hospitable.

Next morn I offered to pay for the oats Bruce and the palfrey had consumed, but the man would not take a farthing.

Father Maurice set loaves and ale before us, and when we and the horses were fed we thanked the priest, mounted our rested beasts, and set off for Standlake and the road to Bampton.

I was some concerned that we might meet Sir John Trillowe's squires along the road. If they had words with Sir Philip they might guess who had freed their prisoner, and where we traveled. On the other hand, they might then also know I served Lord Gilbert Talbot, and not wish to offend such a great lord.

We drew the horses to a halt before Galen House just after noon. Kate took one look at Amice, knew who she must be, and so there would be enough to feed our guests set about adding peas and leeks to a kettle of pottage which was warming upon the coals.

Arthur took Bruce and the palfrey to the marshalsea, and I explained Amice's presence to Kate, Alice, and Osbert while I, Amice, and her children munched upon a maslin loaf and waited for the pottage to be ready. Osbert, I was pleased to see, sat alert upon a bench, and did not grimace when he moved, although he seemed to stir as little as possible.

"What will become of Amice?" Kate asked when I concluded the tale. "She cannot return to her house in Abingdon. Those knaves will seize her again."

"She must remain here until she is no longer threatened. She can assist you with Osbert, and Alice may return to her work at the castle."

Alice seemed crestfallen at this news, but her life there was better than might have been had her felonious brothers had their way. And I knew that Will Shillside, son of Bampton's haberdasher, had an eye for the lass. Few scullery maids have a quarter-yardland to bring to their husbands at the church door, but Alice did.

I had promised Brother Theodore that I would deal with his fistula as soon as I could, and Saturn was now past Aries. I told Kate that I must leave for Abingdon on the morrow, to perform the surgery. I had another reason for the journey. There were questions I wished to ask the hosteler.

Kate was not pleased that I must travel again, nor, in truth, was I. Sir John Trillowe's squires had visited my house and stolen John Thrale's treasure but a few weeks before. Might they return, seeking again to lay hands on Amice Thatcher? I must see that, if they did so while I was away, they would find a harsh welcome. I set out for the castle, found Arthur with his cheeks full of maslin loaf, and told him to organize castle grooms to keep watch over Galen House, night and day, two at a time, until my return.

"Think them squires might want Amice Thatcher back, eh?" he said.

"Aye."

"A man might want Amice, even if she had no treasure," he grinned. Cicily looked over her shoulder and scowled, but Arthur spoke true. Amice was nearly as pleasing to look upon as Kate.

I was crossing the castle yard when John Chamberlain saw me and cried out: "Lord Gilbert wishes you to attend him."

"In the solar?"

"Aye."

My employer was seated in a chair beside the fireplace, deep in conversation with some gentleman guest I had not met. When John Chamberlain ushered me into the solar the visitor stood, excused himself, and departed. When a lord wishes to discuss matters with his bailiff most knights understand that their presence would be an intrusion.

"That villein you helped escape from Sir Philip," Lord Gilbert began, "is he well enough to return him to his lord?"

"Nay. He finds it difficult to stand. Becomes dizzy. And the lacerations upon his back are likely to break open if he bends over."

"How much longer, then?"

"A fortnight... perhaps longer."

"And if I require you then to send him to Sir Philip, you intend to leave my service?"

"I do, m'lord."

Lord Gilbert snorted, turned to the fire for a moment, then, as I was about to ask his leave to depart, he faced me and spoke again.

"By heaven, you're a hard man, Hugh."

"Men who serve you do not often cross you?"

"Nay... only you. A fortnight, no longer. That villein will be returned to Sir Philip, whether he can stand or not.

"Now, what of the chapman found murdered upon my lands? You are yet my bailiff. Have you found the guilty men?"

"Aye, so I believe."

"You believe? You are uncertain?"

"I know who the felons are, and why they beat the chapman to death, but I have not yet the evidence which would convince the Sheriff or the King's Eyre. And the men I suspect are squires to a great knight and may have maintenance."

"They wear his livery?"

"Nay. Perhaps they do not wish it known who they serve."

"Who do they serve?"

"Sir John Trillowe."

Lord Gilbert scowled. "Bah, if his squires did murder upon my lands, his arm will not shield them."

"If I can discover proof of their guilt."

"Well, you have a fortnight to do so, for that villein must be returned and then, unless you reconsider, you will no longer serve me in this matter, or any other, if that is your wish. And by the way, the maid Sybil... her father is coming for her day after tomorrow."

I do not know Sir Henry Montagu, but I suspected that Sir Philip Rede would soon suffer serious embarrassment.

I bowed my way from the solar and returned to Galen House for a dinner of stockfish and maslin loaf, and a chardewarden made of the fresh pears of autumn. I saw that Osbert was much recovered, for he ate his fill and more, although he sat stiffly at the table.

Next morn I left Galen House with the Angelus Bell and met Arthur and Uctred walking up Church View Street to assume their posts as sentinels for the souls who resided in my home.

Shortly after noon I arrived at the New Inn, left Bruce with a stable boy, and with my sack of herbs and instruments slung over a shoulder, sought my dinner at the inn. This was also a fast day, so stockfish was all there was to be had, and as I was late for dinner, what remained had the consistency of shavings from a cooper's drawknife.

I did not linger long over this meal, for the loaf was little better than the fish. 'Tis but a few paces from the New Inn to the abbey gatehouse, between St. Nicholas's Church and St. John's Hospital. At the porter's lodge I asked for Brother Theodore and the porter's assistant ran to fetch him. The monk soon appeared behind his stained linen shroud, and I felt a sense of satisfaction that here was a tormented soul I could help.

The hosteler saw the bag over my shoulder and his eyes brightened. "Saturn is no longer in the house of Aries," he said. "You did not forget my suffering."

"Nay. I am prepared to deal with your fistula – this day, if you are willing."

"I am. What must be done?"

"I have herbs which will help dull the pain. But I must warn you again, as I did when we first met, that the surgery I must do will be painful."

"I have thought upon your words, but I will gladly bear brief suffering if it will end what I have endured for so long."

"Then we may begin. I require a room with a fire, where I may heat a cautery rod, a cup of ale for you, in which I will place herbs to lessen your pain, and an egg. Also some wine."

"The only room of the abbey with a fire, other than the kitchen, is the calefactory. Will that serve?"

"Aye, if the other monks warming themselves there do not mind my work."

The calefactory was beyond the monks' dormitory, attached to the infirmary, where ill and elderly monks might drive away the chill of a winter day. A lay brother kept the blaze in this warming room, and when told of what I intended to do was eager to assist. I sent him for a cup of ale and another of wine. When he returned Brother Bartholomew accompanied him.

Brother Theodore greeted the infirmarer with impolitic words. "Ah, Brother Bartholomew, here is Master Hugh, a surgeon, who is to cure my fistula."

The infirmarer had surely used his store of knowledge and salves to work a cure, to no benefit, and I feared he might resent my intrusion. I thought to deflect any acrimony, so asked the monk what salves he had tried.

"Many ointments, but none have succeeded. A paste of our lady's mantle seemed to reduce the discharge, but it soon returned."

"You have applied adder's tongue?"

"Aye. Also a lotion of bruised betony leaves, which has brought success in other cases, but not for Brother Theodore. What herbs will you use?"

"None. You have tried the best God gives us. If they brought no healing, the fistula must be cut and burned away."

"I have heard of such a remedy, but have no knowledge of the method."

"If you will assist me, you may see how 'tis done. Then, if another brother suffers a similar hurt you may deal with it.

"The first thing is to do what we may to lessen the pain of the surgery. I have pouches of herbs to add to a cup of ale; crushed seeds and the dried juice of lettuce, pounded hemp seeds, and bruised leaves of mandrake."

"Mandrake?" the infirmarer asked with raised eyebrows.

"Aye. 'Tis a powerful sedative, and I will use little. I prefer lettuce and hemp alone when I must cause a man pain, but cauterizing a fistula calls for greater relief than they provide."

I placed a strong mixture of hemp seeds and dried and pounded lettuce in the ale, then added a smaller portion of the fragments of mandrake leaves. Mandrake is a strong physic. Too much of the plant will put a man to sleep so that he will awaken in the next world. And its use is known to cause a man to contemplate females with much appreciation. Such an effect in a monk is to be avoided.

It is my observation that herbs to deaden pain, when taken with ale, are most effective an hour or two after the mixture is consumed. Days grew short, and by the time Brother Theodore would be ready the sun would be low in the west. I requested the infirmarer to assist me in moving a table before a west window, and I asked of him also a clean linen cloth and a feather.

Brother Theodore waited upon a bench for me to announce when the surgery would begin. After an hour or so he began to sway, his eyes drooping, and I judged him ready for the procedure. From my pouch I took a bronze tube nearly as long as my foot and the diameter of my thumb, and an iron rod with a wooden handle, small enough to fit through the tube. I gave the rod to the lay brother and asked him to heat it in the fire, being careful not to allow the flames to singe the handle.

I told the monk to take his place upon the table, and when he had done so I bathed his hurt with wine, then selected from my instruments a small blade. With this I enlarged the ulcer so that I could seek its root. It is often necessary to enlarge a wound before it can be healed, much like the grievances between men, which cannot be repaired until the cause be laid bare and excised. Brother Theodore took this cutting well, but worse was to come.

Next I broke an egg into a bowl, removed the yolk, and with the feather swabbed out the incision with the egg white, using the linen cloth to absorb the blood and pus which issued from the wound. Through all this the hosteler remained silent, nor did he twitch in pain or show any other sign of discomfort. That would soon change.

I allowed the egg white to work for a few minutes, then took the iron rod from the fire. The bronze tube I then inserted into the wound, which caused Brother Theodore to open his eyes in alarm. I told him to close his eyes, and when he had done so I grasped the heated rod by its wooden handle, slid it through the tube, and cauterized the root of the monk's fistula. Smoke and hissing arose from the wound, and the monk, who had seemed near asleep, writhed in pain. This is why the bronze tube is necessary for such a cure. When the heated rod burns away the source of the fistula the patient will jerk and thrash about in torment. The tube prevents the rod from contacting and burning that flesh which is whole.

I dislike causing a man pain, and in such surgery it is tempting to withdraw the heated rod before it has completed the cautery. I resisted the impulse, and continued the treatment until I was sure of the cure. When I withdrew the rod and tube I saw a tear form in the hosteler's eye and trickle down toward his ear.

With what remained of the wine I washed again the incision and cauterized wound. Brother Theodore winced as the wine touched flesh, but held still when I assured him that the worst was past and the surgery nearly complete. All that remained was to take needle and silken thread and stitch the laceration closed.

When I was done I used what remained of the linen cloth to wipe sweat from my brow. The blaze had warmed the room, and my work required much concentration – so much that I did not notice the calefactory filling with observers as I did the surgery. One of these watchers was the obese abbot, Peter of Hanney.

"You did not seek permission for this surgery," he

said as I mopped my brow and looked about the chamber in some amazement at the audience which had gathered there.

"Saturn is no longer in the house of Aries. Is it necessary to ask permission to do good?"

"God visited him with an affliction for the good of his soul, to bring him to humility and patience, which are virtues."

"Aye, so they are." I agreed. I thought to ask the abbot what affliction the Lord Christ had awarded him, that he might be humble and patient, but thought better of it. Too much wit might send me to the abbey dungeon.

"God has provided all that is needful for men," the abbot continued. "If a man suffers an affliction," here he looked to Brother Theodore, "from which no salve or herb will cure him, then it must be that the Lord Christ wishes him not to be cured."

"Or mayhap the Lord Christ sends a man of wit, skill, and experience to effect the cure."

"You claim to act for God?"

"All who do His will act for God."

"And what is God's will?"

"You will find it in Holy Scripture, where nowhere have I read that a man must be required to suffer when relief is possible."

"Whom God loveth, He chasteneth," the prior said.

I was about to reply that when He chooses to chasten the abbot, he should not call for me. I would not interfere with God's lessons nor his expression of love. But visions of the abbey cells came again to me and I held my tongue.

"God is not the only power who may chasten a man," the abbot said. "Be gone, and do not return. You shall treat no man here ever again."

The abbot's doughy face was growing red. I thought it best to make no further reply, so turned to Brother Theodore and the open-mouthed infirmarer, and told Brother Bartholomew to remove the hosteler's stitches in a fortnight.

"Salves?" the infirmarer asked.

Again I was required to explain that I follow the practice of Henri de Mondeville, who learned while in service to men at arms in war that wounds heal best when left dry, and that they should be covered only if it is necessary to do so to keep them clean.

I was sorry to be required to leave the abbey, as I had questions for the hosteler which, I hoped, after he had recovered from the pain of the surgery, he might be able to answer.

Abbot Peter had required that I leave the abbey precincts. I had no option but to do so. The Lord Christ's love for poor sinners is a remarkable thing, but even more mysterious is His patience with ill-tempered saints. The abbot had also commanded that I not return. Before I passed through the abbey gate I was devising a plan to steal back into the monastery to learn what I might from Brother Theodore.

Chapter 14

In the street before the abbey gate I saw a baxter selling pies from a cart, and was reminded how hungry I was. I purchased two, and considered a scheme to return to the monastery while I ate.

As with most monasteries, women of the town are hired to wash the monks' clothing. While I munched upon my pies I wandered about the neighborhood, keeping the abbey gatehouse in view, until I saw a woman pass through the gate and walk across the marketplace toward the bury. I followed.

To my surprise she entered the alley where Amice Thatcher's house stood, walked purposefully past the empty dwelling, and entered the threadmaker's house. I followed, and rapped upon the door.

It was a small house, as are all of those in the bury, so the woman had but a few steps to reach the door and open it from any corner of the place. She drew the door open a crack to see who was there, did not recognize me, and immediately slammed it shut again. The day was far gone, night was near, and honest folk would soon be off the streets.

I pounded upon the door again. I heard voices within, but some time passed before the door again opened. The threadmaker scowled through the opening this time, recognized me, and asked my business.

"It regards Amice Thatcher, Amabel Maunder, and the men who have harmed them."

The fellow opened his door wider and motioned for me to enter. His wife had heard me speak, and said, "You know what's become of Amice an' Amabel?"

"Aye. Amabel recovers from her injuries at St. John's

Hospital. Amice was held captive, but has been freed and is now safe with her children in a town not far from here."

"Captive?" the woman said. "Why'd someone take Amice captive?"

"To discover from her the location of a treasure."

"Amice has treasure?"

"Nay, but the men who took her thought she knew where riches were buried. She does not," I added hastily.

"Who did this?" the threadmaker asked. "An' why do you interest yourself? You said when you was here before you was a friend. Didn't know Amice an' Amabel had such friends," he said, inspecting the quality and cut of my cotehardie.

"The men who took Amice and beat Amabel murdered a man in seeking his treasure. I believe I know who did so, but need more proofs before the Sheriff will act."

"You a friend of the dead man?"

"Nay. I am bailiff to Lord Gilbert Talbot, on his manor of Bampton, where the murdered man was found."

"You need proofs, why do you come here?"

"I believe that there are, in the abbey, monks who may know something of the matter."

"Monks? Then why seek us?"

I turned to the woman. "I followed you from the abbey just now. Are you a servant there?"

"Aye. Wash their clothes."

This was as I hoped.

"The abbot is displeased with me," I said, "so will not permit me to enter the abbey. I cannot question monks if I cannot gain entrance to the place."

"What did you do to offend Abbot Peter?"

"I am also a surgeon. Without the abbot's permission, I treated a monk who suffered from a fistula."

"Brother Theodore? Him who goes about with a cloth over 'is face?"

"Aye."

"You could help 'im? He's one of the few in the abbey who's decent to folk like me."

"His fistula is cured, if all goes well. I need to gain entrance to the abbey to speak to Brother Theodore, but the abbot forbids it. I require assistance."

"From us?" the woman asked.

"From you. Do you return to the abbey Monday?"

"Aye."

"When you leave it, hide under your surcoat a habit you have washed. I will wear it to enter the monastery, and when it has served its purpose you may return it, none the wiser. For this service I will pay you two pence."

The woman peered at her husband in the darkening room, caught some signal from him, and agreed. I arranged to visit the house on Monday at the same time of day to take possession of the robe and cowl.

Two days must pass before I could put my plot into action – time enough to consider whether it be foolish or not. Generally, the wisdom or folly of a deed does not become apparent till after its completion, and so it was that all of the next day no serious flaw in my plan came to me.

Late Monday afternoon the washer-woman appeared with the black robe and cowl, as she had agreed, and I gave her two pennies for her temporary theft. She would be required to wash the habit again, for what I intended would likely leave the garment with a muddy hem.

I thanked the woman, bundled the robe under my arm, and hurried to the New Inn, where, if I did not make haste, I would miss my supper. If any man in the place noted the black woolen fabric folded under my arm he was too busy spooning pottage to his lips to consider what it might be.

By the time I finished my pottage and loaf the night was full dark, and when I left the New Inn I heard the bell of the abbey church announce compline. I would have nearly six hours to accomplish my task before vigils, when the monks would awaken for the office.

The moon would rise later this night, so only starlight showed the way as I walked north past St. Nicholas's

Church, following the boundary wall of the abbey. I soon came to a path leading eastwards, where the precinct was bounded only by the abbey ditch. When I reached a likely place where I might cross the ditch I donned the robe and cowl, then sat with my back against a small tree to give the monks time to return from the church to their dormitory and fall to sleep.

When I had nearly fallen to sleep myself, cold as the night was, I felt sure that the monks were snoring in their beds. I took off my shoes and tied them about my neck, raised the hem of the borrowed habit, and stepped into the dark water. My chauces would be soaked, but there was no helping that.

The ditch was deeper than I had expected and the muddy bed slippery. I was in above my knees before I could change my course and splash toward the bank inside the abbey wall.

I clambered up the bank and shook out the habit. An orchard occupies the north-east corner of the abbey grounds. I made for the nearest apple tree. There I sat, shivering from the effect of the cold water, and drew on my shoes. I waited there in the darkened orchard and watched as the waning moon began to appear through bare tree limbs to the east. After a time, when no man cried out a challenge, I felt ready to put my plan into effect.

My first step from the sheltering tree fell upon something soft, and when my foot slipped from the object I nearly turned an ankle. I thought at first I had trod upon some large, fallen, rotting apple. But not so. Apples do not have fur; dead cats do. Perhaps this feline had been pursuing rats when death overtook it. The discovery startled me, but my mind often works in curious ways, and I thought of a use for the animal. I picked it up by the tail and crept from one tree to another toward the infirmary.

From the infirmary I walked past the reredorter, feeling safe there. If any man saw me he would think a brother about some nocturnal relief. I had drawn the cowl over my head, the shadow would obscure my face, and the cat was grey and not likely to be seen dangling close by my leg.

After I passed between the reredorter and the dormitory, however, I needed to be more careful, for I was entering a space where no monk should be after compline, with or without a dead cat.

My goal was the guest house, and the hosteler's chamber there. To reach the guest house my path lay past the abbot's kitchen. There was a narrow entry between the kitchen and the guest hall which led toward the cloister. I ducked into the shadows of this entry and found the door to the kitchen. It was not locked. I entered, and when my eyes became accustomed to the gloom, found a large iron pot which hung over a cold hearth. I dropped the cat into m'lord abbot's cook pot. With luck the cook would not soon discover it.

The door to the guest hall was just across the entryway from the abbot's kitchen. I prayed that the hinges would not squeal and gently opened the door. The hinges were silent.

Brother Theodore's small cell lay just inside the entrance. I rapped knuckles upon his door firmly enough, I hoped, to awaken him, but not so loudly that other sleepers nearby would be roused from their slumber.

The hosteler was not easily aroused, but eventually I heard the latch of his door lifted. His chamber had a narrow window of glass, so I saw his shape in the open door, and the dim moonlight allowed him to see a man standing before him. But there was not so much light that he knew me.

"'Tis Master Hugh," I whispered.

"You? Hugh? But... m'lord abbot has banished you."

"Aye. Which is why you must bid me enter your chamber and close the door, that we may speak privily."

"Oh, uh, aye. Enter."

The hosteler closed the door behind me and I saw him approach a small table where there appeared to be an open book and a cresset.

"No light," I said.

"Why have you come? The fistula is well. You need not have troubled yourself. I have little pain from the surgery. How did you enter? Whose robe is that?"

I had questions for the hosteler, but thought I would be more likely to learn from him what I sought if I answered his questions first. I told him all, except how I came by the habit – and the matter of the dead cat – for I did not wish to bring trouble to the threadmaker's wife should her part in this become known.

"I have told you how I came here," I said, "and now I will tell why. The woman I brought to the hospital nearly a fortnight past, Amice Thatcher, was sent from the hospital. She was told that her children disturbed those who were ill. That same night two men took her and her children, as I feared might happen."

"Why did they do so?"

"A chapman of the town and she were to wed, but he was found near Bampton, beaten so badly that he soon died. I investigated his death and learned that the man had found treasure – ancient coins of silver, and jewels and golden objects."

"I remember – you told me of this. He was murdered for this wealth?"

"For the location of the find, I think. He would not tell, even when they beat him insensible."

"Where is this hoard?"

"No man knows, nor woman, either. But the men who murdered the chapman thought he might have told Amice where it was hid."

"Ah, I see. Because they were to wed."

"Aye. And somehow they knew of it."

"So now they have her, until she tells what she does not know?"

"Nay, she is freed, and now safe in Bampton."

"Saints be praised."

"She was held in an abandoned plague house in East Hanney."

"Are her captors brought to justice?"

"Not yet?"

"Who are they?"

"I believe they are squires to Sir John Trillowe."

"Him who was Sheriff of Oxford two years past?"

"Aye. Your abbot is Peter of Hanney."

"He is, from West Hanney."

"But the villages are small, and close together. Men in one place would know those who lived in the other."

"Surely."

"Does the abbot receive guests from the villages, old friends who call when they visit Abingdon?"

"Aye. Many brothers are from towns nearby, and m'lord abbot is lenient in allowing visits from family and friends. I am from Lyford, not far from West Hanney."

"Did you know Abbot Peter before you came here?"

"Knew his father and older brothers. I'm nearly twenty years older than m'lord abbot."

"If you were reared near West Hanney, and knew folk from the village, do you know some of the abbot's visitors?"

"Aye, some."

"The day Amice Thatcher was sent away, or the day before, did the abbot entertain guests?"

"Aye, he did, one."

"Did you know the man?"

"Oh, aye, Sir Simon's easy to remember, with his ear standing away from his head as it does."

"Did Sir Simon stay long at the abbey?"

"Don't know. He doesn't stay in the guest range. Stays in the abbot's private rooms."

"Did Abbot Peter have other visitors with Sir Simon that day?"

"Not that I saw... You said the men who slew the chapman are squires to Sir John Trillowe?"

"Aye."

"And when Sir John's son visited the abbey, next day the abbot sends Amice Thatcher away."

The hosteler saw the direction of my thoughts. "Aye," I replied. "Sent out to fend for herself, where men might seize her to seek treasure."

Brother Theodore was silent.

"Sir Simon is Sir John's youngest son," I said. "He'll inherit little."

"So if there was treasure to be had, he'd be as eager as two penniless squires to grab a share," Brother Theodore said.

"Those are my thoughts."

"If Sir Simon is in league with those who murdered the chapman, how will you prove it?"

"I do not know. What I have so far learned might hang a man if he was but a tenant or yeoman, but no King's Eyre would send a gentleman to the gallows on what evidence I have."

"Perhaps it might."

"How so?" I asked.

"M'lord abbot is not popular in Abingdon. Indeed, we brothers take care not to walk alone upon the town streets if we must leave abbey precincts. A jury of Abingdon men might be eager to convict a friend of Abbot Peter."

"But the Eyre meets in Oxford."

"Oh, aye, where Sir John and Sir Simon will have friends, and there will be men who have no interest in anything but a bribe."

"Just so."

"Well, I have told all I know. You must make of it what you can. I wish you well."

"Much thanks for your help."

"'Tis I who must thank you. You said that your fee for treating my fistula would be three shillings. I have no coin, no possessions. Abbot Peter must award the fee."

"He will not do so," I said.

"I fear not. He'll use as excuse that I did not seek his permission for your work."

"It may be nearing time for vigils. I should be away before the office."

Brother Theodore stood from his bench when I rose from mine and bade me Godspeed, and when I had departed his cell closed the door softly behind me. I cautiously moved from the guest house to the entry, tossed the cowl over my head, and walked brazenly past the abbot's kitchen toward the reredorter and infirmary. If any man saw me I wanted to appear as a man about his lawful business, not some skulking culprit trying to avoid discovery.

I had entered the orchard when from the church tower I heard the sacrist ring the bell for vigils. I hid behind the trunk of one of the larger apple trees till I was sure that the monks had assembled in the church. When I heard the sound of the office carrying over the still night air I felt safe in removing my shoes and stepping into the ditch to escape the abbey in the same manner I had entered.

I slept that night in Bruce's stall, cold and wet, or more precisely, wet and cold, since I was cold because I was wet, not wet because I was cold. I piled clean straw in a corner of the stall, burrowed into it, and wrapped the black woolen habit about me to ward off the chill. Sometime in the night I briefly awoke, and, as if in a dream, a scheme to ensnare John Thrale's murderers came to me.

Next morn I returned the soiled habit to the threadmaker's wife, purchased a loaf from the baker, retrieved my sack of instruments from the New Inn, and set out for Oxford. Bruce is not a beast to be hurried, but we crossed the Thames at Southbridge and passed through the New Gate well before midday.

My destination was the castle, and a conversation with Sir Roger de Elmerugg. The Sheriff is an old friend to Lord Gilbert, and I intended to present him with the facts of John Thrale's death and Amice Thatcher's abduction, then propose to him a plan whereby the felons might indict themselves.

I am well acquainted with Oxford Castle, even its dungeon, having spent some days there falsely accused of stealing my own fur coat. Thoughts of the coat reminded me that I would be more comfortable this day was I wearing it, and that it was nearly the season to remove it from storage in my chest and place it again in service.

I left Bruce in the castle forecourt, found my way to the Sheriff's anteroom, and asked the clerk if Sir Roger was in. The clerk remembered me as Lord Gilbert Talbot's man and immediately rose from behind his desk to crack open the door behind him and announce me. The anteroom was empty of supplicants, which surprised me, as the Sheriff is generally besieged by those who seek his favor.

Sir Roger possesses the most impressive eyebrows of any man I know. He invited me into his chamber, asked my business, and as I told him the tale of John Thrale, Amice Thatcher, and Sybil Montagu he scowled till his eyebrows became a single bristling appendage.

"Those squires are surely guilty of murder," Sir Roger said when I had completed the tale. "But Sir John will prevent their punishment, unless you find more proof against them."

"I thought as much, and have devised a plan."

"'Tis near time for dinner. Tell me of it whilst we dine."

Sir Roger keeps a good table. His cook presented the Sheriff and his guests with a first remove of aloes of lamb, pomme dorryce, and parsley bread with honey butter. For the second remove there was a fruit-and-salmon pie, herb fritters, and cabbage with marrow. For the third remove we enjoyed a pottage of eggs, capon farced, and a cherry pottage. I must remember, when my business requires me again to call upon Sir Roger, to do so at the dinner hour.

I told the Sheriff of my scheme while we consumed the meal, and he agreed with but a few modifications. Immediately after dinner I sought Bruce, hoisted my overfed self to the saddle, and set out over Bookbinder's Bridge and past Osney Abbey for Bampton. I arrived at Galen House as the evening Angelus Bell rang from the Church of St. Beornwald, dismissed the grooms who watched there, and sent them to the castle with Bruce.

Whether or not my scheme to seize two murderers

succeeded depended upon Amice Thatcher. After a supper of pease pottage she put her children to bed, and I drew benches near the fire to explain what was needed of her, if the squires who slew John Thrale and seized her were to be impeached for the felonies. She was at first reluctant, as would be the cheese if asked if it wished to be placed in a trap for rats, for the plot would place her in some peril. But when I assured her that her children would be safe in Bampton, and sergeants from Oxford Castle as well as grooms from Bampton Castle would see to her protection, she agreed.

This was with some hesitation, but as she considered how the villains had robbed her of a secure future, she became more agreeable to the role she must play. Snares, to be successful, must be baited.

I was a little surprised that Osbert also seemed averse to the plan. It did not concern him. So I thought.

Chapter 15

That night, as we lay abed, Kate told me that Amice had lately shown much concern for Osbert's care, applying the ointment of pears and moneywort twice each day. I had hopes that the salve would not only help the healing of his wounds, but soften them so that he could bend without opening the scars, both now and in the future.

"She is much concerned for Osbert, and when I told her that he must soon be returned to East Hanney she was woeful."

"The day cannot be put off much longer," I replied. "He is a young man and is healing rapidly now."

"And he has a skilled surgeon to treat his wounds."

After a night in the straw of the stables behind the New Inn I slept well in my own bed. Following a loaf and ale I sought the castle, found Arthur and Uctred, and told them to make ready tomorrow to travel to Abingdon and there meet six of Sir Roger's sergeants. Together nine men should be sufficient to capture two felons if I was successful in luring them to their ruin.

I am usually oblivious to the behavior of females about me. I speak and read two languages in addition to my own; French and Latin. But I have never been much conversant in feminine. This may be considered strange, as 'tis the speech of half the realm. I think I am not alone in this ignorance. So if Kate had not told me of it, I would likely not have noticed how solicitous Amice had become for Osbert's recovery.

Next morn I observed her regard for Osbert. The man was healing well under her care. I would soon have to devise some plan to see him safe from Sir Philip's wrath, but not that day. One scheme at a time.

Early Friday morn, Kate took Bessie and Amice's two children to the castle, there to remain in my old bachelor quarters till this matter was resolved. Osbert was enough recovered that he could remain alone in Galen House, although he could not defend it. If the felonious squires did not swallow my bait and instead returned to Galen House, they would have no reason to do him harm.

After Kate and the children were established in Bampton Castle, Arthur, Uctred, Amice, and I set out for Abingdon. Uctred drove John Thrale's horse and cart, and Amice rode therein, while Arthur and I were once again mounted upon Bruce and the old grey palfrey.

It was important that Amice not be seen returning to her home in the company of three men, so she climbed down from the cart while we were yet a mile from Abingdon and entered the town alone. Uctred followed Arthur and me to the New Inn, and immediately after Arthur dismounted from the palfrey I sent him off to the bury, there to watch over Amice until Uctred, I, and six sergeants from Oxford Castle might join him.

Sir Roger had promised that his sergeants would arrive at the New Inn this day by noon, and he was true to his word. I found the six dining upon a barley pottage, with the crumbs of numerous maslin loaves beneath their elbows.

Their officer, a man of commanding girth and a livid scar across one cheek from some earlier episode of law enforcement, recognized me from Sir Roger's description and stood as I approached his table. He could surely hold his own in any scrap with miscreant squires, but if the culprits took to their heels some other man would need to chase them down. I noted two youthful sergeants at the table who seemed likely to show a good turn of speed, should pursuit be required.

The sergeants were appareled incognito, as I had requested, with no badge or tunic showing that they served Sir Roger de Elmerugg. I told the fellows to follow, and with Uctred beside me, I walked the short distance to Amice's house in the bury. I had given her six pence of Lord Gilbert's coin to purchase barley and pretend to set about her occupation, and when we passed her house I saw smoke rising from beneath a cauldron in the toft. The day was too cool for barley to malt properly unless the water it soaked in was warmed. Arthur leaned against Amabel Maunder's empty dwelling across the street, and joined our group as we continued down the lane to the road from the direction of Marcham and Hanney.

There I assigned two men to begin the watch for Sir John Trillowe's squires. I thought it unlikely that word of Amice's return would reach East Hanney this day, but was not willing to take a chance of being wrong. A sergeant would prowl each end of the lane, occasionally exchanging positions during the day. Four others, and Arthur and Uctred, would conceal themselves in Amabel Maunder's empty house, which they might enter from a narrow alley behind the row of houses that included the neighboring threadmaker's dwelling. Two would watch while the others slept. I would remain in Amabel's house catching what sleep I could while watching Amice's house with the others.

There was the matter of food for nine men. I approached the threadmaker, told him as much as he needed to know of what was happening upon his street, and offered him three pence each day to feed us. This bid he gladly accepted.

There was but one more thing to do. I did not wish to be seen at Amice's door, for I could not know who might be watching. I circled behind houses and came upon her as she poured barley into the cauldron of warm water. My approach startled her, even though she knew to expect my appearance.

I told her where guards were stationed, advised her that I would be in Amabel Maunder's house with the watchers, and bid her continue her work so her actions would be unremarkable to any who observed her closely. I left her with a last admonition: if somehow her abductors should elude our watch and enter her house in the night, she should tell them what they wished to know – that John Thrale found his cache of coins and jewelry in a forest near to an ancient chapel east of Bampton.

Amice looked at me with wide eyes. "Did he so?"

"So I believe."

"You have not found it?"

"Nay, but I believe the treasure to be somewhere there."

Arthur, Uctred, the sergeants and I spent the next three days watching over Amice Thatcher. The sergeants thought this good sport, for watching Amice was a rewarding experience for any man. Each day that passed increased my expectation that felons would soon seek her and the knowledge they assumed she possessed.

I was confident that the men who had slain John Thrale, threatened Kate and Bessie, and held Amice captive would learn of her return. Somehow these squires of East Hanney had learned of her friendship with the chapman, and knew also when she was driven from the abbey guest hall. Whoso had told them of these things would not hesitate to inform the felons of her reappearance. I wished this talebearer would make haste. Days grew shorter and colder, but we dared not light a fire on Amabel's hearthstone, for to do so might give away the ambush.

The third night we watched, one of the sergeants, peering through the ragged edge of the skin which covered one of Amabel's windows, called for me to come to the window.

"There's somethin' movin'."

All through the previous nights we had seen no man upon this lane, not even the beadle, who kept to more traveled streets.

I hastened to the window and watched for some sign of the movement the sergeant had seen. For several minutes I saw nothing, then, emerging from the shadows, a pale form came into view.

"'Tis a dog," I told the sergeant.

While I watched a mongrel hound of chaotic ancestry

followed its nose from one side of the lane to another, searching for something edible.

The animal's search amused me, so I lingered at the window, watching as the scrawny beast ambled past my place. The dog had gone perhaps five or six paces beyond Amabel's house, then, as I was about to turn away, the hound stiffened and turned to look behind. Some sound, perhaps, had alerted it to danger. I followed its gaze and studied the curving lane in the direction from which the beast had come.

I saw nothing, but the dog saw or heard something which caused it unease. It loped away, no longer interested in discovering a meal. I turned to study the lane and saw what had caused the dog to flee.

A lone figure slipped from one shadow to another, hurrying in careful fashion, toward me. Not two? Where was the second squire? Perhaps one remained where the lane joined the main street, as sentinel. I whispered loudly for Arthur, Uctred, and the sergeants to be alert; a man approached.

When the stealthy shape drew near, it hid for a moment in the shadow of the house beside Amice's dwelling, then dashed across the lane and through the door of Amabel Maunder's house. 'Twas the sergeant assigned to watch where the lane joined the main street.

"Three men," he said, "just now halted their horses down there." He pointed in the direction from which he had come. "One has remained with the horses, the others follow after me. I don't think I was seen. They will be here anon."

I told the sergeants to have their daggers ready and kept watch through the tattered skin of the window for a glimpse of the approaching squires. They did not appear.

All we who waited were tense and eager for the capture we expected. When no men appeared slinking about the lane, our taut alertness began to fade.

"You sure you seen 'em?" one of the sergeants whispered to his cohort.

"They was followin' close behind me... moon is risin', so I could see 'em plain."

"Perhaps they are being cautious," I said softly. "But we are ready for them."

We were not, not totally. I watched and waited and grew increasingly uneasy. Arthur, Uctred, and the sergeants shared the emotion. I heard them shuffling feet upon the rushes and breathing heavily, anticipating a fracas and puzzled that it did not come.

I believed the sentry when he claimed to have seen two men enter the bury. Could it be they were about some other, lawful business? If so, why leave a third man with the horses? Such conduct spoke of a desire to make a hasty departure. Men who did no felony would have no need to violate curfew, nor would they be prepared for flight when they concluded their business. Sir John Trillowe's squires were in the bury, of that I was certain, but where, and what did they intend?

I knew their intent: to seize Amice Thatcher again, or force from her the location of John Thrale's treasure. I did not know how they intended to do this, and as time passed I became more and more fretful that somehow the squires had devised a way to approach Amice Thatcher's house unseen.

The alley! Behind Amabel Maunder's house was a narrow passage, weed-grown and rarely used, which gave access to the tofts behind each house. There was a similar alley behind Amice Thatcher's house. My approach through the alley had startled her three days past.

The waning moon was now high enough that the pale tower of St. Nicholas's Church was visible to the south above Abingdon's rooftops. The added light meant that we could see our quarry, but they also could see us. I had no choice. Because of me, Amice's safety was at risk. If the hidden felons saw us and fled, and my snare snapped shut empty, so be it.

I told the others to follow and ran from Amabel's house across the lane to Amice Thatcher's dwelling. I stopped in the shadow of the house, raised a hand to halt the others, and was about to divide them and send half to the front and the other half to the rear of the house when I heard a muffled gasp. The throat which made such a sound was surely feminine. Arthur and the others heard also, the night being still.

We were too late. The squires were in the house. They had come by way of the alley, for I had watched the lane. We might trap them in the house, but they held Amice and would threaten her if we menaced their escape.

I whispered for the sergeants to guard the rear of the house, told Arthur and Uctred to follow me, and ran to the front door.

I had told Amice to bar her doors, and when I grasped the latch the door did not open. But it did move enough to rattle the hinges and thus speak a warning to those inside that someone wished to enter.

I told Arthur and Uctred to remain at the front door and ran to the toft. The sergeants stood at the rear door, hands upon their daggers and ready for a brawl. I tested this door also, and found it barred as well. How had two men gained entrance to the house? Or did my ears deceive me and no suspicious gasp come from the place?

"Amice," I whispered, "Amice... 'tis Master Hugh. Are you well?"

When a response finally came it was not what I wished to hear.

"She is well, but she will not be if you do not depart."

"Who is there?"

"Desperate men. We were told you might lay a snare for us, so we have prepared one for you. There is a dagger at the woman's throat. She will tell us where the chapman's treasure may be found, or you will, or her throat will be slit."

"If you do such a thing you will die."

"The man we serve will protect us."

"Protect you from the Sheriff of Oxford? Sir Roger

has the King's trust, Sir John does not." (I thought it could do no harm to disclose that I knew who they were and who they served). "Are you willing to risk a scaffold in Oxford upon that confidence?"

Silence followed.

"There are armed men at the front and back," I said through the door. "You cannot escape."

"Perhaps. We have the woman."

"If you harm her you will hang, or perhaps there will be a fight here in the bury and you will, regretfully, be slain in the struggle."

"You would have us surrender to you? We may hang should we do so. So if we harm the woman, what greater harm to us? Her death is loss to you, not to us."

The man spoke true. If I could I would see them hang for their felonies. Slaying Amice Thatcher would not increase the penalty.

"You knew we would be watching this house," I said. "Who told you?"

"No man you can harm."

"You will never gain the chapman's treasure."

"Why do you say so? Have you found it?"

My silence was answer enough.

"So you have not," the squire said. "Then we may yet discover it before you."

"Not from the Oxford Castle dungeon."

"We will not be there."

"You believe Sir Roger will not impeach you for your felonies?"

"He will not seize us to do so."

"What? His sergeants stand here at the door."

"Mayhap, but they will not take us. We have the woman."

"You cannot remain in the house forever."

"Aye, but when we depart it will be with the woman, and with a dagger at her neck."

My plan had unraveled like an old surcoat. All because I had not thought of access to Amice's toft through the little-used alley. But how did these vile squires get through her barred door without making some sound I might have heard from my post across the lane?

I could not worry about that for the moment. Later, when Amice was free of her captors, then I could learn from her how they gained entrance.

"Stand away from the door, you and the sergeants. We will leave with the woman, and should any man come within five paces of us, my dagger will pierce her throat."

When I made no immediate reply the man spoke again. "Did you hear? Answer, yea or nay."

"Yea... I heard."

I turned to the sergeants and in a whisper bid them seek the alley behind the toft and hurry to where the lane joined the main street. There they would find a man and three horses. I told them they should not seize the fellow, but if they could, they should work their way close to him and the beasts in the dark, without being discovered.

The sergeants disappeared into the shadows of the alley, and I ran to the front of the house.

"We heard," Arthur said. "Are we to do as the knave said?"

"We must. But as they retreat toward their horses we will follow, five paces away. They must not be allowed to take Amice from Abingdon."

I heard the bar lifted from Amice's door, the hinges squealed, and three figures filed through the opening. The shorter of the two squires led, a dagger in his right hand, then came Amice and behind her the taller of the squires, with one arm about her waist and the other pressing a dagger to her throat. I saw the blade reflect moonlight.

"Stay back," the taller squire demanded, and shoved Amice before him. The stout squire decided 'twould be best to place himself where he could observe us, so moved behind his companion and walked backward, his dagger pointed at me all the while. My arrow wound took that moment to ache, reminding me that I should avoid another perforation.

Thus we traveled, two hundred paces or more, past the silent huts of the bury, no man in either group speaking. The only sound was the scuffling of feet and once, a sob from Amice Thatcher.

As we approached the main street I heard a horse stamp a foot and blow through its nostrils. I studied the night in the direction from which the sound had come, and saw dimly the shapes of three horses. As I watched the animals moved from the shadows into the moonlight.

A rider upon the first horse had seen or heard our approach and led the other beasts to meet the squires and their captive. This horseman wore dark chauces and cotehardie, and his cap was pulled low over his forehead so as to obscure his features, but I knew who it was who awaited the felonious squires.

The rider's left ear showed white in the moonlight, protruding from under his cap as if set in plaster. My excuse for this misshapen ear is that it was the first time I had ever been called upon to reattach such a member. I shall do better in the future. And, in truth, I cared little at the time if Sir Simon Trillowe's features were blemished or not.

I detected movement behind Sir Simon and the horses. 'Twas the sergeants I had sent hurrying through the alley. Sir Simon, the squires, and Amice were surrounded, but the advantage yet lay with those who held a blade to a woman's throat.

Neither Sir Simon nor the squires spoke. They knew the risk they had taken, and had planned what they would do if their scheme was thwarted. The taller of the squires, who held his dagger to Amice's throat, approached a horse and attempted to throw Amice across the beast's neck, before the saddle. The animal did not approve of the business and sidestepped, so that rather than finding herself upon a horse, Amice was pitched face-first into the mud of the street.

Just for a moment the squire's dagger was away from Amice's neck. "At them!" I yelled, and with my own dagger drawn I plunged toward the tall squire so to prevent his seizing Amice again. A dagger used against me could not be laid aside Amice's neck.

What followed was a maelstrom of shouting, cursing men, stamping horses, and one shrieking woman. The squire heard my cry, glanced from Amice, at his feet, to me, leaping for him, saw my dagger glinting in the moonlight, and vaulted to his saddle. The other squire had been mounting his beast when Amice fell, so was in his saddle when Uctred and a sergeant charged after him. From the corner of my eye I saw his dagger sweep before Uctred's approach, and Uctred fell back. Whether or not he had been slashed I could not tell.

Amice hindered my rush to seize the squire who had restrained her. She rose to her knees as I was about to leap over her. I stumbled and nearly fell, which gave the squire time to gain his seat and steady himself. I made for his leg, intending to pull him from the saddle, but his dagger flashed out and forced me back.

From his opposite side I heard a roar, and saw the squire turn. 'Twas one of the sergeants who had run ahead through the alley who was now attacking. I had no time to consider this, however, for at that moment a horse whirled before me and drove me back toward Amice. Sir Simon was the rider, and when he saw me step away from his rush he bellowed to the squires that they must be away, then spurred his horse off down the street.

The squires heard and followed. Arthur had the corpulent squire by a leg, ducking to dodge the wild swings of the fellow's dagger. But when the horse gathered himself and sprang away Arthur was forced to release his hold, else he would have been dragged to some place where he would face three furious men alone, away from others of his force.

Arthur drew himself from the mud of the street, then knelt again to study the road at his feet.

"What have you found?" I asked.

"'Tis the short, fat fellow who rides the horse with the broken shoe. See here."

I squatted beside him and saw in the moonlight the shape of the broken horseshoe which had so vexed us.

The ambush had been a failure. Amice Thatcher had nearly been seized from under my nose, the squires had got away, and Uctred was holding his right arm with his left and I thought it likely I would need to stitch up a wound.

My explanation for this debacle is that I spent a year in Paris studying surgery, not the capture of felons. All men seek to excuse their failures; why must I be different?

Our horses were stabled at the New Inn. By the time we retrieved them and set off in pursuit our quarry would be halfway to East Hanney and Sir John Trillowe's protection. The only man who could pry the felons from his custody slept in Oxford Castle. I resolved to travel there at first light and seek Sir Roger's aid. He would not be much pleased to be required to journey to East Hanney, but he has no love for either Sir Simon or Sir John.

I gathered the sergeants, some of whom had set off afoot following the squires, as if they would chase mounted men, and found Arthur inspecting Uctred's arm. 'Twas too dark, with only the waning moon for light, to see how badly the groom was slashed. The sleeve of his cotehardie was neatly sliced, and I felt the damp of blood there and saw a dark stain upon the fabric. It seemed more than a scratch, but not so deep a gash as to warrant concern. At Amice Thatcher's house there would be a cresset to give light enough to see and deal with the wound. I told the others that was where we would go first, and set off into the bury.

The ten of us crowded into Amice's small house, and she lit two cressets from coals yet glowing upon her hearthstone. In their light I saw that Uctred's laceration was not deep, yet required stitching if it was to heal properly.

The threadmaker would not appreciate being awakened at midnight, but I thought a length of his finest linen thread would serve for Uctred's cut, and a threadmaker is likely to have a needle or two about his house. I was correct on all counts. The threadmaker was not pleased when he opened to my insistent pounding upon his door, his thread was of excellent quality, though not so fine or strong as silk, and he did possess several needles.

I had no herbs to dull Uctred's pain, and Amice's barley was not yet malted and was many days from becoming ale. Uctred seemed not to mind. He took off cotehardie and kirtle and waited stoically in the cold while I drew the edges of the wound together with six sutures.

While I worked, with Arthur and the sergeants looking on, I planned what must next be done. I was little confident that any plan to apprehend the malevolent squires would conclude as I wished, the unsuccessful plot to seize the felons here, at Amice's door, being fresh in my mind. But a man may learn much from his failures, if he is willing.

We must sleep, for the next day would be long and wearisome for all. Although it was unseemly, I told Arthur and Uctred that they and I would remain with Amice for the remainder of the night. The squires were unlikely to return, but I had been wrong before. Arthur nodded and began piling rushes against a wall opposite to Amice's bed.

The sergeants I sent to Amabel Maunder's house, where I was sure they would soon be snoring. I spent much of the next hour upon Arthur's pile of rushes, reliving the events of the past hours, devising useless schemes which might have succeeded. Some time before the morning Angelus Bell I finally fell to sleep.

The threadmaker's wife had loaves and ale enough to break our fast, and when we were fed we set off for the New Inn. Arthur and Uctred I sent to Bampton, with Amice in their care. But before they set out I asked her how the squires had gained admittance to her house.

"They was at the back, in the toft. One of 'em whispered 'e was you. Said as there was a need to speak to me. Thought 'twas you. One man's whisper sounds much like another's."

The squires knew who was seeking them, and how to avoid me. Some man had told them this, but there was no benefit to fretting now about who might have done so.

Arthur, Uctred, and Amice set off toward Bampton, Amice again riding in the chapman's cart. Before they departed the New Inn I told Arthur to go directly to Galen House and leave the cart in the toft. Behind my house I had built a shed, with thatched roof, to keep firewood dry. It was large enough to shelter a small cart horse. I instructed Arthur to tie the chapman's horse there, then take Amice to the castle where she might find safety with Kate.

Chapter 16

The sergeants and I went north, to Oxford. Most folk upon the roads do not like to see seven mounted men approaching, and so make it their business to clear the way for such a company. One man, when we drew near, vaulted a wall and trotted across a harvested oat field as if he had some pressing errand amongst the stubble. King Edward has done much to keep the roads safe, and we in England are not troubled as are the French with marauding bands of unemployed knights and men-at-arms, yet few men ever regret an excess of caution.

Our horses were rested and we traveled fast – as fast as Bruce could manage, he being an ancient beast. We arrived at Oxford Castle before the fourth hour, and I admit that images of the castle hall set for the Sheriff's dinner came to mind.

There was, alas, to be no dinner. When I told Sir Roger of Sir Simon's part in the near recapture of Amice Thatcher, he sent his clerk to have his horse made ready, and to tell the six sergeants to prepare to return to Abingdon and East Hanney. Wheaten loaves and cheese would make our simple dinner.

"Sir John will not risk himself to protect those villains," Sir Roger said between bites of his loaf. "Not when Lord Gilbert Talbot's bailiff saw them attempt to seize a woman."

"And Sir Simon?" I asked, being willing to see my handiwork upon his ear undone on a scaffold.

"He was with the horses? Sir John has enough influence that, even was he with the squires when they laid hands on the woman, a King's Eyre would likely set him free. We may, however, give him a fright." He grinned as he spoke.

Sir Roger was in a hurry, so our dinner was hastily swallowed. The Sheriff, upon his younger, fresher horse, would have set a faster pace, but when he saw that Bruce could not keep up, he slowed. So it was that when we reached East Hanney none of those we sought was to be found.

Sir John Trillowe's manor is more prosperous than that of Sir Philip Rede. Sir John's house is larger, its wall freshly whitewashed, with leaded glass in every window. The roof is of slate, not thatch. Perhaps the fines he levied while Sheriff of Oxford, and which so angered the burghers of the town that they begged King Edward to dismiss him, paid for such a roof.

Sir Roger, with me and six sergeants – who now wore his livery – arrayed behind, pounded upon Sir John's door. A valet opened so soon that I suspect our arrival was not a surprise. The Sheriff pushed past the valet and commanded in a loud voice to be taken to Sir John forthwith. It is likely Sir John heard without the servant informing him.

The valet showed us into a small hall, then trotted off to seek his lord. Neither he nor Sir John appeared soon. 'Tis my belief that Sir John expected the Sheriff's arrival, and was determined to demonstrate that he was yet a man of authority, even though King Edward had set Sir Roger in his place as Sheriff of Oxford.

"Sir Roger," Sir John said warmly when he finally appeared. "How may I serve you? Come from Oxford this day? A long ride." Then, to the valet, who stood behind, "Wine for Sir Roger, and ale, the best, mind you, for his men."

Sir John swept a hand toward me and the sergeants as he spoke of ale, so although I wore no livery it would be ale for me. But the best, mind you.

After voicing these commands Sir John looked to Sir Roger, and with a bland smile awaited the Sheriff's reply.

"You have two squires who serve you. I wish to speak with them."

Sir John shrugged, raised his eyebrows, and said, "I have four squires. Which two do you seek?"

Sir Roger turned to me. "One is tall and slender, and when he does not wear your livery is commonly seen wearing a red cap. The other is short and stout, and wears a blue cap."

"Ah, you seek Giles and Henry. They are not here."

"Where are they?" Sir Roger asked.

"London. Why do you seek them?"

"They have done murder," I said, "and theft, and seized a woman and her children so to demand of her where a treasure might be found."

"Giles? And Henry? Surely not. You are mistaken."

"Last night, near midnight, they tried again to take the woman. Sir Simon aided them."

"Sir Simon? Nonsense. Sir Simon was nowhere near Abingdon last night," Sir John scoffed. "He is in London. Has been for three days now. Giles and Henry accompanied him."

"Abingdon," Sir Roger said. "What has Abingdon to do with Sir Simon?" Sir John had misspoke himself and was caught out.

While we talked I noticed occasional shadows passing before a window. Curious about what this might be, I sidled toward the window until I was near enough to glance through it to the front of the manor house. Between the house and our horses was a group of grooms and valets and tenants, perhaps a dozen or more. Two others arrived as I watched. I saw no weapons, but did not doubt each man possessed a blade concealed upon his person. Sir Roger, his sergeants, and I were badly outnumbered.

Sir John chose the moment to change the subject. "This fellow," he said, pointing to me, "has stolen a man from Sir Philip Rede. He should be arrested for seizing Sir Philip's villein."

Sir Roger looked at me, raising his shaggy eyebrows in expectation of some explanation.

"Sir Philip intended to murder the man."

"Murder? Nay. The man ran off with you. Sir Philip was but disciplining a wicked servant."

"The villein was beaten near to death," I replied, "and the gallows he was to hang upon was standing before his eyes, here, in this village."

"Sir Philip has the right of infangenthef. The man stole property from Sir Philip. A thief may be hanged for his crime."

"He stole himself from a wicked lord," I said.

"Wicked? Because he would not countenance theft of his chattels?"

"Nay. Wicked because he held another knight's daughter for ransom, and the villein he would have slain allowed her to escape."

"So you say. A knight is lord of his manor. You have abetted a theft, and Sir Roger must arrest you for it."

"I may do so," the Sheriff interrupted, "when I have spoken to Sir Simon."

"The lad is not here. I have told you. He was off to London three days past."

"A poor season to travel so far."

"Aye," Sir John shrugged. "But when a fair maid is at the end of the road few journeys are too far."

We were thwarted. Our travel to East Hanney was for naught. I had no doubt but that Giles and Henry were away from East Hanney, and likely accompanied Sir Simon on the road to London, or some other far place. But I doubted that their absence was permanent. And if Sir Simon did travel to London, he had departed East Hanney with the dawn this day.

Sir Roger looked at me, rolled his eyes, then turned to Sir John. "When Giles and Henry return, send word to me immediately. Sir Simon, also."

"Indeed, Sir Roger. I will do so."

A valet arrived with wine and ale, and we slaked our thirst while standing, for Sir John had offered no chair, and our business was frustrated and over. The Sheriff thanked Sir John for his time and turned to the door, which an alert valet jumped to open. I and the sergeants filed out into the cobbled forecourt, passed between the silent men assembled there, mounted our horses, and set our faces for Oxford.

"Tell me more of this villein who fled his place," Sir Roger said when we had left East Hanney behind.

I did so, and when I had done Sir Roger said, "And Lord Gilbert commands that you return him?"

"He does."

"And you have told Lord Gilbert that, if the man is sent back, you will no longer serve him?"

"I have."

"Where will you go?"

"I will remain in Bampton and seek my bread as a surgeon."

"In such a small town?"

"Or remove to Oxford."

"This matter is no business of mine, although I could make it so. If you return to Oxford I will see that custom is sent to you."

"My thanks. I would not lack for patients when your sergeants are required to break up some brawl at an ale house of a Saturday eve."

"Nay," he chuckled. "My lads might send much business your way."

Where two roads met to the west of Marcham I left Sir Roger and his sergeants. They took the road through Marcham to Abingdon and Oxford, and I turned Bruce to the left, for Standlake and Bampton. Bruce was weary and I did not hurry him, so that there was barely enough light to see the spire of the Church of St. Beornwald, dark against the sunset, when I arrived.

I left Bruce at the marshalsea and sought my bachelor chamber off the castle hall. Kate was pleased to see me, but with Amice and her children looking on, my welcome home was more subdued than I might have wished.

My quarters at the castle were too small for two women and three children, and as I was bound for Galen House, Kate would not willingly remain longer at the castle. I carried Bessie, nodding sleepily upon my shoulder, to Galen House, with Kate, Amice, and her children trailing behind.

I was pleased to be home, especially with winter near, but gloom soon overtook me. Galen House was warm, for Osbert had kept a blaze upon the hearth, as I had told him to do, but I could not escape thoughts of my failure to apprehend murderers, nor could I tear my mind from considering what might lie ahead for Osbert.

I had laid a scheme to capture felons, and had failed. I had also a plan to save Osbert from the penalty Sir Philip had awaiting him. Would this design be as flawed as the attempt to catch Giles and Henry? I mistrusted my competence.

Amice and her children were put to their rest upon pallets in the vacant ground-floor room, and Kate took Bessie up to our bedchamber soon after. The house and the town were quiet as Osbert sat with me, contemplating the embers of the fire.

"You've got to send me back to Sir Philip soon, I know," Osbert finally said. "When you goin' to do it?"

"Lord Gilbert told me you must be returned when your back is healed. I will postpone that day as long as possible."

"To what purpose? A few days more of life? I am a dead man. Sir Philip intends to make a lesson of me."

"To keep other villeins from bolting the manor?"

"Aye. Since plague come he an' his father before him has lost half the villeins who worked 'is demesne. What didn't die of plague ran off, now that workers is scarce an' a man can hire out in a town, or mayhap set up as a tenant upon lands of some other gentleman."

"Did you ever think to do so?"

"Often... but I knew what Sir Philip would do did he take me. I only come with you because I knew what would happen to me for allowin' Sybil Montagu to escape. Wouldn't 'ave done so, otherwise."

"Does your back cause much pain?"

"Nay. The salve you made... I can't reach to all places

on me back to daub it on, as Amice could do. Can't bend to touch me toes yet, neither."

"You may never be able to do so."

"Aye. A man in 'is grave don't touch nothing but the dirt in 'is face."

"Perhaps there is a way for you to avoid Sir Philip's wrath."

"Not likely," Osbert sighed. "You 'ave yer lord, an' I 'ave mine, an' they agree what's to be done. There's an end to it... and an end to me. I've set my mind to face what's to come, an' when I'm properly shriven I'll go to meet the Lord Christ as a man."

"Amice will be much grieved."

Osbert was silent for some minutes, staring at the dying coals.

"She said she's lost three good men," he said.

"Three?"

"Aye. Her husband, the thatcher, what died two years past, then the chapman she was to wed. Now me."

"You and Amice have found pleasure in each other's company?"

"Aye. Never thought to find such a woman, an' now I have, 'tis too late."

"Does Amice feel the same? Would she wed you if you were not to be sent back to Sir Philip?"

"Aye, believe so. I've not asked. No reason to do so. I've few tomorrows left me."

"So you wish me to see you back to Sir Philip now?"

"May as well. What's a few more days to a dyin' man?"

"'To everything there is a season, and a time to every purpose under heaven' – so said Solomon."

"Who?"

"Never mind. Perhaps the time for your death is not yet. God may have another purpose for you."

"I wish it might be so."

"Go to your bed. The fire is near out. Tomorrow we will speak more of this."

Next day, at the third hour, after terce, I sought Father Thomas de Bowlegh, one of the three vicars who serve the Church of St. Beornwald. Father Simon and Father Ralph are fixed in their practices, but I thought Father Thomas might, if he knew the circumstances, be more adaptable.

No one may wed until a priest of his parish has read the banns for three consecutive Sundays – this so that if anyone knows why a man and woman should not marry, he will have opportunity to tell the priest of it.

If banns for Osbert and Amice were read out at the Church of St. Beornwald, Lord Gilbert would soon hear of it, and wonder that a man soon to be sent back to his lord, perhaps to his death, should plan to wed without his lord's sufferance. And Osbert's healing went well. I could not keep his recovery from Lord Gilbert much longer.

So when Father Thomas's clerk answered my knock upon the vicarage door I had in mind a desperate scheme to save Osbert, and perhaps Amice as well. If the priest agreed, Osbert would soon be far from Sir Philip's reach, and Amice would disappear from the shire, where Giles and Henry, back from London or wherever they had gone, would never find her to threaten evil did she not tell them of John Thrale's treasure.

Father Thomas has the disease of the ears, so I knew his clerk would overhear our conversation. I was required to trust his discretion, for the matter I wished to raise with the priest must not go beyond the vicarage.

The priest invited me to sit with him on a bench, before the fire, and inclined an ear to me, the better to hear. He knew nothing of the dead chapman, or my pursuit of murderers, and as I wished much from him I thought it proper that he know all of the events which brought Osbert and Amice under the roof of Galen House.

I was sure that the clerk lingered somewhere near the door to hear my tale. This was confirmed when I concluded, for Father Thomas called out for the fellow, and he was in our presence instantly.

"Wine for Master Hugh," Father Thomas said, then

turned to me. "Why do you tell me of this? Is there some matter of the soul which requires my care?"

"Aye, there is. Two people, a man and a woman, are about to flee injustice, and should be wed before they set off upon the roads together."

"This Osbert you told me of, and Amice?"

"Aye."

"But the fellow fled his lord."

"He did. I told you of the evil his lord did, seizing a lass, and how Arthur and I found him, lashed near to death, with a gibbet raised before his eyes."

"And you believe this knight, Sir..."

"Philip."

"Aye, Sir Philip, will slay him for fleeing the manor."

"I've no doubt, nor does Osbert."

"But the law..."

"The law would make murderers of us all, for if we connive in sending Osbert to his lord we will all have his blood upon our hands... and his death upon our consciences."

"I wish you had not told me of this."

"But I did."

"Aye," the priest sighed. "Now what is it you wish of me?"

"Tonight, after the evening Angelus, meet us at the church porch and marry Osbert and Amice."

"But the banns..."

"If they are read Lord Gilbert will learn of it and decide that any man well enough to take a wife is well enough to return to his vengeful lord."

"But 'tis church law."

"Where in Holy Scripture is it written that no man, nor woman, may wed till the banns have been thrice read? Did St. Paul write of it?"

"Nay."

"Men too often reject the requirements God places upon them, and rather place burdens upon other men which God does not."

"But we have always done so."

"Always? I think not. The earliest Christians had no church where they might read the banns, yet they married. Holy Church requires all marriages be public. Kate and I will be present."

"I cannot do this."

"They could set off unwed. Who would know? Making them husband and wife will keep them from sin."

Father Thomas was silent for some time, struggling within himself. I saw his consternation and kept silent. "'Tis most irregular," he finally said. "Father Simon and Father Ralph would never approve."

"I know that. This is why I have come to you."

"You think me more pliant?"

"I think you more just."

"Oh. Well, I must think and pray about this. If you demand an answer now, it must be 'no'."

"Very well, but there is little time to contemplate the matter. Lord Gilbert, if Osbert crosses his mind, may summon me to the castle at any moment and charge me to return him to East Hanney."

"And you will refuse, and resign your post?"

"Aye. Lord Gilbert will find some other to do the work. I will not. Osbert Hanney will die."

"Return at midday. I will give you my answer then."

I was optimistic that Father Thomas would agree to my scheme, so walked to Galen House with lighter heart than when I left it. Although, when he discovered that Osbert was away, Lord Gilbert might dismiss me from my post before I could resign. That troubled me, but I could live with reduced income more readily than with Osbert's mangled corpse upon my conscience.

I gathered Amice and Osbert to the fire, and told them of my scheme. Behind Galen House was a cart, nearly new, and a young cart-horse, the property of John Thrale, which would have come to Amice had he lived a few weeks longer. I could see no reason it should not do so now. I had searched, but found no heirs of the chapman to whom the cart and horse should go. Lord Gilbert needed neither, and would not know they were missing.

"I have this morn spoken to a priest. Do you wish to wed?"

"Aye," Amice answered. Osbert was silent. I waited, and Amice looked to him. Osbert looked down to his hands, which he was twisting in his lap.

"I'll not make of Amice a widow twice," he finally said.

"You need not. I have asked Father Thomas if he will make you husband and wife this night at the church porch. He has promised an answer in a few hours. If he agrees, you must then be ready to flee the town and even the shire.

"The chapman's horse and cart can take you far. If Father Thomas agrees, we will make ready this afternoon, and you may flee in the night."

"But where can we go?" Osbert asked. "Sir Philip will not rest till he finds me."

"Will he go so far as Lancashire to seek you out?"

"Dunno. 'Ow far is that?"

"Many miles."

"But where in that shire could we find safety?"

"My older brother was lord of the manor of Little Singleton, after my father. He died and left a wife and sons when the plague first came, nineteen years past. The oldest lad will by now be lord of the manor, and if he is like other knights he will possess fallow land for which he has no tenants, plague having taken off so many."

"But I have no money for gersom," Osbert said, "nor to buy food for such a journey."

"Kate will send you off with eggs from her hens," I said, and glanced to my wife, who nodded agreement. "Perhaps Father Thomas can be persuaded to offer alms from the poor fund, and provisions from his new tithe barn. And in the castle are stored the goods John Thrale had yet in his cart when men set upon him. If you sell them while on your way north to Lancashire, you will have enough for the journey. There is woolen fabric, buttons and combs.

The stuff is stored with Lord Gilbert's Chamberlain."

I saw Osbert brighten before my eyes, his face like the sun appearing after many clouded days.

"You think the priest will marry us?"

"If he can without the other vicars learning of it, yes, I believe he will."

"What will Lord Gilbert say of this?"

"He will know nothing of the matter. If Father Thomas agrees to meet us at the church porch this night, you must afterward go to your beds, but arise in the night and be gone. If Lord Gilbert asks of you I will then be able to tell him that you fled in the night. This will be no lie."

Kate had listened to this conversation intently, and offered a suggestion. "You must pen a letter to your nephew and sister-in-law," she advised. "Else when two strangers arrive asking to take up a yardland and claiming you sent them, they may not be believed."

"Can you read?" I asked Osbert.

"Nay," he replied. I looked to Amice and she shook her head.

"No matter. Kate's counsel is wise, and I will do so."

Kate had prepared Leach Lombard for our dinner this day. I enjoy the dish, but grew tense as the hour approached when I must seek Father Thomas and learn if he would consent to join Amice and Osbert in matrimony. They might flee even if he would not, but it would be seemly to be wed in such circumstance. In Lancashire no man would know if they were wed or not, but they would. When I left my house after the meal I took with me one of the sacks I use to transport herbs and my instruments when I travel.

Chapter 17

"**N**o man must ever learn of this," Father Thomas said when I sought him after dinner.

"Neither I nor Kate will ever speak of it," I said. (I did not promise not to write of the matter.) "If your clerk holds his tongue, no man need ever know.

"The couple is in great want. Osbert was a villein, owned nothing but his stomach. Amice is a widowed ale wife, and what little she possessed is in her house in Abingdon. She dare not return there. The men who captured her once, and tried to do so a second time, are yet at large, and believe, wrongly, that she knows where treasure may be found."

"What is it you ask?"

"Six pence in alms, and grain from the tithe barn."

The priest left his seat and walked to a table upon which a small, iron-bound chest rested. He produced a key from a lanyard attached to his belt, unlocked the box, and drew six silver pennies from it.

"What more will you ask of me?"

"Tell your clerk to go to the tithe barn after the Angelus Bell tonight and set before the door some sacks of grain, held back for the poor, oats and barley, so they may eat and feed their horse until they reach their destination."

"What is their destination?"

"If you do not know, you cannot tell. But the sacks should be large, for the distance is great."

So Father Thomas reluctantly agreed to meet us at the church door an hour after the evening Angelus. From his vicarage I walked to Catte Street and the home of John Prudhomme, Bampton's beadle. I told him that he might see some folk near the church that night, violating curfew.

If so, he need take no notice. Later he might see a horse and cart quietly leaving the town. This also he should ignore.

From Catte Street I set off for the castle, praying that I could enter the place without Lord Gilbert knowing I was there. He would be sure to ask inconvenient questions did he learn of my presence at the castle.

John Chamberlain was not in his chamber. I knocked upon the door to no response. As his presence was not required for what I intended to do, I pushed the door open and entered.

John Thrale's goods were stacked neatly upon the floor, beside a table. I did not take all of the items. The sack was not large enough, and if all the goods were missing John would surely notice and wonder at the loss. But if only a part of the stuff was gone he might never notice.

John Chamberlain and Lord Gilbert might never know that some of the chapman's goods had been appropriated, but I would. These things, as well as the horse and cart, might have been Amice's had the chapman lived a few weeks longer. But he had not, so I must pray that the Lord Christ forgive me the theft. My conscience was some troubled later, when I thought upon the pilferage, but not so much as it would have been if I had consented to Osbert's death at the hands of an evil lord.

With the sack slung over my shoulder I returned to Galen House and found three anxious people, convinced that Father Thomas had refused and that I lingered at the vicarage, attempting to persuade him otherwise. They were much relieved that their fears were not realized.

I took pen, ink, and parchment and wrote to my nephew, explaining only so much as he needed to know and requesting that he provide land to Osbert, waiting to collect gersom and rents until the fellow was able to harvest a crop. I do not know my nephew, as he was but a lad when I left Little Singleton for Oxford and Balliol College, but most manors are in need of labor and good tenants, so I thought he would prove amenable to allowing Osbert and Amice to settle upon his estate. Perhaps there might be a house, empty due to plague, which could be made suitable for a tenant.

We supped on maslin loaves and cheese, and when we had eaten our fill Kate filled a sack with the leavings. As she did, the evening Angelus Bell rang from the tower of St. Beornwald's Church.

Osbert and I went to the toft behind Galen House and readied the horse and cart for the journey to come.

The hour passed slowly. Amice and Osbert alternated in pacing about the room and sitting upon a bench. Occasionally, when they thought neither Kate nor I saw, they exchanged timid smiles.

"It's time," I said finally. And we donned surcoats – Osbert wearing an old one of mine, for he had none – and set out for the church. I carried Bessie upon my shoulder and Amice's lads followed sleepily behind. They had been put to their bed after supper, and were unwilling to be drawn from the warmth of their pallet into a cold night.

Father Thomas awaited us at the porch, and set immediately to his work. There would be no formality this night; no ring to give, nor coins to distribute to the poor, no dower or dowry announced.

When Father Thomas had asked Osbert and Amice if they wed freely, and of no compulsion, and received their reply, he pronounced them man and wife and led the way into the church. A row of candles flickering to denote souls in purgatory gave some light to the nave. Standing before the altar, Father Thomas spoke a brief mass, presented the eucharist to Amice and Osbert, and announced that the sacrament was done.

Bessie slept through the business, Amice's children yawned, and I thought I saw the mark of a tear glistening upon Kate's cheek as we passed the row of candles while leaving the church.

At Galen House I placed a pallet in the cart upon which the children might sleep. The sack of John Thrale's goods lay in the cart already.

"At the north edge of the town, on the right side of

the road," I said to Osbert, "you will see the bishop's new tithe barn. Before the door there will be two sacks for you, one of oats and one of barley. To find the manor of Little Singleton you must travel north and ask for roads to Preston. At Preston travel west to Kirkham, and when you reach that place Little Singleton will be but a few miles to the north. Folk thereabout will know the way. You have the letter?"

"Aye. How many days travel, you think?"

"'Tis a far journey. A fortnight, perhaps longer if the roads be mud."

Osbert looked to his feet, silent in the dark behind Galen House.

"Don't know what to say," he finally said. "You might 'ave sent me to die... be less trouble for you."

"More trouble for my conscience."

"I've no way to repay."

"Tell my nephew, Roger, and his mother, Maud, that I am well. I have taken a wife, and our Bessie is healthy and growing. Deliver that message and I will consider myself paid well."

"'Twill be done."

"Take no heed of the beadle, if you see him. He has been told you may be on the streets after curfew. Now we must all go to our beds. When you are sure Kate and I sleep, rise and be off."

Osbert and Amice were eager to be away. I was not yet asleep when I heard the door to the toft open. What time of the night this was I could not tell, so if Lord Gilbert asked I might yet honestly say that I did not know.

Kate also lay awake. "They are off," she whispered.

"Aye... and God speed," I replied.

Soon after I fell to sleep, worries behind me for a few hours, and did not awaken until Kate's cock announced the dawn. I was of two minds how I should tell my employer that Osbert was away. I might wait until he remembered that the man was convalescent under my roof, and demanded again to know when he could be sent to Sir

Philip. Or I could this day seek Lord Gilbert and inform him that Osbert was gone.

To give this news today might mean that Lord Gilbert would demand that I organize a body of grooms and pages and set out after Osbert. This I would not do, although 'twould be simple enough to search the roads to the south, toward London, where we would be sure not to find our quarry.

If I waited until Lord Gilbert called me to him he would ask why he had not been told sooner that Osbert was away. I would have no ready answer.

So after a portion of maslin loaf, which seemed tasteless in my mouth, I walked to the castle, found John Chamberlain, and told him I wished to speak to Lord Gilbert.

Lord Gilbert was in the solar, with Lady Petronilla, when John ushered me into his presence. I bowed, and before I could speak Lord Gilbert said, "Ah, Master Hugh. We are well met. I was about to ask for you."

My heart fell at these words, for I was certain he was about to demand that Osbert be sent to Sir Philip forthwith.

"We will soon be away to Goodrich for the winter. How do my tenants and villeins do? Harvest was plentiful this year, was it not?"

"Aye. John Holcutt is much pleased."

"So the poor will see themselves through the winter?"

"A man who has but a quarter-yardland will find it difficult to feed his family even in a year when the harvest is plentiful."

"Oh," Lord Gilbert said, and the eyebrow rose again. "Well, I will leave funds for you to assist the poor while I am at Goodrich and Pembroke, so no man may starve upon my lands this winter.

"And another thought has come to me. The dead chapman, found near to St. Andrew's Chapel, have you discovered the murderers?"

"Aye, I have."

"Has Sir Roger held them for the King's Eyre?"

"Nay, m'lord. They have fled, and we do not know where to seek them. 'Tis said they have gone to London."

"Ah… and the coins the fellow found, do you know where they came from?"

"Nay. Arthur and I searched, but found nothing."

"The fellow's cart and horse, and the goods found in the cart… I've no need of them. You said that the priest of St. Andrew's Chapel wished to have them to help the poor. He may do so. I have no need of coarse wool and crude buckles, nor of such a horse and cart. Sell them, or give the stuff to the poor."

I could not tell Lord Gilbert that I had already done so, but was much relieved to hear him speak these words. My conscience would rest easier.

"One more thing. The villein who fled Sir Philip Rede, is he whole enough to be returned to East Hanney?"

I swallowed, then replied. "He has fled, m'lord."

"Fled?"

"Aye. He knew his fate if he was returned to Sir Philip, so arose in the night and made off."

"What night?"

"Just last night, m'lord."

"So if I sent men after him he might be found? You've probably no idea where he went?" he said sarcastically. I made no reply.

"Well, bolting as he has done solves two problems. I no longer must send a man to his death, and you must no longer leave my service so to soothe your tender conscience. I am glad he is no longer a concern for either of us."

I had not been aware that Lord Gilbert was troubled about Osbert's fate. Perhaps I had misjudged my employer.

For the next months, when the weather was not foul and the ground not frozen, I prowled the forest to the east of St. Andrew's Chapel where I had found John Thrale's horse and cart, and where Arthur and I had discovered the rows of strange stone mounds. Occasionally John Kellet accompanied me, or Arthur, but I brought no other man to the search, and required of John and Arthur that they tell no man of what we did. If folk of Bampton learned that treasure was perhaps buried somewhere in that wood, the forest floor would soon be ploughed as if an army of hogs had been set loose to pannage the place.

I lost interest in the search when spring came. I am yet convinced that the chapman's discovery is somewhere in that forest, upon Lord Gilbert's lands, but no longer trouble myself seeking it. Perhaps, many years hence, some other man may find the hoard. If so, I pray the consequence will not be as it was for John Thrale.

Afterword

In *Bampton Town; Its Castle and the Earls of Pembroke* (a publication of the Bampton Archive written by Anthony Page) we read that "there are traces of (Roman) occupation in the Weald area. A Roman altar has been found, and a quantity of Roman coinage, one coin of which is very rare."

In the fifth and sixth centuries Romanized Britons often fled west before the invading Saxons. Some buried valuables, perhaps hoping to return for them when the invaders had passed. Some of these caches have been found. Who knows how many more await discovery?

The orderly columns of tiles and masonry Master Hugh discovered were hypocausts. This construction permitted Romans to pass warmed air under the floor of a villa, providing heat in winter. A fine example has been unearthed at Chedworth Roman Villa, a few miles west of Northleach.

A few decades ago a medieval longbow was found preserved in the oxygen-free environment of a bog. A new bow was made to its measurements and was found to have a draw weight of 140 pounds. This is about twice the force needed to draw a modern compound hunting bow. So much for the idea that our medieval forebears were smaller and weaker than modern men.

Medieval arrows were as thick as a large man's thumb, and were supplied with iron points up to four inches long, depending upon the arrow's intended use. Such an arrow, more than three feet long, discharged from a bow of 140 pounds draw, could travel more than a mile.

Abbot of Abingdon's St. Mary's Abbey in 1367 was indeed Peter of Hanney. Whether or not he was obese is conjecture, but it is true that he was not popular in the town. Relations between town and abbey led several times in the fourteenth century to lawsuits and riot.

In the early 1960s Peter, Paul, and Mary sang the delightful song, "A Soulin',"

> about children begging for coins and soul cakes at Christmastime. The cakes and begging were accurate enough, but it was on All Souls' Day that children went from house to house seeking the little cakes, not at Christmas.

Many readers have written asking about medieval remains in Bampton and tourist facilities in the area. St. Mary's Church is little changed from the fourteenth century, when it was known as the Church of St. Beornwald. Little remains of Bampton Castle. The gatehouse and a small part of the curtain wall form a part of Ham Court, a farmhouse in private hands. Visitors to Bampton will enjoy staying at Wheelgate House, a B&B in the center of the town. Village scenes in the popular series *Downton Abbey* were filmed on Church View Street, and St. Mary's Church appears in several episodes.

An Uncertain Sleep

An extract from the sixth chronicle of
Hugh de Singleton, surgeon

Chapter 1

Unwelcome guests may be a tribulation, and when they depart 'tis usually considered a blessed occasion. But not so if the visitor is a knight and he departs to make his new home in St. Beornwald's Churchyard.

Sir Henry Burley was a small, ferret-faced man who, in battle at Poitiers more than a decade past, had done some service for my employer, Lord Gilbert Talbot. What this service was I know not. Lord Gilbert said only that it would cost him little to repay the knight's valor. From this brief explanation I judge that Sir Henry had distinguished himself in battle, to Lord Gilbert's advantage. How this could be is a mystery to me, for Lord Gilbert is nearly as tall as me, and is squarely built, while Sir Henry is – was

– small and slender and, I judge, weighed little more than eight stone.

But after nearly a month entertaining Sir Henry, his wife and daughter, two knights and two squires in Sir Henry's service, and several valets and grooms, Lord Gilbert was clearly ready for them to depart. Sir Henry was a demanding sort of man who seemed to delight in finding fault with Bampton Castle and its inhabitants; the garderobe was not perfumed to his liking, and Lord Gilbert's servants did not show him proper deference.

Three days before St. John's Day, in the year of our Lord 1368, Sir Henry went to his bed hale and healthy after enjoying a long evening of music, conversation, and dancing in Bampton Castle's hall. The next morn his valet found him cold and dead.

Shortly after Sir Henry's valet made this disagreeable discovery, I was breaking my fast when a loud and insistent thumping upon my door drew me from my morning reverie. Kate was feeding bits of a wheaten loaf to Bessie and continued her occupation, an early summons not being unusual in Galen House. I am often sought at such an hour, either because of my profession, surgeon, or due to my service as bailiff to Lord Gilbert Talbot's manor of Bampton. My summons this day was because of my training as surgeon, but soon called for a bailiff's work as well.

John, Lord Gilbert's chamberlain, stood before me when I opened the door. I knew immediately some affair of urgency had brought him to Galen House. Had it been some routine matter, a lesser servant would have been sent.

"Come quickly, Master Hugh. Sir Henry is dead!"

Why the presence of a surgeon was required quickly, when the patient was dead, did not seem to have occurred to John, but I did as he bid. I had yet a part of a wheaten loaf in my hand. This I left upon our table, then explained my hasty departure to my wife. Bessie has discovered language, and makes incessant use of the knowledge, often at great volume if she believes her words are not awarded sufficient attention. So Kate had not heard who was at our door or what the reason until I told her.

Usually when I am called to some place where my skill as a surgeon is required, I take with me a sack of instruments and herbs, so as to be prepared for whatever wound or injury I may find. I took no implements this day. Of what use would they be to a dead man?

I questioned John regarding the matter as we hurried down Church View Street to Mill Street, crossed Shill Brook, and approached the castle gatehouse. As we spoke I heard the Passing Bell ring from the tower of the Church of St. Beornwald.

"Lord Gilbert wishes your opinion as to what has caused this death," John said. "The man was in good health yesterday. Complained of no illness. Lord Gilbert, I think, fears poison or some such thing which might cast blame on him and his household."

I reflected. Two days earlier a page had called at Galen House. Lord Gilbert's guest, he said, was unable to sleep. Lord Gilbert wished me to send herbs which might calm a troubled mind and bring rest. I sent a pouch of pounded lettuce seeds, with instruction to measure a thimbleful into a cup of wine an hour before Sir Henry went to his bed.

Perhaps Lord Gilbert worried that the lettuce seed I provided to aid Sir Henry's sleep might have contributed to his death.

"Is there reason to suspect evil in this?" I asked.

"None... but that the man was robust one day and a corpse the next."

"Men may die of a sudden. 'Tis known to occur."

"Aye, when they are aged."

"But Sir Henry was not. I dined with him a week past, when Lord Gilbert invited me to his table. How old was the man?"

"Forty-six, his wife said."

The faces of those who greeted me in the Bampton Castle hall were somber, lips drawn tight and thin. Lord

Gilbert and Lady Petronilla sat in earnest conversation with an attractive woman whom I recognized as Lady Margery, Sir Henry's wife. Lord Gilbert stood when he saw John usher me into the hall, spoke briefly to the widow, then approached.

"I give you good day," I said.

"Much thanks, Hugh, but the day is ill. John has told you?"

"Aye. Your guest was found dead this morning."

"He was. And no sign of what caused the death... which is why I sent for you. A surgeon or physician might more readily see what indisposition has caused this."

"You have seen the corpse?"

"Aye."

"And you saw nothing out of sorts?"

"Not a thing. All was as a man should be when asleep, but for his eyes. They were open. The body is unmarked. Sir Henry was not a young man, but he was in good health yesterday."

"John Chamberlain said you feared poison."

Lord Gilbert shrugged, then whispered, "'Twas but the thought of a moment. We are all baffled. I would not have Lady Margery hear of poison. John," he continued, "take Master Hugh to Sir Henry's chamber." Then to me he said, "'Tis an odious business, I know, to ask of you, but I wish to know if Sir Henry's death is God's work or man's."

"You suspect man's work?"

"I do not know what to think. So I have called for you. Is it possible that the sleeping draught you sent did this?"

"Nay. The seeds of lettuce are but a mild soporific. A man would need to swallow a bucket of the stuff to do himself harm."

Lord Gilbert turned back to Lady Margery and left me to John, who nodded and led me to the stairs which would take us to the guest chambers beyond Lord Gilbert's solar.

Past the solar the passageway grew dark, but at its

end I saw two figures. I recognized one. Arthur, one of Lord Gilbert's grooms, stood at the closed door of a chamber, and another man, wearing Sir Henry's livery and badge, stood with him.

The two men stood aside as I approached, having been notified, no doubt, that I was to inspect the corpse and give reason for the death. I opened the heavy door and entered the chamber, but none followed. Death is not pleasant to look upon, and the three men who stood outside the door were content to allow me to do my work alone.

Sir Henry lay as he had been found, upon his back, sightless eyes staring at the vaulted ceiling and boss of his chamber. Would a man die in his sleep with his eyes open? Perhaps some pain seized him in the night and awakened him before death came.

A cresset was burning upon a stand, where it had been all night should Sir Henry have wished to rise and visit the garderobe. I lifted it and held it close to the dead man's face. Two windows gave light to the room, but they were narrow, and one faced north, the other west, so that the morning sun did not illuminate the chamber.

I first inspected Sir Henry's neck to see if any contusion was there. None was. I felt the man's scalp, to see if any lump or dried blood might betray a blow. All was as should be. I pried open the lips – no easy task, for rigor mortis was begun – to see if Sir Henry might have choked to his death upon regurgitated food. His mouth was clear.

Because Sir Henry was already stiffening in death I assumed that he was dead for some hours before he was found. De Mondeville wrote that rigor mortis begins three or so hours after death, and becomes severe at twelve hours.

A blanket yet covered the corpse. I drew this aside, and with my dagger slit Sir Henry's night-shirt so I might inspect the body for wounds or evidence of blows. There were none.

Beside the bed, next to where the cresset had been placed, was a cup. I held it to the window and saw in the dregs the few remains of the pounded seeds of lettuce which had been in the wine. Was some other potion added to the cup? I touched the dregs with my fingertips and brought them to my lips. I could detect no foreign flavor, although this is not telling, for there are several malignant herbs which leave little or no taste when consumed. Monk's Hood is one. And for this they are all the more dangerous.

The walls of Sir Henry's chamber were of stone, of course, and the door of heavy oak. If he felt himself afflicted in the night, and cried out for aid, he might not have been heard, especially if his call was weak due to an affliction which took his life.

I went to the door, where Arthur and Sir Henry's valet stood, and asked the valet if anyone had heard Sir Henry shout for help in the night.

"Don't know," he replied. "My chamber's in the servants' range. I wouldn't have heard 'im."

"Has no other, those whose chambers were close by, spoken of it?"

"Nay. None said anything."

"It was you who found him?"

"Aye."

"Has anything in his chamber been moved since then? Has Sir Henry's corpse been moved?"

"Nay... but for Lady Margery throwin' herself upon 'im when she was brought here an' saw Sir Henry dead. Lord Gilbert drew her away. Told her he had a man who could tell why Sir Henry was dead. That would be you?"

"Aye. I am Hugh de Singleton, surgeon, and bailiff at Bampton manor. You are...?"

"Walter Mayn, valet to Sir Henry... *was* valet to Sir Henry."

"Two days past I was asked to provide herbs which might help Sir Henry fall to sleep. Was there some matter which vexed him, so that he awoke of a night?"

Walter did not reply. He looked away, as if he heard some man approach at the end of the passageway. A valet is to be circumspect, and loyal, and hold his tongue when asked of the affairs of his lord. The man did not need to say more. His silence and glance told me that some business had troubled Sir Henry. Whether or not the issue had led to his death was another matter. Might a man die of worry? If so, this was no concern of Lord Gilbert Talbot's bailiff.

"Who slept in the next chamber?" I asked the fellow.

"M'lady Margery."

"And across the passageway?"

"Sir John an' Sir Geoffrey."

"They are knights in Sir Henry's service?"

"Aye."

"And they did not speak of any disturbance in the night?"

"Not that I heard. There was lots of screamin' and all was speakin' at once when Sir Henry was found."

I decided that I should seek these knights, and the Lady Margery, if she was fit to be questioned. I told Arthur and Walter to remain at Sir Henry's door and allow no man, nor woman, either, to enter the chamber till I had returned.

Lady Margery I had seen in the hall, so I returned there and found Lord Gilbert and Lady Petronilla comforting the widow. Lady Margery's eyes were red and her cheeks swollen. She had seen me an hour before, but through teary eyes. She did not then, I believe, know who I was.

"Master Hugh," Lord Gilbert said, rising, "what news?"

"Hugh?" the woman shrieked. "Is this the leech who has poisoned my husband?"

Lord Gilbert answered for me. "Nay, Lady Margery. Master Hugh is as competent as any at his business. He has assured me that the potion he sent to aid Sir Henry's slumber could not cause death."

"Of course he would say so. Something did. And Sir Henry took none of the potion until the night he died."

"'Tis of that night I would speak to you," I said. "Sir Henry's valet said your chamber was next to your husband's. Did you hear anything in the night? Some sound which might now, when you think back upon it, have told of Sir Henry's distress, even if in the night, when you heard it, you paid no heed?"

"Nay, I heard nothing. 'Twas the potion you gave which caused his death. It was to bring sleep, you said. So it did, the sleep of death. This man," she turned to my employer, "should be sent to the Sheriff for trial before the King's Eyre for the murder he has done."

"Surely Master Hugh has done no murder," Lady Petronilla said. "If so be his potion brought death, 'twas surely mischance, not felony."

Lady Margery stared skeptically at Lady Petronilla, but said no more.

Across the hall, as far from the grieving widow as could be, yet remaining in the chamber, I saw two knights sitting upon a bench, their heads close together in earnest conversation.

"Sir John and Sir Geoffrey occupied the chamber across the corridor from Sir Henry, is this not so?"

"Aye," Lord Gilbert replied, and nodded in the direction of the solemn knights.

I walked in the direction of his gaze and the two knights stood when they saw me approach.

"I give you good day," I said courteously, although my words were but an affectation, for no such day could be good. "You are knights in service to Sir Henry?" I asked, although I knew the answer.

"Aye," the older of the two replied. "I am Sir John Peverel. This is Sir Geoffrey Godswein."

I introduced myself and my duty, and asked if they had heard any cry in the night, or any other sound to indicate that Sir Henry might have been in distress. Both men shook their heads.

"Heard nothing amiss till Walter shouted for help," Sir Geoffrey said.

"When he did so, you went immediately to Sir Henry's chamber?"

"Aye."

"Who entered first?"

"I did," Sir Geoffrey replied.

"What did you see? Tell all, even if it seems of no importance."

"Walter stood at the door, which was flung wide open, bawling out that m'lord Henry was dead. I pushed past and saw 'twas so."

"Were the bedclothes in disarray, as if he'd thrashed about?"

Sir Geoffrey pursed his lips in thought, turned to Sir John as if seeking confirmation, then spoke. "Nay. All was in order. Not like Sir Henry'd tossed about in pain before he died."

Sir John nodded agreement, then said, "His eyes were open. You, being a surgeon, would know better than me, but if a man dies in his sleep, they'd be closed, seems like."

I agreed. "Unless some pain awoke him before he died."

"Then why'd he not cry out?" Sir Geoffrey asked.

I had no answer.

"When did you last see Sir Henry alive?"

"Last night," Sir John said.

"After the music and dancing," Sir Geoffrey added. "We retired same time as Sir Henry and Lady Margery."

"Did he seem well? Did any matter trouble him?"

The two knights seemed to pause before they replied. Their hesitation was slight, but I noted it.

"Nay," Sir Geoffrey said. "Lord Gilbert had musicians and jongleurs to entertain here in the hall after supper. Sir Henry danced an' seemed pleased as any."

"When he went to his chamber, did he stand straight, or was he perhaps bent as if some discomfort afflicted his belly?"

Again the knights exchanged glances, but this time Sir John spoke with no hesitation. "Sir Henry always stands straight, being shorter than most men. Wears thick-soled shoes, too. Was he bent last eve we'd have noticed, that being unlike him."

"Think back again to this morning, and when you first entered Sir Henry's chamber. Was anything amiss, or in disarray?"

"When a man is found dead," Sir John said, "other matters are trivial. I paid no heed to anything but the corpse." Sir Geoffrey nodded in agreement.

I thanked the knights, bid them good day, and motioned to Lord Gilbert that I wished to speak privily to him.

"What have you learned?" he asked when we were out of Lady Margery's hearing.

"You saw the corpse?" I asked.

"Aye," he grimaced.

"Sir Henry's eyes were open in death."

"Aye, they were. What means that?"

"I do not know, but the fact troubles me."

"Why so? You think violence was done to him?"

"Nay. I examined the corpse. I found no injury. If a man dies in his sleep, his eyes will be shut. I'm sure of this. If Sir Henry awoke, and felt himself in pain, he would, I think, have called out. But no man, nor Lady Margery, heard him do so."

"The castle walls are thick," Lord Gilbert said.

"As are the doors. But between the bottom of the door to Sir Henry's chamber and the floor is a space as wide as a man's finger is thick. If Sir Henry cried for help I think he would have been heard through the gap, unless the affliction had greatly weakened him."

"Mayhap the malady took him of a sudden."

"Perhaps," I shrugged.

"You are not satisfied to be ignorant of a matter like this, are you?" Lord Gilbert said.

"Nay."

"'Tis why I employed you. But you must remember that only the Lord Christ knows all. There are matters we mortals may never know."

Lord Gilbert Talbot, baron of the realm, valiant

knight, now theologian and philosopher.

"You wish me to abandon my inquiry?"

"The longer you continue, the more distress for Lady Margery. If you think it unlikely you will ever discover the cause, 'twould be best to say so sooner than later. Men often die for no good reason."

"There is always a reason, but other men are ignorant of it."

"And you do not like being outsmarted, even by death, do you?"

"Nay. And if I cannot discover what caused Sir Henry's death, Lady Margery will tell all that 'twas my potion which did so."

"Another hour or two, then. Have ready an opinion by dinner."

I promised to do so. As I left the hall Sir Henry's daughter entered, as red-eyed and puffy-cheeked as her stepmother. Lady Anne, I had been told, was Sir Henry's daughter by his first wife, the Lady Goscelyna. The lass looked to be about twenty years old, and was followed by two youths – squires, I remembered, to Sir Henry. The lads were somber, but showed no sign of terrible loss. Lady Anne is a beautiful maid, and probably accustomed to being followed by young men.

I returned to Sir Henry's chamber, nodded to Arthur and Walter, and entered the room. Perhaps, I thought, murder was done here in some manner I had not discovered, and when Sir Henry was dead all marks of a struggle had been made right. But if such had happened, why did Sir Henry not shout for assistance when he was attacked? Whether the man died of some illness, or was murdered, I could make no sense of his silence.

I sat upon a chair, ready to abandon the loathsome task I had been assigned. The Lord Christ gives to all men their appointed tasks, but occasionally I wish that He had assigned another profession to me. My eyes fell upon the fireplace. It was cold, and the ashes of the last blaze of winter had been long since disposed of, but 'twas not the hearth which seized my attention.

A poker stood propped against the stones, and my mind went to a rumor which passed amongst students while I studied at Balliol College. A rumor concerning the death of King Edward II. Mortimer and Edward's faithless queen deposed him nearly a half-century past, and he was taken to Berkeley Castle where, some months later, he was found dead of a morning. Folk living near the castle were said to have heard terrible screams in the night, but, as with Sir Henry, no mark was found upon the King's corpse to tell of violent death.

A red-hot poker, rumor said, was thrust up the deposed King's rectum, doing murder and cauterizing the wound at the same time, so no blood flowed to disclose how the felony was done. And no visible wound was made to indict the murderers.

There had been no blaze in Sir Henry's fireplace, but I went to the hearth to examine the poker nevertheless. The iron bar was dusty with ashes from its last use, which had been as was intended, not to do murder.

I replaced the poker against the wall, but the thought of Edward II's death caused me to consider again Sir Henry's corpse. Surely if a man was murdered as the King was, his screams would have been heard throughout the castle, stone walls and oaken doors notwithstanding.

But what if he was silenced with a pillow over his face? Would that muffle his shrieks? Or might a pillow have been enough to suffocate the man and silence his protest at the same time?

I turned to the door of the chamber to seek Arthur and Walter and conduct an experiment with the pillow. 'Twas then I saw the tiny brown droplet upon the planks. I knelt to inspect the mark, thinking at first it might have been made by a drop of Sir Henry's wine. The color so matched the floor that 'tis a wonder I saw it at all. Some man, or men, did not.

The circular stain was smaller than the nail upon my little finger, and when I scraped a thumbnail across it I was able to lift some of the substance from the floor. Wine will not thicken so. A tiny drop of dried blood lay before me.

Could this be Sir Henry's blood? If so, whence did it come? I approached the corpse, turned it upon the bed, and spread the legs so I might inspect the rectum for some sign of violence. I saw none, although I admit I might have performed the examination more carefully.

When Sir Henry was again upon his back I made another search of the corpse for some wound from which the drop of blood might have come. As before, I found none. Was there some other orifice of a man's body whereby he might be stabbed and murdered, the wound invisible? I had already peered into Sir Henry's mouth and seen nothing amiss. I tilted the head back and inspected the nostrils to see if any trace of blood was there. None was.

Sir Henry was stiff in death, but I managed to turn his head so that I could inspect his left ear. 'Tis all dark within a man's ear, so at first I saw nothing, but it seemed to me that Sir Henry's ear was darker than might be expected. I drew my dagger and with the point teased from the ear canal a flake of dried matter identical to the drop of dried blood upon the floor. If a man died in the throes of apoplexy, would the strain cause an eardrum to burst? I had never heard of such a thing, and Galen and de Mondeville wrote nothing of such a phenomenon.

I needed my instruments. I bid Arthur and Walter maintain their watch, told Lord Gilbert my examination was near complete, and hastened to Galen House. Bessie toddled to me, but I could spare her but a peck upon a cheek before I seized a sack which I keep always ready for a time when my skills are called for.

Often when I walk the bridge over Shill Brook I stop to observe the water pass beneath, but not this day. I hastened to the castle, and at Sir Henry's chamber I selected my smallest scalpel with which to prod the dark recess of Sir Henry's ear. A moment later I drew forth a clot of dried blood.

If an awl is driven through a man's ear, into his brain,

will he die so suddenly that he does not cry out in pain before death comes? I did not know, and do not know yet, for there is no way to make experiment to learn if it may be so.

But I was then sure that Sir Henry was murdered. Some man thrust an awl or thin blade through his ear. If such a wound bleeds much – I had no experience of such a wound to know, and no writer has treated the subject – the felon had mopped up the blood so as to befuddle all who sought to find the cause of Sir Henry's death. They had overlooked one drop.

I must now report this sad discovery to Lord Gilbert, and he must send for Sir Roger de Elmerugg, Sheriff of Oxford. Murder upon Lord Gilbert's lands would generally be my bailiwick, but not when the deceased was a visiting knight. I was pleased that seeking a murderer would be another man's business. Sir Roger entertained other thoughts.